Emma finally dropped to her knees at the grave side, eyes fixed on the bodies of her parents, sobs racking her body.

She didn't recognise the figure that jumped down into the grave.

She watched silently as he took the first of the coffin lids and began screwing it into place over the battered body of her father.

Emma screamed at him to stop, but he merely continued with his task. Sealing the first of her parents beneath the wood, hiding him from her sight.

As the figure reached for the second coffin lid and began fixing that into position, Emma could contain herself no longer. She leapt into the hole beside him, tearing madly at his clothes in an attempt to stop him.

He turned and gripped her wrists, leering into her face. She could feel his breath on her tear-sodden cheeks. He smiled, his eyeballs rolling in the sockets until only the whites showed.

Emma screamed but no sound came forth. He hurled her to one side then continued sealing her mother's coffin. Again she attempted to prevent him completing his task but, as before, he pushed her away.

When he was finished he clambered effortlessly up out of the hole, standing on the lip above her. She tried to follow him but could gain no purchase on the slippery walls of the grave and fell back on to the now closed coffins.

The other mourners had moved forwards so that they ringed the makeshift grave.

Each of tgh with dark earth and, aclods began to rain dow

D1464406

Also by Shaun Hutson

TWISTED SOULS

Shaun Hutson

TIME WARNER
BOOKS

TIME WARNER BOOKS

First published in Great Britain in August 2005
by Time Warner Books
This paperback edition published in April 2006
by Time Warner Books

A CIP catalogue record for this book
is available from the British Library.

ISBN 0 7515 3523 0

Typeset by Palimpsest Book Production Limited,
Polmont, Stirlingshire
Printed and bound in Great Britain by Clays Ltd, St Ives plc

Time Warner Books
An imprint of
Time Warner Book Group UK
Brettenham House
Lancaster Place
London WC2E 7EN

www.twbg.co.uk

This book is dedicated with great respect and affection to my fantastic agent, Brie Burkeman. The only woman I know who can actually smile while she's shouting me down.
(And trust me, that takes some doing . . .)
Thanks, Brie.
If there's one better, I'll be bloody amazed.

Acknowledgements

Here we are again. That time when I thank a disparate (and in some cases desperate) group of people, places and things for something they've done before, during or after the writing of this latest book.

If I've forgotten anyone who should be in here then I apologise. No doubt I'll make up for it in the acknowledgements of the next one. Here goes . . .

Massive thanks, as always, to my publishers. Especially Barbara Daniel, Andy Edwards, Sheena-Margot Lavelle, Carol Donnelly, Cecilia Duraes and everyone else at Time Warner.

A special thanks to my amazing Sales Team. My 'Wild Bunch'.

Thank you to my accountant, Peter Nichols, and everyone at Chancery. Also thank you to Leslie Tebbs and very special thanks to Brian our Bank Manager.

To James Whale, Melinda and also to Ash.

I would like to say a very special thank you to everyone connected with the BBC's *End of Story* programme. Especially to Angus Dixon (maybe I'll see you and Celtic at Anfield next season), to Katie ('can we get clearance for this?'), to Andy ('the lips are having a tantrum') and everyone else who filmed me, sorted out hotels and trains for me and paid my expenses (thanks, Trish). Also to all those who turned up to the workshops and who entered my particular story, thank you very much.

Special thanks also to Meaghan Delahunt.

A huge thanks to everyone at Sanctuary Music and Sanctuary Publishing especially Rod Smallwood, Val Janes, Dave Pattenden and Albert DePetrillo. Not forgetting Maiden themselves. Special thanks to Steve, Bruce, Dave, Adrian, Nicko and Janick.

Very special thanks to all the management and staff at the Savoy Hotel in London who always make my visits feel like I'm coming home.

A massive thank you to Jo Roberts (I don't think your direction is leaden at all, Jo . . .) and Gatlin Pictures for giving me the chance to appear in *Forest of the Damned* and for two of the most enjoyable days of my life. Thank you to all the cast and crew and especially to special effects man *extraordinaire* Nathan McLaughlin (I'm sure I've spelt that wrong, Nathan, sorry) who did such a superb job of decapitating me. Something which many will feel should have been done years ago . . .

To Matt Haslum who must have suffered more phone calls than any editor I've ever worked with and yet still speaks to me. Thanks, Matt and everyone else at Working Partners.

Thanks also to my good friend Martin 'gooner' Phillips.

To Ian Austin, to Zena, Ted and Molly, Hailey, Terri, Rachel and Becki, Nicky and to Sandi at Waterstone's in Birmingham.

The usual thank you to Graeme Sayer and Callum Hughes for their brilliant work on *www.shaunhutson.com* and, as ever, I thank all of you who have visited the site or contacted it and me.

Extra special thanks to October 11 Pictures and Jason Figgis, Jonathan Figgis and Maria (yes, it's that English bloke on the phone again . . .).

Many thanks to Claire at Centurion and everyone else there who's helped me and looked after me in the past few years. Thanks, folks.

I will continue to thank the departed genius of Sam Peckinpah and Bill Hicks. There will never be two flames that burn again with the same intensity.

A huge thanks to Cineworld UK, especially Mr Al Alvarez and a particular thank you to all the management and staff at Cineworld Milton Keynes especially Mark, Martin, Nick, Simon, Terry, the 'ever pert' Teresa, Debbie, Paula, Kojo, Claire, Ty and everyone else I've doubtless forgotten or spelt wrong . . . I'm sure you'll let me know next time I'm in . . . Many thanks as usual from 'Cappuccino man'.

I offer thanks, and always will, to Liverpool Football Club. Especially to everyone in the Commercial Department, Sue, Joanne, Debbi and Kirsty. Also to those in the Bob Paisley suite, especially Steve Lucas and Paul Garner. Many thanks also to my long suffering co-driver, Aaron 'not another traffic jam' Reynolds.

A very special thanks to my Mum and Dad as ever.

I would say thank you to my wife, Belinda, but, as I always say, it seems too inadequate a word. For her strength, her love, her patience and her belief and everything she does, I am eternally grateful.

That goes for that other girl in my life. Even if her taste in music sometimes drives me mad, I love her more than anything in the world and to have her with me the night the mighty Reds beat Juventus at Anfield was one of the greatest moments of my life (the fact that we'd had a quid on Sami Hyypia to get the first goal helped, of course . . .). Every book I write is for her and this one is no exception. This is for my wonderful daughter.

And finally, the biggest thank you of all to you lot, my readers. Old and new. All ages. Many of you have stuck with me from the beginning, many more have joined the ride along the way.

I welcome any more newcomers this time around.

Let's go.

Shaun Hutson

'There is no turning back now you've woken up the demon in me.'

Disturbed

It's only a matter of time before I kill one of them.

I know that. I've known it for a while.

I'm sorry. I've tried to feel differently, but it's no good, and I know that I will kill one of them soon.

I've been hiding this for so long. Burying it deep down inside me, praying it'll go away, but I know it won't.

I see them every day. Little smiling faces. Then one of them cries or screams and I can't stand it any longer and I want them to stop and I want to hit them until they shut up. Slam their heads against a wall until their skulls burst. Or stick a knife in them, or grab them around the neck and squeeze until they are silent. Until their eyes pop.

But when their mothers come to pick them up from the nursery I smile at them and talk to them and wave the children goodbye, when all the time I want to hurt them and I know it'll start all over again the next day.

So I'm leaving.

Don't try to find me. I know you understand why I've got to leave.

I'm sorry.

If I was brave enough I'd kill myself. Perhaps I'd be better off dead.

Sorry.

Forgive me.
Love
Catherine
xxxxxxx

1

The lids of both coffins were gone.

Emma Tate didn't know where. She didn't know who'd taken them or why. She didn't really care. All she knew was that their abscence revealed the lifeless forms within.

Cocooned inside wood and silk, the bodies of her mother and father lay motionless.

Both were wearing the clothes they had died in. Both still bore the devastating injuries they'd sustained in the car crash. Emma could see part of her father's ribcage gleaming whitely through the pulped mess that was his chest. Needle-sharp pieces of glass were still embedded in her mother's face like monstrous acupuncture needles. One particularly large shard had pierced her right eye, burst the orb and drilled through her skull. The blood-stained tip protruded a good four inches from the back of her head.

The bodies had been dumped in the coffins as unceremoniously as rubbish hurled into a skip.

The coffins had been dragged through the mud at the grave side. Not lifted by pall bearers but hauled by their brass handles, leaving furrows in the wet earth right up to the lip of the deep hole in the ground.

It had been crudely dug, the dirt hurled in all directions, as if speed had been of the essence.

Emma shivered in the freezing cold breeze that swept across the cemetery. Her long blonde hair whipped about her face. It stuck to her cheeks where tears had dampened her skin. She brushed it away angrily and staggered helplessly around the grave where her parents lay.

She wondered why none of the other mourners seemed troubled by the situation.

She was curious as to why *they* were all dressed in black and *she* was naked.

As naked as the day she'd been born. Born of the two people who now lay dead below her, ready to be swallowed by the earth.

Friends. Family members. Acquaintances. None of them seemed to care that the coffins had no lids. That the bodies had been bundled into them with so little dignity. They didn't even seem to notice Emma.

She ran up to a number of people and shouted at them but they ignored her and continued to gaze blankly ahead. They weren't troubled by her nakedness. They seemed as oblivious of *that* as to her suffering.

Emma finally dropped to her knees at the grave side, eyes fixed on the bodies of her parents, sobs racking her body.

She didn't recognise the figure that jumped down into the grave.

She watched silently as he took the first of the coffin lids and began screwing it into place over the battered body of her father.

Emma screamed at him to stop, but he merely continued with his task. Sealing the first of her parents beneath the wood, hiding him from her sight.

As the figure reached for the second coffin lid and began fixing that into position, Emma could contain herself no longer. She leapt into the hole beside him, tearing madly at his clothes in an attempt to stop him.

He turned and gripped her wrists, leering into her face. She could feel his breath on her tear-sodden cheeks. He smiled, his eyeballs rolling in the sockets until only the whites showed.

Emma screamed but no sound came forth. He hurled her to one side then continued sealing her mother's coffin. Again she tried to scream at him to stop, once more she attempted to prevent him completing his task but, as before, he pushed her away.

When he was finished he clambered effortlessly up out of the hole, standing on the lip above her. She tried to follow him but could gain no purchase on the slippery walls of the grave and fell back on to the now closed coffins.

The other mourners had moved forwards so that they ringed the makeshift grave.

Each of them was holding a shovel piled high with dark earth and, as Emma screamed again, the first clods began to rain down upon her.

2

She didn't wake screaming from the nightmare.

Emma Tate merely let out a long sigh as she sat upright in bed, her eyes open and staring into the darkness. She blinked three or four times, hoping to drive the last vestiges of the bad dream from her consciousness.

She then swung herself out of bed and padded towards the bathroom.

In the warmth of the bed she'd left behind, her husband stirred slightly but didn't wake.

Emma shivered as she sat down on the toilet and urinated. She could see herself in the mirror opposite. She wasn't naked as she had been in the dream *(as she always was in the dream)* she was wearing a short, baggy T-shirt.

Emma crossed her arms over her chest as she sat gazing at her own reflection for a moment longer, then she flushed the toilet and wandered back into the bedroom.

She listened to the low, even breathing of the form before her for a moment longer, then, sure he was still sleeping, she made her way along the landing towards the stairs.

She cursed the creaking boards as she descended quickly, moving swiftly across the hallway and shutting the kitchen door behind her. She slapped the lights on and crossed to the fridge to retrieve some milk.

She poured some into a mug and stuck it in the microwave.

As she waited for the milk to heat up she glanced back at the door of the fridge. There were two photos Blu-Tacked there. One of her and her husband, taken on their honeymoon eight years earlier. Standing on the white sand beach outside the hotel in Bermuda where they'd married. Emma looking stunning in a white bikini. Above it was a picture of her in a tight-fitting red dress that hugged her lithe form like a second skin. She smiled at the recollection that she had been naked beneath it that night. She complimented herself on the fact that she hadn't put on more than a couple of pounds in the intervening years.

The microwave bell interrupted her musings and she spooned some sugar into the warm milk before seating herself at the kitchen table to drink it.

On the walls all around the kitchen there were photos of her or her husband at some of the places they'd enjoyed holidays. Either photos or mementos of those locations. A photo of her outside the Colosseum. A framed menu from a New York deli. Two charcoal caricatures they'd had done with the Eiffel Tower in the background.

Emma got to her feet and retrieved a packet of cigarettes and a lighter from a drawer beneath the worktop. She lit the Silk Cut and looked down at the ashtray they'd bought at a museum just outside Lisbon.

She took a drag on her cigarette, blowing out a stream of smoke and curled her toes against the kitchen floor, still shivering slightly.

From the cold or the recollection of the nightmare?

'I woke up and you weren't there.'

She turned towards the source of the voice.

Nick Tate closed the kitchen door behind him and sat down opposite Emma.

He was wearing a pair of faded jogging bottoms and holding a towelling robe.

'I thought you might need this,' he said, handing it to Emma.

She smiled and slipped it on.

'I didn't mean to wake you,' she apologised.

'You didn't. Like I said, I turned over and you weren't there.'

There was a long silence as he watched her sipping from the mug of warm milk.

'Same dream?' He yawned, running a hand through his short brown hair.

Emma nodded.

'You know why you're having these dreams, don't you?'

'Tell me.'

She pushed the cigarettes and lighter towards him and he lit one for himself.

'It's stress,' he told her. 'Same as it was the first time.'

'I don't need a psychiatrist to tell me that, Nick. Is it any wonder? It *is* only two years since they died. That memory's still strong. I'm about to lose my job and—'

'Come on, Em, you don't know you're going to lose your job,' Tate cut in. 'You've worked at that record company for nearly ten years now. They're not going to get rid of *you*. They'll start with junior staff. People who haven't put in as much time.'

'We heard that *no one's* job was safe. It's got nothing to do with time worked or anything like that. They're cutting back on staff, Nick. It could be *anyone*.'

'Look, even if the worst comes to the worst, you'll get another job without any trouble. You—'

'It's not as easy as that,' she interrupted. 'It's not just about me.'

8

'Meaning?'

'Your photography business, Nick . . .' She allowed the sentence to trail off, almost reluctant to finish it.

He took a drag on his cigarette.

'Your business, our lives,' Emma continued. 'They're . . . not like they used to be. You know that. You know the money's not there like it was eight, nine years ago. It's harder finding money to pay the bills. We've still got twenty-six grand left to pay on that loan we took out last year and the mortgage went up again last month.' She lowered her head.

'Something'll turn up.' Tate wasn't sure if he was trying to convince Emma or himself.

'And what if it doesn't, Nick?' she demanded. 'What if I lose my job? What if your photography business *doesn't* pick up? What if we *do* have to sell the house?'

'It won't come to that.'

'How can you be so bloody sure?' There was a note of anger in her voice. 'I hate having to live like this. I wake up every morning and I'm terrified. I'm scared of what's happening to us, what could happen to our lives. I don't want to live in fear for the rest of my life, Nick. I can't. If only there was a way out. I wouldn't care what I had to do. I'm sick of being afraid.'

The heavy silence that settled over them was finally broken by Emma. She pointed at the photo of them stuck to the fridge door. 'Remember them, Nick?' she said bitterly. 'That used to be us. When we had money to burn. When we didn't have a care in the world.'

Tate got to his feet, walked around the table and sat down beside his wife. He snaked an arm around her and pulled her closer to him. 'It'll be like that again,' he murmured, kissing the top of her head. 'Things are always quiet at this time of the year. Not so many weddings in January and February. People don't put photographers at

9

the top of their list of priorities. Everyone in my business is in the same boat.'

'You said there might be some work for that catalogue,' Emma reminded him.

'I'm still waiting to hear. Like I said, things are quiet for the first two or three months of every year, it doesn't matter which business you're in. You just notice it more when you're self-employed.'

'And your wife's about to lose her job too.'

'You're not going to lose your job.'

'Can I have that in writing?'

'Open a vein and I'll write it in blood,' he said with as much joviality as he could summon.

'I'm sorry, Nick,' Emma said finally.

'We'll be OK.'

Emma wearily swept her hair away from her face. 'I wish I could believe that,' she murmured.

3

He knew it was cancer. He was convinced.

Jason Skelson lay on his bed looking down at his right leg, aware of the dull ache around the top of the limb. It had spread to his hip during the past two days. Since he'd seen the doctor. It hurt when he walked. It hurt when he lay in certain positions. Jesus Christ, it hurt nearly all the time.

A simple groin strain didn't hurt as badly as this. He'd suffered similar injuries before when playing football. This was different. He'd told the doctor but the silly old bastard had just continued looking dismissively at him.

He hadn't even been impressed by Jason's declaration that he'd been losing weight for the last two weeks.

It *had* to be cancer. And there was nothing anyone was going to do to help him. It'd just spread through his body until it consumed him. At twenty-three he'd die in agony, his protests falling on deaf ears. It had happened to others his age, he'd read about it in newspapers. Seen it on the news. Cancer was no respecter of youth. It wasn't just old people who got it. Why was he the only one who realised?

Why wouldn't the doctor send him for an X-ray?

If he did they'd find the growth. They'd remove it. Save him.

11

In the darkness of his bedroom he ran a hand tentatively over the top of his thigh, using his thumb to probe the area around his groin where the lump was most prominent. He tried to control his breathing, using two fingers now to prod at the flesh beside his testicle.

There was a lump there. No question.

He felt a little nauseous. As he moved his leg he winced in pain. Jason reached across to the drawer of his bedside table and reached inside with a shaking hand. He drew out the Swiss Army knife and pulled the blade free.

He ran the pad of his thumb over the cutting edge, satisfied with its sharpness.

Fuck them. Fuck them all. He'd show them.

He pressed the point of the blade to the flesh close to his right testicle, near to where the pain was the most intense.

Go on. Cut it out. Show them the growth. Show them the pulsating, blackened lump of diseased tissue that's going to kill you.

He closed his eyes, his heart thudding hard.

It won't hurt that much. Better some pain now than to die slowly in agony.

Jason pressed the point more firmly against his skin.

Cut.

He pulled the blade away, perspiration running down the side of his face. Fear filled his stomach like undigested food.

No. He couldn't do it. Not yet.

He needed something sharper. Something that could slice through skin and thick muscle more easily. A blade capable of hacking the lump free.

He would wait. He would find the instrument he sought in time. *Then* he would cut.

12

4

Emma finished her cigarette and ground it out in the ashtray, watching the smoke rise in front of her.

'Come back to bed,' Tate said quietly.

'What for? So I can have the nightmare again? It's *exactly* the same time.'

'Like you said, you're still grieving for your mum and dad. That's only natural. Once we get away—'

Emma cut him short. 'I realise that, Nick,' she told him. 'And I'm looking forward to this break. Honestly. I know we all are. It'll be great spending time with Jo and Pete. Especially as we haven't seen them much since they moved back to England. It's like we're all getting to know each other again.'

Tate nodded. 'It hasn't been easy for them since they got back, Em,' he said.

'Perhaps Pete should have thought about that before he started screwing around in New York.'

Tate shrugged. 'He was like it before they went to the States,' he said. 'The only difference was, he didn't get caught.'

'I should have told Jo he was messing around behind her back.'

'I thought you always said she was the type that didn't want to know if anything like that was happening. What she didn't know wouldn't hurt her and all that.'

'It hurt her in the end though, didn't it?'

They sat in silence for a moment.

'Have you said anything to Jo about *us*?' Tate finally enquired. 'Our situation?'

Emma laughed humourlessly. 'Situation,' she repeated. 'What a lovely euphemism, Nick. She knows about my job being in danger, yes. If you mean have I told her that we're up to our necks in debt, your business is going to pot and I'm scared shitless about our future, then no.' She looked at her husband. 'Have you said anything to Pete?'

'No.'

'Why not, Nick? If you're so confident about us getting out of this, why not tell him?'

'It's our business, no one else's.'

'What's the big deal if they know?'

Tate shook his head. 'There's no reason for them to know,' he murmured.

'You're scared too, aren't you?' Emma said challengingly.

'Everyone's scared of something. I've never failed at anything in my life,' Tate told her. 'I don't intend to start now. If we sell this house, it's like giving up. If I let my business collapse, it's like I've been beaten. I won't give it up, Emma.'

She looked across at him and smiled. 'How are we going to afford this holiday?' she wanted to know.

'Stick it on plastic like most of the fucking population do,' Tate proclaimed. 'Worry about it at the end of next month.'

Again Emma managed a smile before yawning.

'That's another reason we should be in bed,' Tate reminded her. 'Pete and Jo will be here at nine in the morning. You know what Pete's like for time. They said they'd pick us up at nine and you can bet they'll be here on the dot.'

'Nearly everything's packed. We'll be ready.'

Tate got to his feet and walked around to Emma. He began massaging her shoulders gently, allowing his hands to stray to her neck every now and then. She pushed back against him slightly.

'I'm sorry for being such a miserable bitch,' she murmured.

'I'll forgive you, this once,' he said softly. 'Let's just enjoy this holiday.' He continued working his fingers over her flesh. 'Try and forget about what's going on here, at least for two weeks.'

'Forget in the wilds of Derbyshire?' she purred, turning her head slightly to kiss one of his hands when it came in range.

He continued to massage expertly.

'I hope you remembered to pack the hot-water bottles and extra blankets,' Tate said, smiling.

'And scarves *and* thick coats *and* sweatshirts,' Emma grinned.

'It'll be good for us to get away.'

'Even if we come back with pneumonia?'

'Yeah.'

They both laughed.

Emma stood up, her back still to her husband, his hands still kneading the flesh on her shoulders, pushing the towelling robe off. He slid his right hand up inside her T-shirt and cupped her breast, feeling the stiffness of her nipple against the pad of his thumb. Seconds later, his left hand also found its way beneath the flimsy material to her other breast.

Emma turned, looking into Tate's eyes as he continued to gently squeeze and stroke her breasts. Her breathing became more ragged. She ran both her hands down his

15

bare back, sliding them inside the waistband of his jogging bottoms then further down to play her well-manicured nails across his buttocks.

They kissed, Tate moving even closer to her as one of his hands left her breast and glided lightly over her stomach down to the inside of her thigh. He trailed his fingertips across the smooth flesh there.

Emma's right hand slid to his groin and she closed her slender fingers around his rapidly stiffening penis.

'*Now* do you think we should go back to bed?' Tate whispered as he kissed the lobe of her ear.

'What's wrong with here?' she asked, squeezing his erection and playing her thumb over the bulbous head.

'It's cold in here,' he said, smiling.

'We'll warm up,' she told him, stroking his cheek with one hand.

She shrugged off the towelling robe completely and let it fall on to the kitchen table behind her. The chill in the room was forgotten. She felt only a wonderful warmth that seemed to increase with each urgent touch of her husband's fingers.

His left hand was still clasped around her right breast but the fingers of his other hand now found their way to the moist warmth between her thighs. She drew in a ragged breath as he brushed the teasing digits around her swollen clitoris and, in turn, she began to move her hand firmly up and down his shaft.

Emma moved back slightly, raising her slim bottom on to the kitchen table. She lay back, parting her legs slightly.

Tate knelt between her slender thighs then moved his head forward and kissed her moist sex, tasting her. He felt her body shudder as his tongue flicked gently along the outline of her tumescent cleft.

She murmured approvingly as he worked his tongue expertly over her clitoris and her labia, pushing her closer and closer to the release she sought.

Tate finally stood up, the tip of his erection touching her wetness. She looked imploringly at him and nodded almost imperceptibly, closing her eyes in delight as he pushed easily into her. Immediately he began to thrust slowly and rhythmically and Emma locked her legs around the small of his back to pull him further inside.

Her pleasure built rapidly and she looked up to see that Tate's face was contorted as he drew nearer his own climax.

Waves of pleasure swept over her and she arched her back, gasping loudly as she reached her peak. He was moments behind her, his liquid warmth filling her.

She pulled him towards her and kissed him. 'I love you,' she whispered breathlessly.

He planted small kisses on her forehead, the tip of her nose, then her mouth.

'And I love you too,' he told her.

They remained locked together for what seemed an age, as if reluctant to be parted. Welded, by their mutual pleasure, into one.

'*Now* it's time for bed,' she smiled.

'And no more bad dreams,' he whispered.

Emma hoped he was right.

5

Catherine Pearce looked down at the note before her. Read it and reread it.

There were tear stains on the paper near the bottom.

She folded the single sheet and propped it up against the empty vase on her kitchen table, then she made her way slowly upstairs and began to pack.

The last thing she placed in the case was the bottle of Mogadon.

She had more than thirty of the tablets.

It would be plenty.

6

The morning brought grey skies and a steady spatter of raindrops on the windows.

Emma applied the last of her make-up then inspected her reflection in the full-length bathroom mirror. Grey sweater worn over jeans. She noticed a smudge of dust on one of her boots and wiped it away with an index finger. As she passed through the bedroom she picked up her leather jacket from the bed then closed the bedroom door tightly behind her and made her way towards the stairs.

She was in the process of descending when the door-bell rang.

'I'll get it,' she called, hurrying down into the hall and pulling open the door.

Joanne Morton smiled broadly as Emma greeted her. The two women embraced briefly.

'Nick said you'd be here dead on nine,' Emma chuckled.

'You know my bloody old man and his time keeping,' Jo said, following her friend into the hall. 'We've been up since seven. He reckons there could be a lot of traffic on the motorway.'

At thirty-two, she was a year younger than Emma. The copper and blonde streaks in her shoulder-length brown hair seemed to gleam. She was wearing a thick grey coat over tight black trousers and a long-sleeved blue shirt that bore the legend:

JESUS IS COMING; LOOK BUSY

She followed Emma into the kitchen.

'I only finished packing this morning,' Jo explained, glancing around as if it was the first time she'd ever been inside the house. 'Where's Nick?'

'He's nipped next door to leave a spare key with the neighbours. Just so that they can come in and pick up the mail. Stuff like that.'

'And their teenage son can nose around in your knicker drawer,' Jo grinned.

'As long as he washes them after he's used them.'

'You dirty cow,' laughed Jo.

'Morning, campers.'

Peter Morton's voice echoed through the hall.

'In here, Pete,' Emma called, smiling at Morton as he walked through. He crossed to Emma and kissed her lightly on one cheek.

'Hello, gorgeous,' he remarked, running appraising eyes over her. 'Come on, let's get going. We'll leave Nick here then I can have both of you to myself for the fortnight. You can share me. There's enough to go round.' He rubbed his hands together and leered at the two women.

'In your dreams,' Jo said, punching him on the arm.

'Whose piece-of-shit Volvo is that parked outside at this time of the morning?' Nick Tate called as he joined them.

'Piece of shit Volvo *Estate*, you ill-informed bastard,' Morton corrected him. He slapped Tate on the shoulder and smiled. 'All right, mate?'

Nick nodded then kissed Jo. 'I like the hair,' he said, flicking it with one finger.

'Thanks, Nick,' Jo acknowledged.

'For what it cost it ought to look good,' Morton added.

Emma glanced at her husband then forced a smile back into place. 'You get the cases in the car,' she instructed. 'I'll make sure everything's locked up.'

'Anything I can do to help?' Jo asked, watching as the two men carried the Samsonite suitcases out to the car and loaded them into the boot.

Emma checked that everything that needed to be was unplugged. Hurried around the light timer switches, checking once more that each was properly set, then she closed every door firmly behind her, ushered Jo outside and pressed the four digits on the alarm keypad.

'All done?' Jo asked, standing on the pavement as Emma locked the front door behind her.

Emma nodded. 'Let's go on holiday.'

7

The stench from the dustbin was appalling.

Lisa McQuillan wrinkled her nose as she stood in her back garden emptying potato peelings into the large receptacle. She wondered what had decayed inside the bin. The dustmen didn't call for another two days. Whatever lay at the bottom of the container would remain there putrefying until later in the week. A ripped and dirty plastic bag and the remains of a chicken carcases were spread around the small paved area near the bin. It looked as if next door's cat had been scratching around for scraps again. Filthy thing. On more than one occasion, Lisa had also found dead mice in the garden, killed by the obnoxious, moth-eaten ginger menace that her neighbour doted on.

Lisa could never understand the attraction of pets. They left hairs on the furniture. They brought mud into the house. They littered the garden with excrement. In her head she ran through a long list of how unhygienic domestic animals were. They smelt. Their food reeked. The list was endless.

Lisa was thankful that winter at least saved her from the added annoyance of flies. She would have been quite happy to forgo the pleasures of spring and summer just to avoid the constant presence of the vile insects. Now, at least, she was spared the added distraction of the six-legged, disease-carrying pests as she scraped the last of the potato peelings into the bin and put the lid back on, securing it with a large stone she picked up from the garden. Perhaps that would dissuade that cat from poking its nose in there again.

She retreated back inside the house, pulled off her rubber gloves and began washing her hands, running hot water over them. Slowly and meticulously, she worked soap over every square inch of flesh, barely noticing that her skin was beginning to turn pink from the heat of the water. Steam began to form clouds around her in the kitchen. Finally, satisfied that every last germ had been removed, she switched off the taps and dried her hands.

She reached up and scratched her head, inspecting beneath her nails when she'd finished.

Two of her friends had children at one of the local schools and they'd both complained of nits in the class. Lisa wondered with horror if she might have acquired some of the filthy insects while visiting their homes.

She scratched again and examined the matter beneath her nails.

Nothing there. No lice. No eggs. Nothing.

She washed her hands again, taking slightly longer this time.

Then the itching began. At the crown of her scalp, right on her hairline.

Lisa raked it with her nails and looked for any signs.

She swallowed hard.

There was something small and black beneath her index fingernail.

Lisa shuddered and stuck her hands beneath the water that was now flowing fast from the hot tap. She barely seemed to notice that it blistered her flesh.

She dried her hands again, aware once more of an infernal itching, again close to her hairline.

The housework would have to wait. A thin sheen of sweat had already slicked her face and neck. She hurried upstairs to wash her hair.

The itching continued.

8

'Stupid old bastard. Look at him.'

The BMW in front of Morton's Volvo stopped suddenly, brake lights flaring madly.

'I bet he only bought the fucking thing a week ago,' Morton rasped, flicking the windscreen wipers to double-speed as the rain began to fall even more heavily. 'What is it with old people and flash cars? They buy the bloody things then can't drive them. Have a look when we go past, I bet he's wearing a fucking hat as well.'

Morton accelerated, moved into the outside lane of the motorway and drew up alongside the BMW. He, Emma, Jo and Tate all turned to look at the driver of the other car.

They all cheered as they passed, noticing the checked cap sported by the man behind the wheel.

'Told you,' called Morton, speeding away.

They drove for some way in silence until Jo spoke.

'We should have rented this house in the summer,' she said. 'The village will be dead at this time of year.'

'Good,' said Morton. 'It'll be more relaxing.'

'It'll be bloody cold too,' Jo muttered.

'Jo, it's a luxury home, not a fucking wattle and daub

hut,' Morton corrected her. 'I know it's up north but even *they've* got electricity now, you know. *And* central heating. I could be wrong but I think this place *even* has an indoor toilet.' He shook his head dismissively.

Tate leant forwards slightly and adjusted the volume on the stereo.

'. . . *There's a secret place, I like to go . . .*'

The sound of guitars and drums thudded inside the Volvo.

'. . . *Everyone is there, but their face don't show . . .*'

'Turn it down, we can't talk with that on,' Jo protested.

'We're going to be talking to each other for the next two weeks,' Morton reminded her.

'. . . *If you step inside, you can't get out . . .*'

'Turn it down,' Emma echoed, grinning.

Tate reached forwards again, this time easing the volume to a barely audible level.

'That's better,' Emma told him.

'The house has got a CD player,' Jo said. 'And a video and DVD. I've brought a few films with me.'

'If you even attempt to put fucking *Love Actually* on that DVD at any time during the next two weeks you're sleeping outside,' Morton said.

'What did you bring?' Jo wanted to know.

'A bit of light relief,' Morton told her. '*Cum-guzzling Sluts* Part 2 and *Schoolgirl Orgy* Volume 12.'

'Seen them,' Tate yawned.

The car sped on up the motorway.

9

The car park of Leicester Forest East services was reasonably quiet. The rain had eased to a curtain of drizzle. Other visitors, some newly arrived, were still seated in their cars. More, returning from the buildings, were clambering back into their vehicles ready to resume their journeys. Emma looked around and wondered where they were all going.

Emma, Jo, Tate and Morton all stood briefly in the fine rain then sprinted for the main entrance.

Morton ran a hand through his hair then looked around for the signs to direct him to the toilets.

'Right, I'm off for a piss,' he announced. 'Can you get me a coffee and a cake or something? Anything that looks remotely edible.'

As he made to step away, Jo moved closer to him. 'Is that *all* you wanted to stop for?' she asked, her voice low, her expression fixed in hard lines.

'Just get the coffee,' he hissed, pulling away from her.

'I'll come with you,' Tate said, walking over to join him.

Emma and Jo wandered through to the nearest of the food service areas.

'It's going to be a great holiday if the weather's like *this* for two weeks,' Jo said, glancing out of the huge picture

27

windows that overlooked the motorway. Rain was coursing down the glass.

'At least we're getting away,' Emma countered. 'We'll be together for a couple of weeks. I know we've all been busy but we haven't spent more than a day or two together since you and Pete came back from New York.' She picked up a tray and slid it along the metal track in front of the counters.

The two women paused beside a chilled cabinet to regard the array of cakes and pastries inside. They selected one each for themselves, then something for their husbands.

Close to the till, Emma ordered two teas and two coffees. She paid then carried the tray towards the waiting tables, narrowly avoiding a collision with a small child who was hurtling round and round a table nearby.

'Bloody kids,' Jo sighed, also stepping out of the child's frantic path. She looked back over her shoulder disdainfully at the youngster. 'Why can't people keep their sprogs under control in public places?'

Emma set the tray down at the first available table and began to remove the cakes, cups and battered metal tea and coffee pots.

Jo lit up a cigarette and puffed on it.

'You all right?' Emma asked.

'I hate long drives.'

'We should be there in an hour or so, depending on the traffic. It's been heavy so far I know, but—'

'To be honest, I'm not sure I should have taken this time off work,' Jo cut in.

'It's a bit late for that now, isn't it, Jo? They've got a temp in until you get back, haven't they?'

'Yes, but it's not the same. You can easily replace a secretary for a couple of weeks but *I'm* a personal assistant. My boss is used to the way I work and I know how he likes things done.'

'You're just scared he'll find out you're not indispensable.'

Jo took another drag on her cigarette then chanced a sip of her coffee. She winced. 'That's bloody strong,' she muttered, adding more milk.

The child that had been dashing frenziedly around the table had finally stopped and was lolling back and forth on his chair. His mother pushed a glass of Coke towards him which he promptly knocked over.

Jo shook her head.

'Do you ever think about the one you lost?' Emma enquired, seeing that her friend's eyes were fixed, albeit contemptuously, on the child.

'Why dwell on it? That was more than eighteen months ago, Emma. *I* don't think about it. Why should *you*?'

She looked away from the child. 'What about you and Nick?' she wanted to know. 'Any plans?'

'Not at the moment. We've still got plenty of time.'

'Sod's law.'

Both women turned as they heard a familiar voice. Their husbands sat down beside them.

'What is?' Emma wanted to know as she poured Tate a cup of tea.

'I *always* get the cubicle where some bastard's had a curry the night before *and* can't be arsed to flush,' smiled Tate.

Emma hit him on the arm. 'That's disgusting, Nick,' she said, trying to sound outraged. 'We're about to eat.'

'Better now?' Jo asked, looking at Morton.

'Yes thanks,' he sniffed.

Jo eyed him irritably for a moment. They ate and drank in silence.

'Jo was just worrying that she'll be missed at work,' Emma said, disturbing the brief peace.

'Her boss'll definitely miss her,' Morton exclaimed. 'She

wears the shortest skirts in the firm.' He slid one hand under the table and caressed her thigh.

Emma and Tate laughed. Jo didn't join them. She kept her eyes fixed on her husband for a second longer then turned away from him slightly, pushing his hand from her thigh.

Morton shifted impatiently in his seat.

'Do you want me to drive the rest of the way, Pete?' Emma offered. 'Give you a bit of a rest?' She sipped her tea.

'He wouldn't trust you, Emma,' Jo sneered. 'He doesn't even like me driving it.'

Morton regarded his wife in silence for a moment then looked at Emma. 'You're not insured, Emma,' he smiled. 'So, thanks for asking, but sorry.' He drained what was left in his cup.

Morton glanced briefly at Jo who took a final drag on her cigarette then stubbed it out. She walked off, heading towards the shop. Morton waited a moment then followed her.

'You two go back to the car,' he called. 'We'll be there in a minute.' He handed her the keys.

Emma nodded.

'Jesus Christ, Nick,' she sighed, keeping her voice low. 'If those two keep on sniping at each other like they have been since we left London this is going to be a *great* holiday. It's unbearable. They're like different people to the ones we used to know. I can sort of understand it after what's happened but . . .'

'I know,' he said. 'But I'm sure it'll get better.'

'I hope you're right.'

'Come on,' he urged. The two of them paused for a second then sprinted through the drizzle towards the waiting Volvo.

Morton saw them clamber into the vehicle then he

walked up behind Jo, who was picking up some bars of chocolate.

'Ready?' he said, trying to sound cheerful.

'How many lines did you do while you were in the toilet, Pete?' she snapped.

He smiled.

'I asked you not to bring that shit with you,' she reminded him.

'Scared you'll want some too?'

'I don't need it like you do.'

'I don't need it. I like it. And you liked it too. Remember?'

'That was then.'

They reached the till. Jo put the chocolate on the counter.

'Pay for those,' she said flatly. 'I'm going back to the car.'

Morton held her gaze a second longer then watched as she walked off.

10

The teddy bear had been a present from one of the children in her group.

As she drove, every now and then, Catherine Pearce glanced at the small stuffed toy that she'd propped on the dashboard.

It looked back at her with its sightless glass eyes and more than once she saw her reflection in those blind orbs.

The little boy who'd given it to her would be at the nursery today. He would probably ask where she was.

Lovely little lad. Quiet. Polite.

She could picture him in her mind's eye as she guided the car down the motorway.

Tom.

Bright blond hair. Always smiling. Always polite. Not like some of the other children. They weren't like him.

She gripped the wheel more tightly and glanced across at the teddy once again.

Not like little Tom.

She was still staring at the toy when the lorry skidded into her path.

There was a terrible high-pitched screech of brakes. The smell of burning rubber filled the car.

She never had a chance.

11

'What are you going to photograph when we get to Derbyshire, Nick?' Jo asked.

'Whatever takes my fancy,' Tate told her. 'This isn't a working holiday.'

'I'm glad it isn't,' Emma echoed. 'I just want to try and relax for a couple of weeks.'

'It'll be great,' Morton offered. 'I've been looking forward to it ever since we booked it.'

'You could photograph me,' Jo said, running a hand exaggeratedly through her hair and licking her lips seductively. 'I've always fancied being a model.'

'One of the girls where I work did a bit of modelling,' Emma revealed. 'She did foot and leg work. She used to have her feet photographed. For shoe ads and stuff like that. No one ever saw her face.'

'I love a woman with sexy feet,' Morton mused, gazing wistfully out of the windscreen.

'You love *any* kind of woman, Pete,' Jo offered.

Morton ignored her comment.

'That was one of the things that first attracted me to Jo. She had a pair of those strappy sandals on and I thought how sexy her feet looked. That and her sparkling personality.'

'Yeah, you *always* go for personality, don't you, Pete?' Jo intoned.

Again their eyes met briefly.

The car was coming to the top of an incline now, close to cresting the rise it was climbing.

'What first attracted you to Emma, Nick?' Jo enquired.

'Her laugh,' Tate said.

'*You* said it was because I wasn't wearing a bra,' Emma grinned.

The car finally reached the top of the rise.

Morton hit the brakes.

'Oh my God,' Emma breathed, gazing out of the windscreen.

12

It was impossible to know how long ago the accident had happened.

There were two police cars parked on the hard shoulder, blue lights flashing. Another was stationary across the white line that separated the inside and middle lanes. There was an ambulance on the hard shoulder too, facing the oncoming traffic. Emma could hear sirens from further away. Other emergency vehicles were approaching the carnage from both directions.

All of them surveyed the destruction before them.

A lorry, portions of its nearside front tyre, cab and container scattered across the motorway like deathly confetti, had skewed across the road, smashed through the central reservation and jack-knifed. The damage couldn't have been more comprehensive if someone had put five pounds of explosive in the pulverised juggernaut.

Two cars on the northbound carriageway had hit it. Both were crushed almost beyond recognition. The metal of their bonnets was twisted and concertinaed like silver foil. There was even more devastation on the southbound side of the motorway.

There were dark skid marks across all three lanes going

north, where drivers had tried frantically to avoid each other. In most cases they had been successful. Except for the three battered vehicles now blocking the two inside lanes northbound.

Traffic on the southbound carriageway was jammed solid. One unmoving mass of metal. All three lanes gridlocked.

Policemen were moving about among the wreckage on both carriageways, some gesturing wildly at each other. More of them were gathered around the stricken lorry and pulverised cars.

'There's still someone inside that silver car,' Emma said softly, transfixed by the devastation.

Even from where they sat, all four of them could see that there was a figure trapped in the front seat of a Ford on the opposite side of the motorway. It was difficult to tell if it was a man or woman. Whoever it was, there seemed to be no way of getting them free of the wreckage.

'Looks like the lorry had a blow out,' Morton muttered.

Emma suddenly shuddered involuntarily and pointed at something on the scarred tarmac of the southbound carriageway. 'Oh God, look,' she said, her voice cracking.

There was a small teddy bear lying in the road.

As she lowered her window the smell of petrol and scorched rubber seemed to fill the car, carried on the breeze.

On the grass verge next to the hard shoulder, two figures had been laid out, covered by bright orange blankets.

'Nobody's going to walk away from that,' Morton said.

Jo was sitting quietly, gazing intently at the scene, her lips moving slightly as if she was reciting some inaudible litany to herself.

'Shall we see if there's anything we can do?' Emma croaked.

'Like what?' Morton wanted to know. 'Help scrape the poor bastards off the road?'

'There's nothing we can do, Em,' Tate echoed.

'Except sit here and wait until the motorway's cleared,' snapped Morton. 'We could be here all night.'

'Jesus Christ, Pete, is that all you can think about?' Jo barked, suddenly roused. 'People are dead and all you're worried about is being stuck in a fucking traffic jam!'

'Just leave it, both of you,' Tate interjected, raising a mediatory hand.

'Great,' sighed Morton. 'So we sit here watching them pull corpses out of there. The lane's clear on this side. Why the hell can't one of those coppers wave the traffic on, get it moving?'

Emma saw two more ambulances and a fire engine heading down the hard shoulder on the opposite carriageway. Seconds later, the unmistakable sound of rotor blades filled the air and she looked skyward. The air ambulance slowly descended.

Up ahead, several drivers and passengers from other waiting vehicles had clambered out on to the tarmac and were standing watching the grisly proceedings.

'That could have been us,' Emma insisted. 'They could have been putting us in one of those ambulances.'

'Thanks for that cheery thought, Emma,' said Morton sardonically.

A heavy silence filled the car.

13

The needle was lying on top of the polished wood of the bar.

Jack Howard saw it glinting in the light and wondered how it had got there.

Fallen from a handbag perhaps? Two women had been seated at the bar at lunchtime, sipping glasses of white wine. Howard remembered serving them himself. One of them could have dropped it.

He wondered why he hadn't noticed the needle before now. He'd wiped the bar down after closing but there'd been no sign of it then.

The thin spear of polished metal was about two inches long.

Howard stood gazing down at it for a moment before he finally picked it up with his thumb and forefinger and rolled it gently between the digits.

He held it there a second longer then gripped the blunt end and drew the needle slowly over the flesh on the back of his hand.

The veins there looked thick and swollen. Howard placed his hand, palm down, on the bar and continued to draw the needle point over the outline of the vessels with great gentleness.

He had seen many needles in the last two years. Mostly of the hypodermic variety. Most connected to drips inserted into various parts of his brother's body.

Howard looked up for a second, gazing into empty air, the image of his brother filling his mind.

The last time he'd visited him in the hospital in Derby he'd had needles in the crooks of both arms, the backs of his hands and even one in his leg. They each delivered fluid from the many bottles that surrounded his bed. Everything from saline to morphine. Another drug to prevent bedsores. Howard hadn't asked the names of the drugs. It didn't seem to matter what they were. Only that they kept his brother alive.

Or at least the semblance of his brother. Not the vital, energetic person he'd grown up with. Not any longer. The figure that occupied the bed in Derby Hospital was kept alive by the needles inserted in him. Sustained by the drugs and chemicals that seeped along clear tubes. They glistened like extra veins and arteries that hung from the drips all around him.

Howard hated those needles. Hated what his brother had become. What the accident had reduced him to.

He lifted the sewing needle he held in his own fingers and inspected the point once again.

It would penetrate flesh with ease.

Jack Howard drew it along his thumb, over the knuckles and to the nail. He held the point against the edge of his nail, teeth gritted.

He ran it back and forth then allowed the tip to touch the tender flesh beneath the nail, wincing at the slight pain he felt.

Was that what his brother felt?

Howard held the needle there a moment longer, applying a fraction more pressure, his hands shaking slightly.

Then he pushed.

The needle pierced the sensitive skin beneath his nail and he kept pushing, driving it deeper until the point was as deep as the quick of his nail. The outline of the metal looked dark under his thumbnail.

He held up his thumb, blood welling up around the needle like a red tear in a punctured eye.

More than half an inch of the thin steel shaft was buried beneath his thumbnail now. He pushed down on it a little harder.

14

The banks of black clouds that gathered threatened a downpour and also signalled the coming of night. Emma glanced at the bruised sky then at her watch, every joint seemed to be aching from the amount of time she'd spent inside the Volvo.

More than once all four of them had, like so many other drivers caught in the traffic jam, climbed out of the car to stretch cramped limbs. Standing in the freezing wind that blew across the motorway gazing at the activity before them or back towards the ever growing queue of vehicles.

'We've been sitting here for more than two hours,' Morton groaned, twisting his neck slowly from side to side, the beginnings of a headache gnawing at the base of his skull.

'Imagine how long the tailback is by now,' Tate offered, climbing out of the Volvo once again and peering back at the seemingly endless array of motionless vehicles. Bumper to bumper, their headlights stretched away as far as he could see.

Jo was leaning against one side of the car smoking a cigarette. She shivered as a particularly strong gust of wind whistled across the carriageway.

'I just want to get moving,' she said. 'Get away from here.'

'It won't be long now,' Tate told her with an air of certainty. He looked in the direction of the emergency vehicles. 'It looks as if they've nearly finished.'

Three large flatbed trucks and a crane had been used to remove the remains of the crashed vehicles. The victims had long since been taken to hospitals (and morgues) and the sky where the air ambulance had come and gone was now clear except for the scudding clouds.

Emma accepted a cigarette that Jo offered her.

Neither of the women spoke. They seemed drained. Unable or unwilling to do anything other than smoke.

Tate waited a moment then wandered back to the driver's side and peered in.

Morton was seated behind the steering wheel, eyes fixed on a tall policeman who had arrived at the scene earlier on a motorbike. It was he who now spoke something into a radio fixed to his jacket.

Other uniformed men moved across to the coned-off area that blocked the outside and middle lanes of the motorway. The police Land Rover that had been parked across the inside lane moved slowly towards the hard shoulder.

'Hey, get in,' Morton called. 'I think they're letting us go.'

As the others clambered back into the Volvo they saw the policeman removing the plastic cones from the outside and middle lanes. One of the uniformed men was waving the traffic on the northbound carriageway forwards. The vehicles at the front of the queue started their engines and began to move off.

Morton followed, gradually building up speed when he could.

'Thank Christ,' he murmured under his breath.

Not much else was said for the next hour.

15

Adam Wilby stood outside the bedroom door for a moment, the scent of soapy water from the bowl he carried catching in his nostrils.

He stood there for what seemed like an eternity (*Trying to find the courage to enter? Had it come to that?*) then gently pushed the door and walked in.

No point in knocking.

Wilby stood at the bottom of the bed and looked at the motionless form of his wife lying before him.

She was sleeping. At any rate her eyes were closed.

Open or closed. What was the difference?

There was a thin string of mucus dribbling from one corner of her mouth. Wilby put down the bowl of water, leant close and wiped the clear fluid away with his hand-kerchief.

She stirred slightly and looked at him and he smiled at her. She was still beautiful.

His Rachel. His wife. His love.

The accident had done nothing to distort her perfectly formed features. All the damage was *inside*.

The massive destruction suffered by portions of her brain that had reduced her to a helpless parody of her former self. The rending of three of her cervical vertebrae that had made all but the most rudimentary movement virtually impossible.

At thirty-two, she was incapable of walking more than four steps unaided. Powerless to feed herself. And yet she was still *his*. Still the woman he had fallen in love with. The one he had lusted after in the beginning.

And still did now.

He tried to drive the thought from his mind as he gently pulled back the sheet to uncover her. He saw her looking at him with those blank eyes. Saw himself reflected in pupils as dead as those of a stuffed toy.

Wilby took the flannel from the bowl, wrung it out and wiped it gently across her face. He did the same around her neck then he paused for a second before undoing the bow at the front of her nightdress. He pulled the garment open and looked down at her body as he had done so many times in the past. Before *and* after the accident.

He held the flannel in one shaking hand and lovingly wiped her right breast, working the damp material around her nipple, his eyes fixed on that pink bud. It stiffened, he assumed, from the slight chill in the air. It had happened before.

A reflex.

Wilby moved to the other breast and repeated the procedure, aware of the growing erection pushing against his jeans.

She was staring at the ceiling, no emotion on her face.

A little more saliva trickled from the corner of her mouth.

He wiped it away before wringing out the flannel once again and drawing it down over her belly towards the triangle of tightly curled hair between her legs.

He gently pushed her legs apart and washed her labia, the throbbing of his penis now almost unbearable.

Wilby looked again at her face. As she exhaled, a bubble of air formed in the mucus on her lower lip.

He looked back at the fleshy folds of her vagina, moist with the warm water he had wiped over them. With infinite care he drew one index finger through the slippery warmth.

She's still yours. You still want her. No matter what. Is that what you're afraid of?

He felt a single tear roll down his cheek as he dried her, fastening her nightdress again, pulling the sheet back into place. He would finishing washing her later.

Wilby left the room quickly, closing the door behind him. He leant against the wooden partition, eyes screwed tightly shut.

He slid to the floor and wept.

16

The road that led towards the town of Roxton was a collection of bends and dips that cut through and across the countryside intrusively. In fact, in many places, it seemed as if nature herself was fighting back at the invasion of tarmac across her soil. Morton was forced to slow the car down to a crawl on several occasions, to negotiate particularly tortuous parts of the road.

Very little traffic seemed to be coming in the opposite direction and they counted fewer than half a dozen vehicles travelling away from the town and the area surrounding it.

'How do they make a living around here?' Jo wondered, gazing out of the side window.

'Farming, I suppose,' Tate answered.

'Perhaps they all work from home, like Pete,' Emma offered. 'A whole village full of website designers. That's a scary thought.' She smiled. 'Especially if they're all like Pete.'

'I bet they can all play the banjo,' Morton said.

'What's that supposed to mean?' Tate asked, smiling.

'Oh, come on, it's well known,' Morton insisted. 'Small communities like this, they're full of inbred families. It's like a hobby for them.'

'What's that got to do with banjos?' Jo wanted to know.

'*Deliverance*,' Tate told her. 'Remember the film? The kid that played the banjo was inbred.'

'And you reckon they'll be like that?' Jo said, prodding her husband in the back.

'Could be,' Morton mused. 'Big teeth. Crossed eyes. Difficulty forming coherent sentences. Knuckles dragging on the ground.'

'No,' Tate grinned. 'That's Geordies.'

Again the sound of laughter filled the car.

'It used to be a mining community,' Emma said. 'I was reading about it.' She fumbled in her handbag once again and pulled out a slim paperback. 'It's all in here. A guide to this part of the country. Roxton's in it. It tells you all about its history.'

'I didn't think there were mines this far south,' Morton mused.

'There's tin mines in Cornwall,' Jo interjected.

'Yeah, *tin*, not coal,' Morton contradicted. 'I think they mined lead around this area too.'

'The mine itself was about three or four miles away from the village, apparently,' Emma told them. 'We could go and have a look at it while we're here. If there's anything still standing.'

The others nodded agreeably.

It was in that split second that something ran into the road.

17

Morton stamped on the brake and knew immediately that he'd applied too much pressure.

On the rain-sodden road, the tyres tried to bite but couldn't. The Volvo skidded violently to one side, heading towards the low stone wall that skirted the road.

Lumps of granite seemed to loom up in the twin beams as the car left the tarmac and hurtled on to the grass verge that ran alongside it.

Morton twisted the wheel, teeth gritted, pumping the brake with his foot.

In the back, the two women both grabbed the seats in front of them, bracing themselves for what they felt would be an inevitable collision.

Tate pushed himself further back in his seat as the Volvo shot across the grass, mud spraying up behind it.

Morton turned the wheel once more, his left hand grabbing at the handbrake and wrenching it up.

The rear end of the Volvo swung round and banged into the stone wall with a sickening thud.

The entire vehicle reverberated with the impact but, to the relief of all inside, it had come to a halt a few feet from the wall it had hit. Morton switched off the engine.

'Fucking hell!'

'Everyone all right?' Tate asked anxiously, turning to look at the two women on the rear seat.

Jo nodded slowly.

'I'm OK,' Emma whispered, her eyes still tightly closed.

'Pete?' Tate continued.

'Yeah, I'm all right,' Morton told him, running a hand through his hair. 'What the fuck *was* that?'

'It must have been an animal of some kind,' Tate told him, opening the door.

'Where are you going?' Emma wanted to know.

'We'd better check if there's any damage to the car,' he replied, hauling himself out into the rain. He was joined a moment later by Morton.

Both men moved hurriedly in the driving rain, ducking down to inspect both sides of the car. Tate crouched and tried to see beneath it.

There was a large dent in the passenger side of the vehicle where it had hit the wall. The hubcap of the rear offside wheel had come loose and rolled through the mud at the roadside. He could see paint on the stone wall, some of which had been knocked down by the impact. There was smoke coming from the exhaust and Tate again crouched low on the wet earth to look more closely.

'There's some damage to the exhaust, Pete,' he said.

'How bad?' Morton wanted to know, wiping rain from his face.

'Hard to tell.'

Both men stood up, looking in the direction of the woods on the other side of the road, then Morton headed back towards the driver's side of the car and clambered in.

Tate waited a moment, his gaze still fixed on the thickly planted trees then he too climbed back into the Volvo.

Morton started the engine and guided the car back on

to the road. 'We'll have to get it looked at tomorrow.' He winced, rubbing his side.

He spun the wheel, mud spraying up behind the Volvo as he accelerated forwards.

18

Lisa McQuillan turned the immaculately clean and sparkling tap on the shower and stood watching the cascading water for a moment before undressing. She pulled on her bathrobe and fastened it around her slim waist, glancing at her reflection in the mirror as she turned.

She folded her clothes carefully then placed them in the large wicker basket in one corner of the spotless bathroom.

There was a clear plastic lining to the linen basket that Lisa had placed there herself shortly after purchasing the object. It was replaced every day during her rigorous cleaning ritual.

She padded back across to the shower and tested the temperature of the water with the back of her hand. Another moment or two and it would be warm enough for her to step beneath.

While she was waiting, Lisa looked back into the linen basket at the jeans, underwear and T-shirt she'd removed and decided there was no point in leaving them there overnight.

She stepped into her slippers, fished out the laundry and hurried downstairs to the washing machine.

Lisa smiled to herself. By the time she was out of the shower, the washing would be done.

Two birds with one stone.

It would give her some extra time as well. She had decided to wipe down the kitchen worktops again before settling down for the night. And, she thought, it wouldn't hurt just to run the duster over the living room surfaces too. Perhaps just hurry around with the hoover too? They were the two rooms she used the most. They were where the dirt collected most readily.

She made her way back upstairs, checked the shower temperature once more and shrugged off her robe, stepping beneath the cleansing spray.

The water soaked her hair and splashed over her body and she smiled as she felt it on her skin.

She swallowed hard when the itching on her scalp began once more.

Lisa reached for her shampoo and squirted some out on to her palms. She massaged it into her hair, rubbing particularly hard at the crown of her scalp where the maddening itch was most prevalent.

It wouldn't stop.

She rubbed harder, her heart beating a little faster.

Nits. It had to be nits.

Lisa gouged one perfectly manicured fingernail into her scalp and dragged it back and forth with such force she winced, but she continued until the maddening itch subsided a little.

The suds from the shampoo dropped in white blobs around her feet and she continued to scrub away at her scalp.

She adjusted the temperature with one hand, easing the heat of the water up.

The hot water would kill the nits.

And still she scratched relentlessly at her scalp.

Even when the water around her feet began to turn red. She barely noticed the blood that was running down

52

her face, spots of it hitting the pristine whiteness of the shower tiles and flowering scarlet before it was washed away.

Lisa continued to tear at her scalp.

Blood continued to rain down around her feet.

But at least the itching was subsiding.

She looked at the nails of one hand and wondered for fleeting seconds what the translucent slivers of matter were hanging from beneath her fingernails.

The realisation that it was lacerated skin from her torn scalp didn't matter to her.

She continued to scratch.

Jason Skelson sat naked on his bed, the magazine open before him.

The girl in the picture had her legs open, two fingers pressed to the slippery lips of her vagina. Her eyes were half-closed in a look of desire, her mouth open. If she'd been in the room with him now that mouth would have been ready to accept his erection. To caress it with her tongue. To massage it with those pouting lips.

Only there was no erection.

Jason held his flaccid penis in his hand, looking down at it despairingly.

He squeezed his lifeless organ, turning the pages of the magazine with his free hand. Other girls stared out at him. All with that welcoming, beckoning look. Some on all fours. Others with their legs spread wide. One had a large dildo pushed into her vagina.

He felt nothing from his penis. No twitching. No tingling. All he felt, all he was aware of, was the ache in his groin.

The lump.

He picked up the magazine and hurled it to one side angrily.

Impotence. That was a symptom of cancer, wasn't it?

He looked down again at his penis, so soft and useless in his fist.

A lump. Impotence. Lack of sexual desire. The discomfort. He knew what was growing inside him. He knew.

And soon, others would know too.

He would prove it to them.

19

He could barely stand to look at his reflection.

George Wilby had washed and shaved with the same care as usual but, as was always the case, he had tried to prevent his gaze straying any lower than his neck.

He rubbed his back with one hand, cursing his rheumatism. The weather didn't help. Cold and damp always exacerbated the condition and the elements had been particularly harsh these past few weeks.

He made his way into his bedroom and stood in just his underpants, waiting to dress, knowing that the full-length mirror on his wardrobe door would allow him a view of his entire body should he choose to inspect it.

Wilby sucked in a deep breath and turned towards the mirror. Even after all these years (forty-two now, wasn't it?) he still had difficulty gazing at his torso and the marks upon it.

As if to gaze upon the flesh was to relive the memories of how it had come to be the way it was now.

Wilby felt sadness more than anything when he looked at his body. At the burns that had disfigured most of the flesh on his torso, upper arms, back and buttocks.

The skin was dark red in places, pink in others. As smooth

as glass where hair refused to grow upon it and had done ever since the day of the accident. How many times had they told him he was lucky to be alive? How many doctors had pored over him as he'd lain in that bed as a youth in his early twenties?

Their platitudes still rang in his ears to this day. The words they had used.

Grateful. Thankful. Lucky.

He touched the twisted, gnarled flesh on his chest and stomach with one index finger. Its texture reminded him of tree bark. The skin had contracted beneath the ferocity of the flames, scabs forming instantly over oozing blisters only to be stripped away again by more flames.

Wilby could remember the fire as if it had happened yesterday. He could still feel the excruciating agony as it had enveloped him. He recalled the way he had looked down at himself and watched himself burning. How his flesh had peeled off like old paint from a dilapidated wall.

He turned and looked at his back. If anything, the damage that had been wrought by the flames was even worse there. The fire had stripped away his flesh and muscle almost to the bone near his pelvis. The backs of his legs were similarly disfigured as far as his calves. Down to the ankle of his left leg.

It was a miracle he'd survived, they'd said.

Miracle had been another of their favourite words.

Wilby stood and stared at his body for a moment longer, at the welts, the twisted discoloured flesh and wasted muscle. Then, very slowly, he opened the door of his wardrobe and took out one of the shirts that hung there. Once it was on and tucked into his immaculately pressed trousers, there was no sign of the burns.

No one would know they were there apart from those who knew him and what he'd suffered.

He closed the wardrobe door and looked at himself now that he was dressed.

Those who knew.

He smiled wanly then began combing his thinning hair.

20

Roxton was built on a valley floor. Lightly wooded slopes rose gently to the north and south of it. To the east the ground approaching the uplands ascended at a sharper angle, the buildings there apparently clinging on none too confidently to the side of the escarpment. The west was a gentler incline but more thickly overgrown with trees.

The four occupants of the Volvo felt something akin to relief as the thick blackness of the road they had followed from the motorway finally gave way to the artificial twilight provided by street lamps and the many lights shining in the windows of the houses and shops they passed.

Emma spotted a couple of small pubs, a number of shops and a restaurant as they drove along the immaculately kept thoroughfares. Despite the driving rain, Roxton looked as if it had a welcoming feel.

As they drew closer to the centre of the town they all saw a large green.

'Anybody fancy stopping off for a quick drink?' Morton asked.

'Let's just get to the house, Pete,' Jo protested. 'Unpack, unwind a bit.'

'Just a thought,' her husband said almost apologetically.

'It's not a bad idea, Jo,' Tate added.

'Let's just keep going,' Jo insisted, looking at Emma as if for support.

Morton slowed down slightly. 'Come on now,' he said. 'I'm asking for a vote. Who's for stopping? Just a quick drink, get our bearings in this bloody rain before we push on for the house.'

'Fair enough,' Tate said.

Jo sighed.

'Emma,' Morton asked, 'what about you?'

'It can't hurt,' Emma said, looking at Jo.

'You're outvoted, Jo,' Morton said triumphantly. He steered the Volvo into the small car park outside the pub that bore the name The Snipe. He found a space with ease and switched off the engine.

'We're going to get soaked,' Jo said, gazing out at the rain.

'Then we'll have to run, won't we?' Morton said, pushing open his door slightly. 'Ready?' They all copied his action. Emma felt the cold droplets hitting her face as she peered out into the night.

'Go!' shouted Tate. He and the two women ran for the main door of the pub, Morton in hot pursuit. He stabbed the key behind him at the Volvo, locking it electronically.

They stumbled into the sheltered porch outside the main door.

'If they all stop talking and look at us hungrily, we leave,' said Tate, grinning.

'Agreed,' Morton smiled.

'Let's just get inside,' Emma urged. 'It's freezing out here.'

They hesitated a moment longer, then, led by Tate, walked into the pub.

The warmth enveloped them like welcoming arms.

Emma looked around the inside of The Snipe and immediately moved towards the roaring log fire blazing away in the hearth. Jo followed while Morton and Tate wandered across to the bar to get the drinks, nodding amiably at two younger men playing pool.

A couple in their forties were seated at one of the tables in an alcove near a window. Two more men, both in their thirties, were seated at the bar, one of them poring over a newspaper. He glanced briefly at the newcomers then returned to his paper.

There was a man sitting close to the fire, gazing distract-edly into the dancing flames. Emma guessed he was in his early sixties. Stocky but powerfully built. He looked comfortable in the high-backed leather chair. There was a large antique mantrap over the fireplace. On either side of it weapons were mounted. Long, broad-bladed cavalry sabres from a bygone age.

Emma and Jo moved nearer to the fire, aware that the older man in the leather chair was now looking at them.

'It's freezing out there,' Emma told him, as if he didn't already know.

'It's been like that for the last couple of days,' the man answered. 'We had some snow last weekend, mainly on high ground though.'

'We're not disturbing you, are we?' Emma asked, warming her hands.

'Help yourself, love,' the man smiled.

'Do you live in Roxton?' Emma queried, warming herself.

'Just down the road.' He nodded towards the main door of the pub as if the simple gesture would somehow illu-minate his abode for the two women. 'Lived here all my life.'

'We're from London,' Emma told him.

'I could tell from your accents.' He smiled. 'Are you staying in the town?'

'No. We've rented a house near here for a couple of

weeks,' Emma offered, rubbing a hand through her hair. 'It's called Springbank.'

'I know it well,' he told them. 'About three miles north of here. We get a lot of people coming and going from there but usually in the summer. It's a beautiful place. My son works as one of the gardeners there. He's up there two or three times a week in the spring and summer. His wife used to be one of the housekeepers before her accident.' He lowered his voice and gazed into the fire. 'A horse threw her. She suffered brain damage.'

'I'm so sorry,' said Emma quietly, a little taken aback by the man's candour.

'My son looks after her as best he can,' Wilby said, attempting a smile. 'Neighbours help out too and a nurse goes in a couple of times a week. But it's hard for him. She was only your age.' He took a sip of his drink then looked at each woman in turn. 'Sorry to go on. That's a habit some of us have in these parts. We'll talk to anyone as if we've known them all our lives. Bore them silly.'

Smiling, Emma introduced herself and Jo. The man rose quickly from his chair, more sprightly in movement than he'd looked in appearance. He shook hands with both of them.

'George Wilby,' he announced. 'Glad to meet you.'

He was about to sit again when Tate and Morton arrived carrying the drinks.

'This is Mr Wilby,' Emma explained by way of introduction.

'George,' he corrected her.

They completed the greetings then all sat down once more.

'Your wife says you're from London,' Wilby said, holding his drink in one large hand.

'Drove up today,' Tate told him.

'I never liked big cities much,' Wilby confessed. 'Always

too many folk with no time for each other, that's how *I* see them.'

'Is it true that everyone knows everyone else's business in a village?' Morton asked.

Wilby regarded him appraisingly for a moment. 'It depends whether that business is worth knowing or not,' Wilby told him flatly. He looked unblinkingly at Morton then took another sip of his drink. 'Besides, Roxton's too big to be a village. Only tourists call it that.'

The fire spat sharply to break the momentary silence and a log tumbled from the pile in the middle of the blaze. Wilby leant forwards, picked up a pair of brass tongs from the hearth and set the log back into place. Then he rubbed his hands together and sat down again.

'What do you do in the town, Mr Wilby?' Emma wanted to know.

'Well, *now* I do as little as I can get away with,' Wilby told her. 'Before I retired I worked up at the mine, like most men around here did when they were younger.'

'When did it close?' Emma enquired.

'About twenty years ago. Same time as most others did.'

'It must have hit the town pretty hard,' Tate said.

'Men who'd been in work all their lives were on the dole,' Wilby replied. 'The men around here had always worked that mine. Every generation knew there'd be a job waiting for them there when their time came. It was all anyone from Roxton knew. There were a few farms around about the place, but it was mining that kept us going. Men came from miles around to work that pit. And then,' he clicked his fingers, 'it was all over. Gone.'

'What did the locals do for work after it closed?' Tate asked.

'Lots of the younger people moved away to begin with. Older ones, like me, we just had to make the best of what there was left.'

'What did *you* do?' Emma asked.

'I got some work on one of the farms around here. Odd jobs here and there. And the Coal Board paid us off when the mine shut,' Wilby told her. 'Not much though. Not enough to compensate for a life spent more *under* the bloody ground than above it – excuse my French.' He finished his drink and set the glass down on the table next to him. 'Mind you, I was luckier than most.'

'Lucky in what way?' Morton asked.

'*I'm* still alive.'

Emma shuffled uncomfortably in her seat and moved nearer to her husband.

'For everyone that came out of that mine in reasonable health, there was another two with lung cancer or some-thing like it,' Wilby informed them. 'The women of the men who were killed in the accident got a pension of sorts.'

'Killed?' Emma said. 'How?'

'A week before the mine closed,' he said, still peering at the fire, 'there was an explosion. The roof of the tunnel we were working in collapsed. I was on that shift. So was *he*,' Wilby gestured towards the bar where a tall, thin-faced man with grey hair was polishing glasses as he chatted to a customer. 'Twenty-three men died that morning.'

'And you say it was an explosion?' Emma persisted.

'Build-up of gas, maybe. Nobody ever told us. No one ever knew for sure. Or if they did, they didn't say.' He inhaled almost painfully at the recollection.

'Dear God,' murmured Emma.

'God?' Wilby said, a slight edge to his voice. 'He was nowhere to be seen *that* bloody morning, believe me.'

'And they couldn't save any of the others?' breathed Emma.

'Twenty-seven men went down that morning, four of us came back up,' he told them. 'The mine's about a mile from the house you're renting. The buildings are still intact. Even the cage and the lift. The mechanism still works. Like a monument to the poor sods who were killed that day.'

There was another long silence, finally broken by Tate. 'Listen, we're going to have to get going,' he said, almost apologetically.

Morton nodded and also got to his feet. 'Yeah, long journey,' he added. 'Come on, girls.'

'It's nice to have met you,' Emma said as they turned to leave. 'Perhaps we'll see you around while we're here.'

'I've no doubt of that,' Wilby smiled. 'You enjoy your stay.'

He watched as the four of them stepped through the main doors of the pub, out into the covered entryway beyond.

Shortly afterwards he heard the car's engine burst to life.

'What did they want, George?'

George Wilby looked up to see the tall, thin-faced man looming over him.

'They're staying at Springbank for a couple of weeks,' Wilby told him, nodding gratefully as he saw that the tall man had brought him another whisky. He set it down on the table then seated himself opposite Wilby.

'Much appreciated, Jack,' Wilby said, sipping at the golden fluid.

Jack Howard, at fifty-nine, was two years younger than Wilby. He reached towards the poker propped in the hearth and stirred the logs around, watching as fresh flames sprang upwards.

'What had they got to say for themselves?' Howard enquired.

'Not much. They seem like most of the others who stay at the house. Money to burn, I shouldn't wonder.'

'What were you talking about?' Howard asked.

'The town. The mine.'

'What did you tell them?'

'No more than they needed to know. I mentioned the accident but that was all.'

Howard raised his eyebrows questioningly.

'What kind of bloody fool do you take me for?' Wilby snapped, glaring at his companion. 'What did you *think* I was going to tell them?'

'I just asked, George. Things slip out sometimes when you're talking. When *anyone's* talking.'

'Not about *that*,' Wilby rasped.

He turned and looked back at the fire. A log had again fallen into the hearth. Once more, the older man leant forwards to retrieve it.

This time he didn't use the tongs. He merely picked up the blazing lump of wood in one gnarled hand and replaced it gently in the middle of the fire.

As he sat back he wiped soot from his palm, his face wrinkled in pain. Some burnt flesh came away too.

The two men looked silently at one another for a moment longer then Howard got to his feet and wandered back towards the bar.

The fire continued to blaze in the grate.

21

It was peculiar.

There was no other word for it.

The pathologist sat gazing down at his notes and looked at what he'd written and, once again, the word popped into his mind.

Peculiar.

He might mention it when the police spoke to him again but, he reasoned, what possible relevance could it have?

All the victims of the accident on the M1 had been brought to the same hospital that afternoon. All the injured had been or were now being treated in operating rooms and wards. All the dead had been examined by himself and his companion.

The driver of the lorry (his body still covered by a rubber sheet on one of the metal slabs in the morgue) hadn't been to blame. No excess alcohol or drugs had been found in his system. His only failing in life was that he had suffered from Type B diabetes. But, as far as the pathologist had been able to ascertain, the man hadn't fallen asleep at the wheel or slipped into a diabetic coma.

Unfortunately, the accident had been caused by what the police were forced to call unforeseen eventualities.

A tyre had blown out and the lorry had gone out of control. Simple as that.

The pathologist sighed and glanced across at the other body still on a slab.

It was the woman who had been killed. Crushed to death by the impact of the lorry. She had suffered horrendous head and upper body injuries. If there had been a saving grace it was the fact that she had most certainly died instantly.

He ran his gaze over his report once more then got to his feet, that single word still sticking in his mind like a splinter in soft flesh.

Peculiar.

He crossed to the body of the woman and looked down at it, the silence inside the morgue broken only by the slow, insistent dripping of a tap from one of the nearby sinks.

The pathologist had found traces of Mogadon in her bloodstream, taken the night before, he had deduced.

But that wasn't what had struck him as peculiar.

It was perfectly understandable. She couldn't sleep. She took sleeping tablets. A simple equation. A bottle of tablets, complete with her name and address had been found in her handbag, along with plenty of other means of identifying her.

No. There was something else. Nothing sinister, just peculiar.

That word again.

He lifted her right hand and looked at the nails, or more particularly, at the dark matter beneath them.

It had been examined by his companion. Verified by one of the labs earlier in the day.

The pathologist gently lowered the hand then walked around the slab and inspected the other appendage. There was more of the dark matter beneath her nails there and again he wondered why or, more to the point, *how* it had come to be there.

Catherine Pearce, victim of a road traffic accident, had coal dust beneath the fingernails of both her hands.

22

'Look, you can see the house,' Emma said excitedly, pointing in the direction of an imposing-looking building at the end of the curved driveway. It had become visible in the glow of several security lights that had burst to life.

The whitewashed edifice was visible between the trees that grew on either side of the drive and a sense of anticipation began to spread among all four occupants of the car.

More security lights, some set on the walls themselves and others perched high on metal poles, flashed to life, illuminating the area in front of the house. Cold white light bathed the tarmac and glinted on the bonnet of the Volvo.

'Here at last,' grunted Morton, turning off the engine and clambering out.

The rain, he was delighted to note, had subsided into little more than drizzle.

Emma didn't seem bothered by the elements. She gazed up at the house then looked around at several small outbuildings.

Jo joined Emma and the two women walked towards the main door of the house.

'Let's have a look around tomorrow,' Tate called. 'We

can't see anything in the dark anyway. You two go in. We'll get the luggage.'

Jo fumbled in her handbag and found the key which she'd tucked, for extra security, inside a small envelope. There was a piece of paper attached to the key ring and it bore a four-digit number.

As she opened the front door, the air was filled with the sound of an alarm.

Jo slapped on the nearest light, checked the four digits scribbled on the piece of paper and jabbed the appropriate ones on the keypad nearby, switching off the alarm. Emma stepped into the hallway of the house and smiled broadly.

'It's beautiful,' she beamed, wiping her feet on the mat.

The two women gazed approvingly at their new surroundings then smiled at each other.

Tate walked in with the first of the cases, set it down and nodded. 'Very nice,' he said before disappearing back into the drive to collect more luggage.

Emma looked around her, still beaming. Immediately in front of them were two white painted doors. To the right was a third, firmly closed like the others. To their left, a narrow corridor revealed more closed doors hiding other rooms.

The staircase, which was also to the left of where they stood, rose to a galleried landing high above them, as yet still in darkness.

Tate walked back in with another case, followed by Morton, who dumped the two he was carrying and closed the front door behind him with a loud bang.

'The housekeeper must have been in earlier today to put the heating on,' Jo mused, touching one of the radiators.

'So, this is home for the next two weeks,' Tate said, looking round.

Emma smiled at him.

*　　*　　*

Of the four bedrooms in the house, the two main guest rooms both overlooked the valley that sloped away from the building.

As Emma finished unpacking, Tate walked through from the en suite bathroom, his toothbrush in his mouth. He crossed to the French windows that opened out on to a narrow balcony and unlocked them.

A cold wind swept into the room, carrying drizzle with it and he hastily closed the windows again.

Emma smiled, crossing to him, taking the toothbrush and wiping some white foam from his lips. 'Are we really going to drive back into Roxton to eat?' Emma asked.

'Pete and Jo think it's the best idea too. It's our first night. None of us want to be cooking, do we? A nice meal. Some drinks. Relax a bit. It'll be a good start to the holiday.'

Emma nodded.

There was a knock on the door.

'Come in,' Emma called.

Jo peered around the door then walked in.

'Ready?' she asked.

She hadn't bothered to change either. Merely applied fresh make-up.

'See you downstairs,' Tate called, picking up his wallet from the bedside table.

'Come on,' Emma murmured. 'Let's go.'

The two women walked out of the room together, then the four of them made their way out to the waiting car. Tate set the alarm and locked the front door behind them. The Volvo moved off in the direction of the road that led back to the town.

23

Samantha Ryan had no idea how long the baby had been crying. All she knew was that it *felt* like a long time.

Please stop.

She waited a moment longer then turned up the volume on the television.

The wailing of the child was still audible, even above the din of the TV.

Sam finally hauled herself out of her chair and stalked up the stairs, leaving the television blasting. As she reached the landing she slowed her pace, aware of the insistent cries of her baby.

Please stop.

For three weeks it had been like this. Ever since she'd returned from hospital. Neither of them had enjoyed a decent night's sleep since the little boy's birth. She was sure that the neighbours would complain eventually. The flat where she, her boyfriend and her son lived was above the antiques shop where she worked. If enough people complained she could lose the flat *and* her job.

And then what?

Sam was sure that there must be something wrong with the child. Something the hospital hadn't detected.

It wasn't natural.

If her boyfriend had been here to help her then it might have been easier to cope but he wasn't here, was he? No, he was working in Leeds for three days. Just like he'd been in Stockport before that. And Bury. And Wolverhampton. She'd already tried to phone him on his mobile but it had been switched off.

Where was he? Why wasn't he answering? Why couldn't he tell her how to shut the fucking baby up?

She paused on the landing, the strident shrieking of the child ringing in her ears.

'I'm coming,' she called, wiping a tear from her eye.

Just a little respite. Please.

'All right, Jack, Mummy's here,' she called as she walked into the small spare room that passed for a nursery. She crossed straight to the cot and lifted the child out.

The little boy's screams persisted.

'Ssshhh,' she said, with as much reassurance as she could manage. 'Are you hungry?'

You fed him an hour ago, he can't be hungry.

The child continued to shriek.

Sam held him closer to her.

The crying subsided slightly and she began walking back and forth, patting the little boy's back. His screaming became deep racking sobs as he gasped for breath.

She finally laid him on his changing mat and checked his nappy.

Clean.

He began crying again but stopped momentarily as she picked him up once again.

That glorious silence.

She felt another tear run hotly down her cheek.

Sam rubbed his back again, felt his body jerk slightly then she was all too aware of the hot vomit that drenched her neck and soaked into the material of her sweatshirt.

73

The child screamed even more loudly.

Sam began to cry uncontrollably.

'Be quiet,' she said, trying to hide the desperation in her voice.

More screaming.

'You'd better shut up,' she whimpered.

She put him down on the floor and knelt beside him, wiping vomit from his face with one hand.

'Jack. Be quiet.' Her voice rose in volume. 'Jack.'

He screamed and thrashed on the floor next to her.

There was a soft hissing sound. Liquid faeces voiding into a nappy.

'I'll change you,' Sam sobbed, undoing the nappy to reveal the reeking waste inside.

She looked down at the child's face and at the gently throbbing area at the front of his skull.

The little boy continued to scream.

Sam put her fingers on the fontanelle and felt the pulsing beneath.

'Jack, be quiet,' she shouted. 'Be quiet.'

Still he screamed.

'SHUT UP! What do you want me to do?' She looked into the child's eyes as if seeking an answer there.

She pushed harder against the pliant flesh on the crown of his little skull.

'Shut up,' she sobbed.

She pushed down with greater pressure, her whole body shaking madly.

Sam wondered how hard she would have to press before her fingers tore through the soft flesh and into her child's brain.

The smell of the open nappy filled her nostrils.

He continued to scream.

24

'I think we're the last ones,' Emma said, looking around the dining room of The George and Dragon to see that no other guests remained. She raised her wine glass and took a sip.

Morton held up the bottle. 'Anyone else?'

Jo pushed her glass towards him.

'Steady on, Jo,' he grinned. 'You know how you get when you've had too much to drink. We don't want to keep Emma and Nick awake all night, do we?'

'All night, Pete?' Jo quipped. 'I should be so lucky.'

The others laughed.

Morton looked up and saw that the young waitress who had served them was glancing across at their table. She was in her late teens, her shoulder-length brown hair tied in a loose pony-tail. The tight black trousers and immaculate white blouse that she wore accentuated her stunning figure and she walked with elegance and grace when she approached.

'Can I get you any desserts?' she asked, order pad at the ready. She looked at each of them in turn with her large green eyes.

'Just a coffee for me, please,' Emma announced.

The others ordered the same. Only Tate paused, considering the menu she'd handed him.

'I'm going to take a chance on the fudge cake, please,' he said, handing the menu back to the waitress. 'It's not *too* fattening, is it?'

'Why, are you on a diet?' she asked, smiling. Then she took the menu from him, turned and swept gracefully off in the direction of the kitchen.

'She's a pretty girl,' Emma noted, taking another sip of her wine.

'Nice to know I've made an impression,' Tate joked.

'Well, why *shouldn't* you, Nick?' Jo offered. 'You're a good-looking bloke.'

'Now I *know* she's pissed,' Morton interjected.

Jo shot him a steely glance.

The waitress returned a moment later with the coffees and Tate's cake which she set down carefully before him.

'I hope you like the cake,' she said, preparing to retreat once more. However, before she could, she was joined by a tall, powerfully built man in his fifties dressed in a charcoal-grey suit. He walked briskly across to the table and smiled warmly at the four diners.

'Was everything all right for you?' he asked.

They all burbled away about how good the meal had been and the man smiled even more broadly.

'That's what I like to hear,' he said. 'I won't have to sack the chef just yet then?'

'Is it your restaurant?' Emma enquired.

'Yes, it is,' the man told her. 'My name's Mark Jackson. This is my daughter, Lisa.' He nodded in the young woman's direction. 'Are you the people renting Springbank?'

'Does news always travel so fast around here?' Morton wanted to know.

'It's easy to spot new faces when you've lived here all

your life,' Jackson assured them. 'How long are you here for?'

'Two weeks,' Emma told him.

'Welcome to Roxton,' he said. 'I hope we'll see you in here again during your stay.'

'I'm sure you will,' Emma assured him. 'The food was excellent.'

'Thank you. It's a matter of knowing your customers,' Jackson said. 'Being aware of the kind of clientele you're going to get in. It'd be no good a restaurant like this serving nouvelle cuisine or anything too fancy. If people want *that* they'll go looking for it somewhere else.'

'Have you always been in the restaurant business?' Emma wanted to know.

'No. Before I took over this place I worked at the mine.'

'It's a bit of a strange career move, isn't it?' grunted Morton. 'Miner to maître d'.' He chuckled at his own joke.

'I'm a quick learner,' Jackson said flatly. 'And my wife had been in the catering business for ten years. She steered me right. She was the real brains behind all this.' He made an expansive gesture with his hand. 'Wasn't she, Lisa?'

Jackson's daughter lowered her gaze and nodded almost imperceptibly.

'Get her out here,' Morton said, reaching for the wine bottle. 'We'd like to congratulate her.'

'She died of a heart attack three years ago,' Jackson told them.

'Oh, Christ, I'm sorry,' Morton sighed.

'You weren't to know,' said Jackson. He sucked in a deep breath. 'I bought this place with the pay-off the Coal Board gave me. I've had it for almost fifteen years now. We're doing all right, aren't we?' He looked at Lisa who nodded and smiled before wandering off to clear some tables on the other side of the room. 'I've got two full-time staff and Lisa helps out in the dining room. I even do some of the preparation in the kitchen myself.'

'You say you worked down the mine?' Emma offered. 'We met someone in the pub earlier who did too.'

'Was it George Wilby by any chance?' Jackson enquired. 'He's a permanent fixture in that place is George.'

'He told us about that terrible accident that happened in the mine,' Emma continued.

Jackson shot her a steely glance. 'What did he tell you?' he snapped.

'About the explosion,' Emma informed him. 'The twenty-three men who were killed. He said only four got out that day.'

Jackson relaxed slightly. 'That's right,' he murmured reflectively. 'George and myself. Jack Howard, who runs The Snipe, and Adam Wood. *He's* got his own business in Roxton too. He sells antiques, paintings. That kind of thing. If you want to know anything about Roxton, ask Adam. He's a bit of a local historian. He paints too. He's got a studio at his house. Sells his paintings from the shop. He did most of the ones in here.'

'What about *that* one?' asked Emma, pointing at a large panoramic canvas depicting St George riding a magnificent white horse, battling a particularly repulsive-looking dragon while a dark-haired maiden looked on, chained to a tree.

Jackson smiled. 'He gave that to me when I took over the restaurant,' he informed them. 'Because of the name of the place, you know. I wanted something traditional.'

'It's very good,' Emma noted.

'It's a bit gory for a dining room,' Jo added, pointing at the gouts of blood that had been painted spraying from the dragon's shoulder.

'No one's ever complained before,' Jackson said, a little

sharply. He looked at each of them in turn then stepped away. 'I'll get your bill.'

'Do you think that's our cue to leave?' Tate asked.

Emma nodded but Morton hesitated.

'I haven't finished my coffee,' he protested.

'We'll have one when we get back to the house,' Jo told him. 'Come on.'

They all got to their feet and headed for the restaurant exit. Jackson was standing in the small lobby area clutching their bill.

Emma picked up her handbag and followed slowly behind, pausing again to look at the large painting of St George and the Dragon.

It wasn't, she decided, a dragon that the knight was fighting, but something more hideous. As she looked more closely she saw that where it should have had claws it sported what looked like misshapen human fingers. The head was wide but almost bulbous. Not long and saurian as was usually depicted. It was swollen. Replete with the kind of corruption that showed vividly in the rheumy eyes. In fact, the features of the monstrosity were more twisted humanoid than reptilian. The image peered back at her.

She looked too at the image of the maiden chained behind the beast.

Slim and slightly built. Brown hair. Green eyes and high cheekbones. The semi-naked figure bore a striking resemblance to Lisa Jackson.

Emma paused for a moment longer, wondering if the likeness had been intentional on the part of the artist. After all, from what Mark Jackson had said, he and the painter had worked together, been friends.

Would a friend paint such an alluring image of another's daughter? It didn't seem (what was the word?) *right.*

She looked again at the painting, struck by the expression on the face of the young girl. It was not fear displayed

79

on those finely chiselled features, but longing. The lips slightly parted, the eyes half-closed, the face flushed with a glow more akin to sexual desire.

Emma heard her name being called and finally walked out.

Hidden inside the kitchen, peering furtively through the slightly open door, Lisa Jackson watched her go.

25

Adam Wood had no idea how long he'd been working. Time seemed to have lost its meaning. It usually did when he was in his studio. Everything other than what he created with his paints seemed insignificant. Such was the case now. He knew it was late (well after midnight) but he didn't care.

All he was aware of was the smell of oil paint strong in his nostrils and the image that rested before him on the canvas.

Wood made two or three brushstrokes, then stepped back slightly to contemplate his work.

He reached for a cloth and wiped his hands, nodding approvingly as he looked at the painting.

It was a massive eye but contained within the black iris of the orb there were other, smaller images. Figures. Some were lying on the ground, others were running. All of them bore the same looks of horror and fear on their faces and Wood closed his eyes for a second, the vision rushing up again from his subconscious. A vision that had inspired this painting and one that would remain with him for as long as he lived.

He'd been young when it had happened. It seemed a

hundred years ago. And yet he could still remember the sights, the sounds and the smells from that day: the first lumps of earth and rock that had fallen from the roof of the tunnel, the warning shouts of other miners; shouts that had degenerated so quickly into screams of terror; and the smell of urine, sweat and blood that had mingled with the fusty, cloying stink of coal dust.

He remembered seeing the man next to him crushed beneath tons of falling rock. Wood could recall that no matter how fast he had tried to run, and no matter which direction he had chosen, the ceiling of the tunnel had come crashing down to block his escape.

They had told him later that the entire structure had caved in almost as far back as the lift shaft itself.

Wood also remembered them telling him how lucky he'd been to survive, pinned beneath tons of earth and stone, enveloped by a darkness so total it seemed to him that he had been blinded.

Apparently one of the pit props had prevented much of the debris from simply burying him alive. The earth and rock that had fallen around him had formed a kind of air pocket which had enabled him to breathe until he had been rescued.

Wood could still remember lying there in the dark, unable to see a hand in front of him, occasionally distracted by the calls of dying men. Of those who hadn't been as fortunate as he had.

He rubbed his eyes as if to wipe away the memory then he looked at his canvas again.

At that one huge eye he'd painted with its tortured, terrified souls at its centre.

The leading figure had his own face.

And it was that visage that bore the most intense look of fear.

Wood smiled to himself.

He reached forwards with one thumb and felt the damp oil paint against the pad of his flesh.

He rubbed his thumb backwards and forwards over the face of the figure, blurring it. Distorting it.

There was no fear there now.

Again he smiled.

26

'Do you want a hand with that, Emma?'

Emma turned her attention from the boiling kettle to see Morton standing in the kitchen doorway.

'You can carry a couple of these mugs,' she said, pouring hot water on to instant coffee.

Morton nodded and walked across to the worktop where she stood. 'Nick's still mucking about with the DVD player in the living room and Jo's watching him,' he said. 'What do you reckon to the house?' He watched as she spooned in sugar where required. He ran appraising eyes over her, his gaze drawn to her shapely legs.

'I think it's great,' she told him. 'It's a lovely place. I can't wait to have a good look round tomorrow. I feel too tired to go exploring now.'

'It's been a long day.' He took two of the mugs of coffee and made his way back towards the living room. Emma followed.

Tate was sitting cross-legged in front of the television screen pressing buttons on a remote control.

Emma sat down on the sofa next to Jo who had kicked off her shoes and drawn her legs up beneath her. There was a glass of red wine on the small coffee table beside her but she forsook that, momentarily, in favour of the coffee that Emma handed her.

'I'm going to bed when I've finished my coffee,' Emma announced. 'I'm shattered.'

'Good idea,' Jo chorused.

Tate also nodded and hit another button on the remote. He found a news programme.

Emma suddenly sat forwards, pointing at the TV screen and its flickering images.

'. . . *An accident on the M1 earlier today caused a thirty-mile tailback and led to traffic being delayed for up to twelve hours. The accident, involving a lorry and several cars—*'

'That's the one *we* saw,' Emma remarked, watching footage of the jammed traffic.

'. . . *The families of all those involved have been informed and police have released the names of those killed in the accident. The lorry driver, John Blackmoor, came from Wolverhampton and the owner of one of the cars involved, Catherine Pearce, was from Roxton in Derbyshire . . .*'

27

As he made his way up the stairs, Mark Jackson could hear the sound of the shower. He smiled as he heard Lisa singing quietly to herself as she washed.

Downstairs, everything was silent. Doors and windows locked and secured. Alarm set.

He'd be up again at six, helping to prepare for another day's business.

He paused momentarily outside the bathroom door then made his way across the landing towards his room. He glanced at the framed wedding photo of himself and his wife then, as he drew level with the picture, he touched the polished glass that covered her face.

Lisa had inherited her mother's good looks, he mused.
Lisa.

He stopped at the door of his daughter's room, the spurting water of the shower still clearly audible.

Jackson drew in a deep breath then pushed the bedroom door open and walked in.

The floorboards creaked loudly and he stood still for a moment, as if fearing that his intrusion might be detected.

There were posters on the walls. Actors and pop singers watched him silently as he moved slowly around the bed.

CDs were piled on the floor close to a small bedside unit that bore a stereo. Her mobile phone lay beside it.

On the door of the wardrobe there were several photos Blu-Tacked to the wood. A couple of Lisa and some of her friends. One of Lisa alone, looking stunning in a short black dress. Some taken in a photo booth. There was one of Lisa and her mother. Both smiling out at him.

Jackson opened the wardrobe door and looked in at the clothes hanging there. They smelt fresh. Newly washed. He reached out a hand to touch a sweatshirt that hung before him.

There were more photos on the inside of the wardrobe door. More of Lisa alone or with friends. Ticket stubs from concerts. The paraphernalia of a nineteen-year-old's life.

He turned back towards the bed where several stuffed toys sat sentinel on either side of the pillow. She had thrown her clothes on to the bed as well. Her uniform.

Her underwear.

Jackson's breathing was heavy now as he reached for the discarded bra and picked it up. He felt the material, rubbed his thumb over the cups, pausing at the centre where he knew her nipples had been.

His penis grew stiffer.

He put down the bra and reached for her knickers, glancing briefly across at the photo of her in her black dress. His daughter was smiling.

Jackson felt the hairs at the back of his neck rise. The aching in his groin became more intense. He rolled the flimsy material of the knickers between his fingertips then raised the crotch to his face and inhaled her scent, his eyes closed.

He pressed the gusset to his mouth and licked the musky cotton.

Down the hall he heard the shower being switched off.

He dropped his daughter's knickers back on to the bed and hurried out of her room and across the landing to his own where he closed the door, leaning against it.

Seconds later he heard her padding back from the bathroom, then the soft click as she shut her bedroom door behind her.

He remained against the door, trying to control his breathing, aware of the ache in his groin.

His eyes were closed tightly.

He could still taste her on his tongue.

28

Emma Tate moved closer to her husband and pressed her head against his chest.

'Shall I tell them to shut up?' he whispered, suppressing a laugh. 'If Jo doesn't keep it down half of Roxton will be complaining.'

'No,' Emma giggled, playfully jabbing him in the ribs. 'Anyway, it sounds like they're enjoying themselves too much. Don't stop them now.'

'As long as they don't take *too* much longer,' Tate insisted.

They both lay in the darkness, the sounds of pleasure drifting from the other main guest room amplified by the stillness inside the house.

'It sounds as if Pete can do *something* right,' Tate said into the darkness. 'I was beginning to wonder.'

'I know,' Emma sighed. 'I thought they might have, I don't know, calmed down when we got here.'

'I'm sure they will. I mean, that sounds like a good start.' He nodded in the direction of the sexual symphony and smiled. 'I was going to ask you if you fancied trying to keep *them* awake for a while,' Tate grinned.

They slid beneath the covers and huddled more closely together.

Outside, the mist was thickening as the temperature fell even further.

Peter Morton exhaled deeply and ran a hand through his hair. He lay back on the pillow, watching as his wife reached for the cigarettes on her bedside table and lit one.

She took a couple of drags then, balancing the Silk Cut on the edge of the ashtray, retrieved the half-empty glass of red wine next to it.

Morton ran appraising eyes over her as she drank. Her tousled hair, the reddish-pink flush that still coloured her neck and chest. She made no attempt to cover her breasts and she was aware that his roving gaze had settled on her still erect nipples.

'What are you thinking about?' Jo asked him, noticing his gaze upon her.

'Nothing. I was just looking.'

'Did you used to look at *her* like that when you'd finished?'

'Who?' he frowned.

'You know who, Pete. Don't be a smart-arse.'

Morton sighed. 'Where the hell did *that* come from?' he asked wearily. 'You haven't asked me anything about that for ages.'

'About your affair, you mean?'

'I'm going for a piss,' he told her, swinging himself out of bed.

Jo followed, standing at the half-open door puffing at her cigarette. 'So, what *did* you do after you'd finished fucking her?' she persisted. 'Cuddle up to her? Tell her how gorgeous she was?'

'We've been over this a hundred times, Jo. Wasn't that one of the reasons we went to marriage guidance or Relate or whatever the fuck it's called? So we could forget all about what happened? Learn to deal with it?' The toilet flushed and Morton emerged, brushing past her. 'Just let it go.'

'As easy as that?'

Morton crossed to the wardrobe and slid the door open. Jo watched him reach into a jacket pocket and remove a small envelope.

'And that's your way of coping?' she questioned, watching him spread the cocaine thinly on the dressing table nearby, shaping it into three neat lines.

'Each to his own,' he said, snorting the first line.

She climbed into bed and lay watching him as he finished the last line and wiped the granules of white powder from his nostril.

'I've got plenty more if you want some,' he said flatly.

'You take it, Pete. Take it *all* if you want to.'

She reached for the switch, clicked off the lamp and turned her back on him.

Darkness filled the room.

29

Emma stood with her arms crossed, watching the kettle, waiting for it to boil.

A watched pot never boils.

That was how the saying went, wasn't it? Some old wives' tale she remembered. Right up there with *Don't put all your eggs in one basket* and *Too many cooks spoil the broth*.

She smiled to herself, wondering why these weird archaic phrases had suddenly popped into her mind.

Still the kettle refused to boil.

Emma pulled her robe more tightly around her, shivering slightly. The heating in the house had switched off automatically three hours ago. She glanced at the wall clock on the other side of the large kitchen.

3.41 a.m.

She'd nodded off earlier but then woken suddenly from a dream that she couldn't remember. For more than thirty minutes she'd lain awake, finally slipping quietly out of bed to stare from the large windows in the bedroom down into the mist-shrouded valley below.

Emma couldn't remember how long she'd sat watching the gently swirling banks of fog as they were buffeted by the breeze but her vigil had done nothing to tire her and send her back to the warmth of the bed where her husband still slept.

Finally she had made her way downstairs, moving in darkness so she didn't disturb anyone else in the house. Now, she continued to watch the kettle, the fluorescents in the ceiling buzzing every now and then.

There was a sharp crack from behind her.

Emma spun round, startled by the noise.

It came again. This time not as loud, and she realised what it was. She reached for the drawstring on the window blind and pulled.

There was a laurel bush close to the kitchen window and a sudden gust of wind had sent its uppermost branches flapping at the glass.

She looked out at the bush, watching as the broad leaves danced at the prompting of the wind then she lowered the blind once more and returned her attention to the kettle.

Still not boiling.

She sighed impatiently and decided to fill her time more constructively. There were plates, cups and glasses in the sitting room that they hadn't bothered to clear away before retiring to bed. Emma padded out of the kitchen and across the hall towards the sitting room. As she passed the bottom of the stairs she glanced up, satisfied that she still hadn't disturbed anyone.

In the sitting room she collected as many glasses as she could carry and took them back to the kitchen where she placed them in the sink before returning for the plates. She stacked them and balanced the cups on top then took one last look around the large lounge before flicking off the lights and making her way back towards the kitchen.

It was as she stepped through the door that she felt the chill.

For a moment, Emma's breath caught in her throat.

The back door was wide open.

It swung lazily on its hinges, cold air rushing into the house like water through the holed hull of a ship.

Emma crossed hurriedly to it, pushing it shut, sliding the bolts back into place at the top and bottom of the door and locking it.

She was still wondering how the hell it had opened when her attention was caught by something on the floor near the back door.

Dark marks led across the tiles towards the hall.

As she looked more closely she saw that they were footprints.

The kettle bubbled away on the worktop, finally coming to the boil. Steam began to pour from its spout but Emma wasn't interested. Her attention was fixed on the single set of footprints.

She knelt and touched them with one shaking finger.

Wet earth. She could smell its musty odour. Emma got to her feet again and followed the footprints into the hall, seeing that they led towards the door beyond the lounge. There was another sitting room there. Larger, more ornate. She could see smears of mud around the door handle.

For a moment she considered shouting up to the others, alerting them to what she had found, but instead she crossed the hall slowly, eyes fixed on the door, stepping in the prints as if trying to retrace previous steps.

Her feet were exactly the same size as the footprints.

She put her hand on the dirty door handle and turned it, pushing open the partition and stepping into the room, slapping at the light switch.

There were three figures seated on the sofa in the larger lounge.

Her mother, her father and, between them, naked, a figure identical to herself.

Emma's eyes bulged madly in their sockets.

The figure that looked like her had one hand deep in

the riven torso of her father, fingers gently stroking the swollen and putrescent intestines. The other was buried to the wrist in the torn face of her mother, the digits moving beneath the flaccid skin, making it appear as if the features were undulating.

Emma screamed.

Her shrieks of terror woke everyone in the house.

30

George Wilby sat bolt upright, eyes wide and staring into the darkness of his small bedroom.

He sat motionless for a second then swung himself out of bed with unusual speed for a man of his years.

He hurried down the stairs to his hallway, paused a moment to suck in a couple of deep, excited breaths, then reached for the phone.

Jack Howard was already awake when the call came. Sitting in the bar of The Snipe, a small whisky before him, he walked to the phone behind the bar and grunted agreeably as he listened to the voice at the other end of the line. When he finally replaced the receiver there was a slight smile playing on his lips.

Mark Jackson wondered if the ringing phone had woken his daughter. He held the receiver to his ear.

'I'll call him now,' he said flatly, pressing two fingers down on the cradle, killing the incoming call.

He jabbed digits on the phone pad and heard a familiar voice at the other end. 'Adam, it's Mark.'

'I know why you're calling,' Adam Wood told him. 'The others know about it too, don't they?'

'Yes.'

'We'll meet tomorrow. At my house.'

There was a long pause finally broken by Wood. 'Do you know these people?' he enquired.

'I've met them,' Jackson told him.

'Tell me more tomorrow.' He hung up.

Jackson replaced the receiver, switched off the bedside lamp and lay back down, but sleep eluded him. It was as if someone had injected him with adrenalin. He lay on his back and stared through the darkness at the ceiling.

31

'That must have been one hell of a fucking nightmare last night.' Peter Morton dipped some bread into the yolk of his fried egg then bit into it.

Emma nodded and sipped her coffee. 'Yeah, it was,' she said. 'Sorry I woke you.'

'It wasn't your fault, Emma,' Jo said, reaching across the breakfast bar where they were all seated to squeeze her friend's hand.

'I've been having the same dream for months now,' she confessed. 'Always about my mum and dad. I thought the change of surroundings might have helped but . . .' She allowed the sentence to trail off and sipped more coffee.

'Did you manage to get back to sleep all right?' Jo wanted to know.

Emma nodded. 'Eventually,' she said, running a hand through her hair.

Outside, a thin curtain of rain was sweeping across the valley as it had been ever since they'd all clambered out of bed.

'I'd say let's all go out for a drive and help you forget about what happened last night but this looks like it's in for the day,' Tate said, getting up and peering out of the window.

'I need to get the car looked at,' Morton reminded him. 'See if there was any damage done that we couldn't see.'

'You and I can drive into Roxton, Pete. Find a garage,' said Tate, seating himself at the breakfast bar next to Emma. He slid an arm around her waist.

Morton nodded.

'What about you two?' he asked, looking at the women. 'What are you going to do with yourselves while we're gone?'

'We'll find something,' Jo shrugged. 'I don't feel much like going out in this anyway.'

'If it clears up we can always go for a walk.'

Jo nodded.

'Let's have dinner here tonight,' Emma suggested, smiling broadly.

'Great,' Morton agreed. 'What's the number of the take-away?'

'I mean Jo and I'll cook.'

'I thought we were supposed to be on holiday,' Jo murmured.

'All right, *I'll* cook,' Emma continued.

'I'm only joking,' Jo assured her. She looked at the two men. 'You two drive into Roxton, pick up what Emma and I need then you can bring it back. While we're preparing everything you can see to the car.'

32

'Has the nurse been in today, son?'

Adam Wilby nodded. 'She came this morning,' he said quietly. 'Gave Rachel a bed bath. Changed the sheets. A few other things.' He turned away from the motionless figure of his wife and stared distractedly out of the bedroom window.

George Wilby gazed down at his daughter-in-law, finally reaching out to touch her cheek softly with his hand.

'Come on,' he said, turning away and sliding an arm around his son's shoulder. 'Let's have that cup of tea you promised me.'

The two men made their way down the stairs to the kitchen where Wilby seated himself at the table, watching as his son filled the kettle and put milk and sugar into two mugs.

'I don't know how much more of this I can take, Dad,' Adam said without turning.

'How much of *what*?' Wilby wanted to know.

'This. Everything. Rachel. The whole bloody business.' He gripped the edge of the sink with both hands and lowered his head, his shoulders slack.

'You knew what it was going to be like, son,' Wilby told him.

'I know that, but it doesn't make it any easier.'

There was a long silence, finally broken by the older of the two men.

'So what do you want to do? Put her somewhere? A hospice?'

Adam Wilby shook his head. 'And let her waste away surrounded by strangers? No. I'll never do that.'

'Then what else *is* there, Adam?'

The younger man turned slowly to look at his father, his face pale.

'She's still my wife, Dad,' he said quietly. 'She's still the woman I fell in love with. I want her here with me but I'm scared.'

The older man sat up, his eyes suddenly more alert. 'What of?' he asked.

'Of what I *still* feel for her. Sometimes I wish the accident had damaged her face as well as her brain. Made her ugly. Made her repulsive. It would have been easier. But when I look at her I still want her. And I know that's wrong but I can't help myself. And it's getting to the stage where I can't hide those bloody feelings any more.'

He turned away as the kettle boiled, suddenly not wanting to face his father any longer.

The older man said nothing. He merely looked impassively at his son's broad back.

Adam Wilby placed a mug of tea in front of his father then sat down at the kitchen table opposite him.

'There's nothing wrong with what you're feeling, Adam,' Wilby told him.

'My wife's a brain-damaged vegetable and I still want to fuck her and you say there's nothing wrong!' There was anger in the words. He sipped at his tea, burning his lips on the hot liquid but not caring.

'And what did you want me to say to you, Adam? That you're sick? That you're a pervert for what you're thinking?

That you're wrong to be afraid of these feelings? Sorry, but I'm not going to do that. Perhaps you're right to be scared of these feelings, perhaps not. I don't know, I'm not a bloody psychiatrist. Like you said, she's still a beautiful woman. No one's saying you're wrong.'

Silence descended once again.

'God help me for saying this,' the younger man finally muttered. 'But perhaps it'd have been better if she'd died.'

'Don't ever say that, son.'

'This wasn't the way it was meant to be, Dad. You know that. I just don't know how much longer I can take it.'

George Wilby got to his feet and walked around the table to his son. He put a hand on his shoulder and squeezed hard. 'You'll get through it,' he said reassuringly. 'Somehow. You'll find a way. A way that's best for both of you.'

The younger man didn't answer.

The kitchen was silent again.

33

'I almost feel guilty doing this,' Emma smiled, sipping at her glass of wine.

'Don't,' Jo told her, raising her own glass in salute. 'We can't do anything until Pete and Nick get back anyway, so cheers.'

The two women drank.

Emma shifted her position on the sofa and looked around the sitting room. 'It's a beautiful house, isn't it?' she said.

Jo nodded in agreement.

'I wonder what the owner does for a living?' Emma murmured.

'Something that allows him to be away from Derbyshire in February,' Jo muttered, refilling her glass. 'I envy him for *that*.'

'Come on, Jo. At least it's a break. And it's good for the four of us to be together again.' She regarded her friend over the rim of her glass and smiled. 'You and Pete certainly sounded as if you were enjoying yourselves last night.'

Jo nodded slowly and ran a hand through her hair. 'I told Pete,' she protested.

'It wasn't Pete who was making the noise. It was you.'

Jo's smile faded and she swallowed more of her wine. 'Just making sure I've got my scent back on him,' she said venomously.

Emma regarded her warily for a moment.

'Do you want to talk about it?' she asked finally.

'About what happened when we were in the States? About Pete's affairs? Why not? What do you want to know? Do you think I'm stupid for staying with him? Do you think I should have thrown him out?'

'You did what you thought was right. I mean, the two of you are still together. It proves you're strong enough to get through it.'

'It proves we're both too bloody scared to make the break, Emma. That's all it proves.' She drank some more wine. 'He was doing it before we moved to the States.'

'Having affairs?' Emma asked, attempting to sound surprised and hoping that her show of ignorance was convincing. 'How did you find out?'

'He told me. When it all came out, he confessed to others. I think I suspected. I just buried my head in the sand, hoped he'd stop.'

'You must still love him though.'

'I'm not sure I ever *did*.' She drained what was left in her glass and refilled it again. 'Not the way you're *supposed* to love someone. You know, all that butterflies in the stomach, excited when you meet them crap. I never had that with Pete. I *needed* him. I still do. And now I hate myself for that.' She reached for a cigarette and lit it.

'You thought enough of him to get married.'

'Perhaps I just convinced myself that what I was feeling was love. Pete had a good job. We both did. He was ambitious and so was I. He understood what I wanted out of life. I needed a man who'd support me in what I did.

Back me up. He was prepared to do that. I *settled* for Pete.'

'Perhaps if you hadn't lost the child it would have brought you closer together.'

Jo laughed humourlessly. 'I didn't lose it, Emma,' she said flatly. 'I got rid of it. After I found out about his affair, I didn't want his child inside me. I didn't then and I don't now. Ever.'

'But Pete *wants* kids, doesn't he?'

'Then he can have them with one of his slags because he won't be having them with me.'

'Have you told him how you feel? About kids?'

'Perhaps I should, but then, if I did, he might leave and who would I have in my life then? He's better off not knowing.'

'Jo, if things are *that* bad between you then why stay together? You're only thirty-two. You've got plenty of time to find someone else if you want to. You can't go through life like that. It's not fair on you *or* Pete.'

'Why should I worry about being fair to him, Emma? Do you think he ever considered *me* when he was fucking around behind my back?' She regarded her friend evenly. 'What would *you* do if you found out Nick was having an affair?'

'I don't know. I'd want to know why, I suppose. I think it's impossible to say unless you're in that position.'

'So you can't ever really know what I'm feeling, can you?'

The two women regarded each other silently for a moment.

Emma felt as if she was looking at a stranger.

'It's about loss,' Jo continued quietly. 'Loss of trust. Loss of self-confidence.'

'I know about loss,' Emma said firmly. 'I know what it's

105

like to lose someone you love. I suppose that's something *you'll* never understand, Jo.'

Silence descended once more inside the large room. And outside, the rain hammered down even more heavily.

34

She heard the fly before she saw it.

Lisa McQuillan was instantly aware of the somnolent buzzing in the kitchen as she wiped down one of the gleaming worktops.

She spun round, her gaze flicking back and forth as she sought out the insect.

It landed on the kitchen table and wandered about in erratic circles for a moment before taking off again.

Lisa shuddered.

Filthy thing.

God alone knew where it had been. What kind of rotting waste it had been crawling over before it flew into her kitchen carrying its germs.

She watched it land on the lamp shade where it stroked its compound eyes with its front legs then remained still, as if it was watching her.

A fly in January. Where had it come from? They all died off in the winter, didn't they?

Lisa scratched her head involuntarily. The very sight of the loathsome insect was enough to make her feel uncomfortable.

There was a bowl of fruit on the worktop nearby. She

watched as the fly buzzed down from its perch on the lamp shade and settled on an apple.

Lisa grabbed the cloth she'd been using to wipe the sink and flicked it at the fly which promptly rose into the air again, buzzing loudly.

Ignoring the six-legged intruder for a moment, she picked up the apple it had landed on and hastily dropped it into the bin, then she returned her attention to the fly.

It had landed on the window sill above the sink. Its bloated blue-black body was even more noticeable against the gleaming white tiles. It remained there and, as she approached it, Lisa was surprised at how large it was. It was easily the size of a thumbnail. A corpulent monstrosity replete with dirt and disease.

She whacked at it with the cloth once more and, again, her aim was bad. The fly rose into the air and buzzed around her head.

Lisa backed away.

The insect flew straight at her and, for one terrible moment, it actually landed on her head. She let out a gasp of revulsion as she felt it touch her skin, scuttling quickly into her hair. She slapped at her own scalp, desperate to drive the fly away.

For interminable seconds she spun round frantically, not sure if the insect had flown off or not. She ran both hands through her hair, raked her scalp with her nails so hard that flesh came away.

Then the fly was airborne once again.

It flew away from her, bounced off the kitchen window and then disappeared out into the hall.

Lisa sucked in a deep breath and looked round at the window sill where the fly had been sitting. There was a small yellowish mark on the tile where it had been.

Excrement or vomit?

She knew that flies spewed fluid on to their food to liquidise it before consuming it.

She hurriedly wiped the yellow mark away with the cloth then binned it. That done, she spun the hot tap on and washed her hands thoroughly. As she dried them she looked around the kitchen. It would have to be cleaned again. There was no telling where the fly had been before she'd noticed it.

She scratched her head, repulsed by the fact that the fly had landed on her scalp and, even more intolerably for Lisa, crawled into her hair.

And she knew it was still in the house.

Somewhere.

35

'There's some damage to the exhaust, a bit of a dent just above the wheel arch and it needs some paint where you pranged it.'

Peter Morton nodded as he watched the mechanic wipe his hands on his oily overalls.

'It could have been a lot worse, Pete,' Nick Tate said.

'We can do the work if you want,' the mechanic continued, wiping his nose with the back of his hand and leaving a smear of oil on his top lip. 'It'll only take a day or two.'

'Thanks,' Morton murmured. 'I'll think about it. Have you got a card?'

The mechanic looked vague for a moment.

'With the garage number on?' Morton continued. 'So I can ring you and book the car in when I'm ready.'

'Oh, right, yeah, I'll go and get you one,' the younger man told him, heading off towards the glass-fronted office of MotorShop.

The garage was on the outskirts of Roxton, set among a number of small warehouses and industrial units, many of which were empty. Tate and Morton had driven past it on their way to the town earlier in the day. Now they sheltered beneath the glass canopy outside the reception area watching the rain that was still falling heavily, bouncing off the cars parked on the forecourt of the garage.

'It'll be cheaper than London,' Tate commented, taking a last drag on his cigarette and grinding it out beneath his foot.

Morton nodded.

The mechanic returned a moment later and pushed a business card in Morton's direction.

'The number's on there,' he said. 'And I've written my name on the back so you can ask for me when you want the work done.'

Morton turned the card; JASON SKELSON was written in biro.

'Thanks,' Morton said. 'I'll be in touch.' He pocketed the card and both men walked to the waiting Volvo, climbed in and drove off.

Jason Skelson watched them go then turned and headed back into the reception. He glanced at the young woman sitting there behind the desk, engrossed in a conversation. 'Just going to the toilet,' he told her, taking her thin smile as an acknowledgement.

As he entered the cubicle towards the back of the building, Jason winced at the pain from his groin. It seemed to be bearable when he was walking, but as soon as he stopped it returned with a vengeance.

Cancer. No fucking doubt.

He unfastened his overalls and dropped his jeans, seating himself as comfortably as he could on the toilet seat. The pain seemed to redouble.

For a second he closed his eyes, then he moved two fingers tentatively towards the part of his groin that ached so badly.

He pressed, feeling the lump that he knew was there.

111

The growth that was expanding daily within the muscle of his thigh, spreading through tissue that it devoured as its destructive cells multiplied.

Jason reached down to the pocket of his jeans and took out the Stanley knife. The blade glinted in the bright light of the single unshaded bulb that hung over the cubicle.

That's it. That's the kind of sharpness you need. It'll cut through flesh and muscle easily.

He hefted the blade before him, his hand shaking slightly, his breath ragged.

With infinite slowness he touched the needle-sharp point to his groin, just below his right testicle. It wouldn't take much pressure to cut. Three or four carefully placed incisions and he could expose the growth. Another two or three and he'd have it out.

Then they'd all believe him.

They'd *know* he'd been right all along.

He gripped the Stanley knife more tightly and prepared to cut.

The banging on the cubicle door made him drop the blade.

'Come on, Jason,' a voice called from the other side of the partition. 'What are you doing in there? Having a wank? Thinking about that new receptionist, are you?'

He heard chuckling as he grabbed the blade and slipped it back into the pocket of his jeans. He pulled them up quickly, refastened his overalls and flushed the toilet.

As he stepped outside he saw one of his colleagues disappearing back out into the reception area of the garage.

'Come on,' the same voice called.

Jason crossed to the sink and washed his hands then he splashed his face with water, standing motionless for a moment studying his reflection in the glass. When his breathing had slowed, he walked out.

His leg still hurt.

When he touched his pocket he could feel the Stanley knife inside.

36

Nick Tate put the last of the shopping into a plastic carrier bag and smiled expectantly at the cashier.

'One hundred and six pounds, thirty-four, please,' she told him.

'Jesus,' murmured Tate, reaching for a credit card.

'I told you we should have got a takeaway,' Morton offered, ensuring that the bottles of wine and spirits were standing carefully in the cardboard box he'd selected for them.

'Having a party, are you?' the cashier asked, swiping Tate's card.

'You could say that,' he told her.

There was a loud electronic beep and the cashier smiled apologetically. 'It won't accept your card, sir,' she said.

'Try this one,' muttered Tate, handing her another from his wallet.

The same electronic beep cut through the air.

'Here, let me,' Morton interrupted, passing over one of his own.

Tate could feel the colour burning his cheeks. He looked away from the cashier, reaching instead for several bags of shopping. He watched as Morton signed the customer copy and tucked it back into his pocket with the credit card. They thanked the cashier and wandered away from the checkout.

'Sorry about that, Pete,' Tate murmured. 'A couple of clients have been late with their payments. The bank obviously hasn't processed them yet.' The lie fell easily enough from his lips.

'Don't worry about it,' Morton said, the box of drink jammed beneath one arm. 'Let's get a coffee before we go back, shall we?' He nodded in the direction of the cafe area of the supermarket. There were half a dozen people sitting there. Two women watched them as they dumped their shopping at the table furthest away from the other customers. Tate bought coffee for them both and the two men sat down wearily.

'I couldn't do this shopping lark every fucking week,' Morton admitted.

Tate merely sipped at his coffee.

'Nick, tell me to mind my own business if you want,' Morton began. 'But is everything OK?'

'What do you mean?'

'With work and that. I mean, your photography business is still doing well, isn't it?'

'Yeah, absolutely fine. Why do you ask? If it's that shit with the credit cards . . .'

'I was only asking. It's just that Jo said something about Emma's job. Cut backs at that record company where she works and—'

'Everything's fine, Pete,' Tate said, a little too forcefully.

Morton shrugged. 'Sorry if I touched a nerve,' he declared.

'It's fine,' Tate repeated. 'Everything's great.'

The two men drank their coffee, the muzak and low buzz of conversation that drifted through the air the only accompaniments to their thoughts.

'Fuck it,' Tate grunted. 'Everything's *not* fine. Yeah, Emma's worried about losing her job and my business is dying on its arse. It has been for the last year or so. I keep telling Emma that everything's going to be all right, but I'm not sure if I'm trying to convince her or myself. I think she looks at you and Jo and it just rubs it in.'

'Sorry about that,' Morton said, a note of sarcasm in his voice.

'She sees what you've got and it reminds her of how good *we* used to have it. To tell you the truth, Pete, we're hanging on by our fucking fingernails at the moment and I can't see things getting any better. She's scared we're going to lose the house and I don't blame her.'

'Then why not be honest with her? Tell her *you're* scared too.'

'You're the last one to be talking about honesty, aren't you?'

'What the fuck's that supposed to mean?' snapped Morton.

'The reason you came back from the States. The other women.'

'What is this? Dear fucking Deirdre? Why not forget photography and take up being an agony aunt? If you're going to start lecturing me about what went on in New York you can save your fucking breath.'

'You were the one who brought up honesty, Pete. People who live in glass houses and all that shit.'

'Yeah, all right,' Morton said dismissively. 'Point taken.' He took another sip of his coffee. 'So, what *are* you going to do about your future?'

'What the hell *can* I do? I just have to hope that the work comes along. And quick. But I can't tell Emma what I'm feeling.'

'Being strong for both of you, eh?'

'You make it sound wrong.'

116

'I admire you for it, Nick. I'm not sure *I* could do it if I was in your position.'

'What about you and Jo?'

'How long have you got?'

'Two weeks. While we're all here together.'

Morton smiled but it never touched his eyes. 'We get by,' he said, pouring himself more coffee. 'But I still wonder what my life would be like without her. The first time I had the thought I felt guilty. That's passed now.'

'What thought?'

'I wondered what would happen if Jo died.'

37

Tate gaped at his friend and sat bolt upright.

He was about to say something when Morton continued, his voice low and conspiratorial.

'When we started discussing my affairs with the bloody therapist or counsellor or whatever the fuck they call themselves, *I* was the one that was angry. I hated Jo because *she'd* stopped me doing it. It took me a long time to get over that anger. To stop hating her.'

'Did you ever think about leaving her?'

'Never. I never loved any of the other women. Not the way I love Jo, but I *did* wonder what life would have been like without her, and it seemed easier to imagine her dead. If she'd been dead then I wouldn't have had to face all the arguing and the crying and the pain that *I'd* caused.'

Tate regarded his friend evenly.

'That sounds weird, I know,' Morton confessed. 'When she lost the baby that all changed. My *feelings* for her changed.'

'She lost the baby after she found out about your affair?' Tate asked.

'She might have lost it *because* of that. The stress and

pressure that I put on her. I blamed myself for her losing the baby. If I could change anything it'd be that.'

'You could have another one.'

'Perhaps we will. I want that as much as anything I've ever wanted in my life. It just hasn't happened yet.'

He drained what was left in his cup. 'Fucking hell,' he said, smiling. 'They must have put something in this coffee. We're sitting here pouring out our feelings like a couple of tarts. The girls will be wondering where we are.'

'They're probably doing exactly what *we've* been doing. Talking.'

The two men got to their feet, retrieved their shopping and headed out towards the Volvo. It was still raining but the morning's downpour had now eased to drizzle.

'Drive through the town on the way back, Pete,' Tate said, loading the shopping into the car. 'We might as well have a look around while we're here. Besides, there's something I want to do.'

'Come on, Jo. It's stopped raining.'

Emma stood at the back door of the house looking out over the large paved area behind it and the huge garden that lay beyond.

She glanced up at the sky, unperturbed by the banks of grey cloud still scudding threateningly across the heavens.

'It's still spitting,' Jo remarked.

'We won't even notice it. Come on, let's explore.'

'We've got two weeks to explore, Emma.'

Jo's words fell on deaf ears. Emma pulled on her coat and stepped out on to the patio. She walked across to the low stone wall that surrounded it. A wide staircase of granite steps led down to the well-manicured lawn and the garden stretched away even further towards a tall privet hedge. Emma could see trees waving beyond it. Behind the thick screen of poplars and firs the valley sloped upwards and away into gorse, heather and densely overgrown forest.

Jo hesitated a moment longer then joined her friend, still clutching her glass of red wine.

'It's cold out here,' she protested, fastening her own coat.

'No it isn't, it's bracing,' Emma corrected her, smiling.

Jo closed the back door, put her wine glass down on the large wooden table nearby and ventured across to join Emma who was already heading for the steps.

As she looked back she saw that French windows also opened out from the dining room on to the patio. She thought how wonderful the house must look in summertime, silhouetted against the sky with the sun sinking slow and bloody beneath the horizon.

For now it still looked suitably imposing. As if it had risen up out of the valley incline to dominate everything around it.

Both women pulled their jackets more tightly around them as they walked, greeted by a gust of chill wind.

'Are you sure you still want to explore?' Jo said, digging her hands in her pockets, the heels of her boots sinking into the gravel path that led away from the bottom of the stone steps.

Emma's answer was to wander a few paces ahead of her friend. She turned, smiled, then walked on. Jo caught up with her and they made their way along the path that turned at right angles to the left and right but also continued straight on, cutting a track through the wide lawn.

'By the look of it, the gardeners still come during the winter,' said Jo. 'The grass looks as if it was cut recently and everything looks tidy.'

'Didn't that old bloke in the pub say his son worked up here?'

'Who? Mr Wilby?'

'George, you mean,' Emma said, smiling with mock reproach.

They walked past flowerbeds and onwards towards the high privet hedge.

'He seemed friendly enough,' Emma noted. 'All the locals have so far. I suppose they see loads of people who rent this place coming and going during the year.'

'Didn't he say his daughter-in-law had worked here too, the one who'd been involved in an accident? Brain damage he said. Poor girl.'

'At least she's still alive.'

Emma spoke the words with such vehemence that Jo stopped walking momentarily and looked at her in surprise.

'Not like my parents,' Emma continued, gazing ahead of her. 'I'd put up with hospital visits or having to look after them, but I never got that choice. They were killed in the crash. They died on some stretch of fucking motorway a hundred miles away from me.'

Jo caught up with Emma and lifted a comforting hand but she hesitated as she went to place it on Emma's shoulder. Her friend continued walking, looking straight ahead.

'*I* never had the chance to say goodbye,' Emma continued venomously. 'Or sorry.'

'What did you have to be sorry for, Emma?'

It was Emma's turn to stop walking.

She stood motionless for a moment, the wind whipping around her, her hair blowing in the powerful gusts.

'I was never as close to them as I should have been,' she said quietly. 'I loved them and I know *they* loved *me*. But I never spent enough time with them. After my dad had a heart attack I swore that I'd ring them every week, visit them as often as I could, but as time passed it never happened. Now I miss them terribly but there's nothing I can do about it. You know that old saying about not knowing what you've got until it's gone? That's true. So true.' She wiped a tear from her cheek. 'The only place I can see them now is in my nightmares and I'm as incapable of helping them in those as I was in real life.'

'You shouldn't be so hard on yourself, Em.'

'Shouldn't I?' Emma snapped.

She dug in her pocket for her cigarettes and lit one, the wind almost blowing the lighter flame out.

'Everyone thinks that way when they lose a parent or someone they love,' Jo remarked. 'They always think there's more they could have done or things they should have said.'

'Really?' Emma said caustically. 'Well, in my case there *was* something I could have done. If it hadn't been for me, they'd still be alive.'

She stalked away.

Jo hesitated a moment then followed.

'They died in a car accident, Emma,' Jo said, hurrying to catch up with her friend. 'You weren't to blame for that.'

Emma finally slowed her pace. She sucked in a deep breath and gazed briefly up at the sky.

'The car they were driving when they were killed used to be mine,' she said quietly. 'I sold it to them.'

'That still doesn't make it your fault.'

'Sold it to them, Jo. I took two thousand pounds from them. From my own parents.' She ran a hand through her hair. 'They needed a car, *I* needed the money. The car should have been checked over more thoroughly before I sold it to them. But they trusted me.'

'Why shouldn't they?'

'I'd been complaining to Nick for weeks before that I didn't think the brakes were working properly. That they needed checking. He said he'd take it into a garage for me. Then my mum and dad told me they wanted a car. Just a runaround. They never went more than about ten miles at a time in their old car. Just shopping and visiting friends.'

She leant back against the patio wall. 'I sold them my car knowing the brakes were faulty, Jo. I should have warned them. It's just that I thought, with them only using the car for short runs, that the brakes would be all right.'

'Brakes fail on short trips too, you know,' Jo offered.

Emma nodded angrily. 'I know that,' she snapped. 'I know.'

'I still think you're wrong to blame yourself for their deaths.'

'If I'd got the brakes checked and fixed they'd still be alive.'

'You don't know that.'

Emma felt tears forming in her eyes. 'There isn't a day goes by that I don't feel guilty,' she announced. 'That I don't think about them. I don't think I'll ever be free of that guilt. And I don't think I deserve to be.'

38

'Swing it in there, Pete.'

Tate jabbed a finger in the direction of a parking space in the main street of Roxton.

Morton brought the Volvo to a halt outside a baker's shop, aware that Tate was gazing fixedly at the building next to it.

'And you're going to get what you want in there?' Morton asked.

'Let's go in and have a look around.'

Both men clambered out of the car and stood on the pavement for a moment looking at the frontage of the shop. A sign above the door announced quite simply: FINE ARTS AND CRAFTS.

Two stone gargoyles about three feet high squatted on either side of the shop's main entrance. One window was full of paintings, maps and photographs of Roxton and the surrounding countryside. The other bore two canvases displayed against white linen.

One showed a church with the sun sinking behind it. The subject of the other was difficult to discern at first glance, but as Tate stepped closer to the window he could see that it was a pair of coal-grimed hands cupped together to form a shaft within. There was a miner inside the shaft, in the distance, visible only by the light of the lamp he carried.

'Very regional,' Morton smiled.

Tate pushed the door and a bell sounded above him. It rang again when he closed it.

Both men looked around.

The shop was large but crammed to overflowing with every kind of tourist memento imaginable. A revolving stand of postcards stood near to one of the counters and Tate pulled a couple free and inspected them. Scenic shots of Roxton.

Morton moved to the counter on their right, his footsteps echoing on the bare wooden floor. He gazed down through the freshly polished glass at some of the many pieces of jewellery that were laid out there. Rings. Earrings. Brooches. Cufflinks. Most were made from the same dull-grey metal but there were more expensive pieces forged from gold and silver. Some had stones set into them.

The walls on both sides of the shop, however, were dominated by more paintings, ranging in size from cameos to one canvas that Tate guessed must have been a good twelve feet long.

Two thick velvet curtains at the back of the shop parted and a young woman emerged, smiled at the two men and took up position behind the left-hand counter, close to the till. The smell of joss sticks wafted in behind her.

Samantha Ryan regarded the two newcomers appraisingly for a moment then spoke. 'Hello,' she said wearily. 'Can I help you?'

'We're just browsing,' Tate told her. 'I'm looking for a gift for my wife.'

'Ahh, isn't that romantic?' Morton chided, joining him.

He looked at Samantha, noticing the dark rings beneath her eyes.

'What kind of thing were you looking for?' Sam asked almost robotically.

'I'll know when I see it,' Tate told her.

She nodded distractedly. 'If you want to see some of Mr Wood's other paintings, you can go through to the show-room,' she informed them, nodding in the direction of the curtains through which she'd appeared.

'Did he do the ones in here?' Tate asked.

'Yes. He makes some of the jewellery too. *And* he sculpts.'

'A man of many talents,' Morton murmured, looking down into the counter behind which Sam stood. 'He didn't make those too, did he?' He pointed at a couple of large mugs with a picture of a coal miner on it and the words 'WELCOME TO ROXTON' painted on it.

'No,' Sam told him. 'We buy those in. Like all the local trinkets. They're made in Roxton though. A couple of small businesses produce them.'

'I bet you weren't even born when the mine was oper-ating, were you?' Morton asked, inspecting some porcelain models of pit ponies.

'No,' she told him. 'But my grandad worked there.'

Tate wandered towards the back of the shop, stopping to look at one of the smaller paintings behind the counter.

'It must get boring around here for someone your age,' Morton noted, smiling at Sam.

The gesture was wasted on her.

'It depends what you want to do,' she told him flatly. 'There are clubs in the towns nearby. I've got a baby so I'm not interested in that kind of thing any more.' Her expression darkened as she spoke.

'Boy or girl?' Morton enquired.

'Boy. His name's Jack. My mum looks after him during the day while I work here.'

Thank God. It gets me away from him for a few hours. Better than nothing.

126

'A little boy,' Morton repeated. 'That's nice.'

Sam nodded unenthusiastically.

If only you knew.

Tate paused beside the curtains at the rear of the shop for a moment then pushed them apart and walked through.

'Pete,' he called from behind the thick velvet. 'Come and look at this.'

'I'm going to get that for Emma,' said Tate, pointing at one of the framed offerings in the back room of FINE ARTS AND CRAFTS.

Morton nodded, his attention attracted by the paintings in the room rather than by what Tate was gesturing towards.

Again, the size of the canvases varied greatly. As did their subject matter.

'How much is that, please?' Tate asked as Sam Ryan joined them.

He was pointing at a framed map that showed Roxton and its surrounding countryside.

Sam consulted the price tag on the back of the frame and told him.

Tate nodded, hoping that the credit card he selected would cover the cost.

'The house you're renting is on there.'

The voice made both men turn.

Adam Wood was sixty. A stocky man with bifocals and a bald head. He had a warm smile and nodded a greeting to both of his customers before watching as Sam took down the map and laid it on the counter.

'You own this shop,' Tate stated after the older man had introduced himself.

'For more than eighteen years,' Wood told them.

'Do you sell many of your paintings?' Tate enquired.

'Enough.'

'We saw the one you did for The George and Dragon,'

Tate continued. 'It was the guy who ran it who told us about your shop.'

'That was good of Mark, putting some business my way,' Wood smiled.

'Did he tell you that we were renting the house?' Morton wanted to know.

'He mentioned it.'

'Word travels fast in a small town, eh?' Morton continued.

Wood regarded him silently for a moment then turned his attention to the map that Sam was about to wrap.

'That's the house,' he said, pointing at a spot on the road leading out of Roxton.

'And the mine is just beyond it,' Tate noted, tapping the glass with one index finger.

'About a mile away, just over the ridge, through the woods at the back of the house. There's a path that runs past the back of the house which leads straight to the workings. All the buildings are still standing.'

'You were one of the ones who got out that day of the explosion,' Morton said, as if telling Wood something he didn't already know. 'One of the four.'

Wood nodded.

'I said to the guy in the restaurant that it seemed a weird change of job for *him* after being a miner,' Morton continued. 'You could say the same for *you*.'

'I was painting long before I opened this shop. When the mine closed I thought I'd try and sell some of my paintings. Along with a few other knick-knacks. We do all right, don't we, Sam?' He smiled at the young woman, who nodded and continued folding tissue paper around the map. 'It's busier during the summer months, but we get by.'

'Some of your subjects are a bit, what's the word, diverse?' Morton noted. 'What's that one of?'

The canvas showed an eighteenth-century battle scene.

Several dozen red-coated English troops were engaged in combat with some savage-looking Scots.

'During the Jacobite Rebellion in 1745, the Scottish army advanced into England as far as Derby,' Wood said, warming to his subject. 'Most of them turned back but a few bands of stragglers went their own way. Attacked some of the villages near here. Some got within five miles of Roxton before they were wiped out. That's what that is. The English troops slaughtered them all.'

'That's a cheerful subject for a painting,' Morton mused.

'Are all your paintings to do with Roxton and its history?' Tate interjected.

'Not *all* of them,' Wood told him. 'The other ones I keep at my house.'

'Not fit for public consumption?' Morton queried, a slight note of sarcasm in his voice.

Wood regarded him evenly. 'They're more personal,' he said.

The two men observed each other silently for a moment.

'Well, my wife will love this,' Tate offered, holding up the now gift-wrapped map. 'I'll send her in for a look around.'

'You do that,' Wood smiled. 'Tell her I'll be waiting.'

Tate nodded then he and Morton said their goodbyes and wandered out of the shop, Tate holding his gift firmly under one arm. He placed it carefully on the back seat of the car and Morton guided the Volvo out into the traffic again.

From inside the shop, Wood watched them go.

39

The grave had been dug earlier that morning in Roxton's cemetery. Regulation depth and width.

It yawned open like a hungry mouth, waiting to swallow what would be delivered into it the next day.

There was no headstone or marker of any kind as yet. Just a small metal plate set into the ground that bore a number.

Rain had collected in the bottom of the grave. It had formed small puddles that now rippled with each fresh droplet that fell.

Children hurrying by on their way home from school passed the cemetery and looked at the array of headstones and markers with curiosity. Some even waved at the vicar who wandered out of the church occasionally to inspect the grave, as if he feared it might have closed up. Collapsed in upon itself as the rain became heavier.

He had presided over a number of funerals since taking up his position as Roxton's priest. He loved the peacefulness of the town and the friendliness of its inhabitants. Most of them he knew by their first names.

That was why it saddened him when he had to speak words he knew only too well over one of their graves. He would speak those words the following day over the grave of Catherine Pearce.

There would be a respectable turnout of mourners. She had been a popular woman in Roxton. They would give her a good send off.

The vicar managed a smile at that thought and the knowledge that she was going to a better place. He would comfort her relatives with that if he could.

Many of the children she had cared for in her post at the nursery had already left sympathy cards at the church for her.

A good woman. She would be missed.

He looked down into the grave one last time then wandered back into the welcoming dryness of the church.

40

'Maybe you were right about Derbyshire in February,' Nick Tate said, looking out of the kitchen window and watching the rain sheeting down.

'No I wasn't,' Emma told him, slipping her arms around his waist. 'I'm glad we came.'

He turned, smiled and kissed her.

'And thanks for my present,' she said, nodding in the direction of the map.

'Well, we always used to collect mementos when we went somewhere, didn't we?'

She kissed him again then turned back towards one of the worktops where half a dozen bottles of wine and several bottles of spirits stood like well-regimented troops.

'Do you think you got enough drink?' Emma asked, smiling.

'We thought it was better to have too much than not enough.'

They both laughed.

'When Jo comes down I'll go and get changed,' Emma said.

Tate inhaled deeply. 'If it tastes as good as it smells it'll be great,' he offered.

'By the time we've drunk that booze, none of us will care what it tastes like,' Emma mused.

'You can't lay off that shit for even one fucking night!'

Jo looked angrily at her husband as he pressed an index finger to his right nostril and, with the left, hoovered up the line of cocaine he'd chopped on his bedside table.

'Give it a rest, Jo,' he said, wiping his nose. 'Are you going to lay off the drink for tonight? I don't think so.'

He chopped another line.

'What do you think Emma and Nick would say if they could see you?' she grunted.

'I doubt if they'd give a fuck.'

'It wouldn't matter to you if they did, would it?'

'No.' He sniffed then ducked and inhaled the next line. 'Didn't you tell Emma all about my problem this after-noon while you were talking about me?' Morton wanted to know.

'What makes you think we were talking about *you*?'

'Were you?'

'It's none of your business what we were talking about. That's typical of you, Pete. You think you're so fucking important that you're always the subject of every conver-sation. What about you and Nick? Are you telling me you didn't have a little chat while you were out?'

'Listen, let's just try and enjoy tonight, shall we? Let's just try and enjoy the rest of this fucking holiday.'

'Well, did you?'

'We talked, yeah. I've got to talk to someone, Jo.'

She looked at him irritably and checked her reflection in the mirror, fluffing her hair up with one hand.

'I'll be down in a minute,' Morton called.

Jo ignored him. She was already heading for the bedroom door.

41

George Wilby sat gazing into the fire as if hypnotised by the dancing flames. He finally moved his chair back slightly and took a hefty swig of his beer. He thought about moving, going and sitting by the bar so he could chat to some of the other regulars in The Snipe. Perhaps he'd watch the two younger men who were playing darts. He might even have a game himself. In the end he decided to stay where he was, the heat from the fire strong on his face.

'You all right there, George?'

The voice startled him and he turned to see Jack Howard standing beside him. The landlord looked at the older man then at the fire.

'I asked if you were all right,' he repeated.

'I'm fine, Jack.'

'Come and sit at the bar.'

Wilby shook his head. 'I'm all right here,' he insisted.

'Have it your own way then,' Howard said, turning to walk away.

'What time are we leaving?' Wilby said quickly, shooting out a hand to grab Howard's arm.

'In an hour or so. It'll take a bit longer to get to Adam's

house in this weather. I'll come and let you know when it's time.'

Wilby nodded and continued staring into the fire.

He watched her with the same unblinking stare with which a predator watches its prey.

Mark Jackson stood near the entrance to The George and Dragon watching his daughter as she moved gracefully from table to table.

Business was always slow in the winter and this particular night was worse than usual. He'd given the other two waitresses the night off and just the chef was working in the kitchen. They could cope.

And when the time came for him to leave, Jackson would allow his daughter to take over. To handle the one other reservation that was pencilled in for that evening. She was more than capable.

His daughter.

His Lisa.

She smiled at him as she disappeared into the kitchen to fetch an order.

He smiled back then glanced at his watch. Another fifteen minutes and he'd set off.

Adam Wood moved assuredly in the darkness.

Years of having worked below ground, he told himself. The blackness of the night was as welcoming as the sometimes impenetrable gloom he'd toiled in every day when working in the mine. He felt comfortable in it. That was why he lit only candles in his sitting room. Enough of them to bathe the lounge in a dull yellow light that cast long deep shadows. He had placed them on the mantelpiece, the sideboards, even atop the television.

When he was satisfied that the light was sufficient he made his way back upstairs to one of his spare rooms.

135

The contrast to downstairs couldn't have been more marked.

The upstairs room was illuminated by strip lights that flickered with such cold brilliance that Wood practically winced as he walked into his studio.

When he was working he needed light. He needed to be able to see every nuance of colour and texture, every detail of what he committed to canvas.

And so it was now.

He crossed to his easel and studied the portrait there.

The painting hadn't taken long. Less than a week from the beginning to the stage it was at now and in another hour or so it would be complete. The others would have arrived by then and he would show them.

Wood kept his eyes on the portrait for a second longer, then reached for a brush and set about completing his work.

42

'That's bullshit, Pete. Absolute bullshit.' Nick Tate shook his head dismissively and took another sip from his wine glass.

'Well, *you* tell me what kind of future there is for anybody who lives in Roxton,' Morton countered from the other side of the table. 'I'm talking about youngsters. Teenagers growing up.'

'It's a beautiful place,' Emma offered, glancing sideways at Morton.

'How do you know, you haven't even seen it yet,' Morton told her.

'I've seen enough of it. It's a lovely environment. The people are friendly.'

'Of course they are, it's in their fucking interest to be friendly,' Morton snapped. 'Their only source of income comes from tourists. If they piss off the visitors what the hell have they got left? When the mine was here it was a different matter, but that all changed when it closed down.'

'Some people are just naturally friendly, Pete,' Jo interjected. 'Not *everyone* has an ulterior motive.' She drained what was left in her glass, smiling at Tate as he refilled it for her. She reached out a hand and squeezed his arm.

'Whatever,' Morton said wearily. 'I'm just saying that it

must be fucking boring living in a place like Roxton if you're young. It's all right for the older people here, what do *they* care? I mean, they want it quiet, don't they? They're just counting down the time until they fucking die.' He sniggered. 'It's like God's waiting room.' He paused for a moment then took a mouthful of his dessert.

The dining room of the house was impressively large with its huge oak table and open fireplace (although the room, like the remainder of the house, was heated by radiators). There were Lalique vases and ornaments sparkling on the wooden mantelpiece and the gleaming antique furniture further enhanced the feeling of opulence. A huge chandelier hung above the dining table. The heavy curtains were drawn wide but there was nothing to see beyond the rain-spattered windows apart from the darkness of the night.

Emma had finished her own food, satisfied with what she and Jo had prepared and also delighted with the reaction from their husbands. Copious amounts of drink had been consumed and Emma already felt pleasantly light-headed. She noted, with a smile, that Jo and even Tate himself were slurring their words very slightly on occasion. She wished she'd put extra Alka-Seltzer on their shopping list. She had a feeling they were all going to need it the following morning. Nonetheless, she refilled her own glass and drank.

'So what you're saying, Pete,' she began, 'is that anyone living in a place like Roxton, or *any* small town anywhere in the country, should leave before they're twenty-five?'

'Earlier than that,' Morton told her. 'Yeah, it might be a nice place to grow up. It might be very picturesque. The people might be wonderful, but I don't see what small-town life has to offer anyone once they get to about twenty.'

'Offer them in what way?' Emma enquired. 'Are you talking about work prospects, stuff like that?'

'You're judging them by your own standards, Pete,' Tate

138

said. 'Just because *you'd* be bored living here doesn't mean that *they* are.'

'So you're telling me that the girl we saw this afternoon, the one who works in that antiques shop, is happy?'

'She seemed happy enough to me.'

'She's trapped and she knows it. And what makes it worse is that she can't do anything about it.'

'Trapped?' Tate said, smiling. 'That's a bit melodramatic. From what she said, her family live here. She's got a kid. Perhaps she's got everything she wants here.'

'Then she's got no ambition,' Morton said dismissively.

'In *your* opinion,' Tate countered. 'Like I said, you're judging the people who live here by your own standards.'

'Pete hasn't *got* any standards,' Jo said, looking across the table at her husband. 'Have you?'

'Shut up, Jo,' Morton said quietly. 'I'm trying to talk.'

'Don't tell me to shut up, you pompous bastard,' Jo rasped.

'All right, leave it,' hissed Morton, raising his hand.

'Like Nick said,' Emma cut in, anxious to defuse the situation, 'it's all a matter of opinion.' She glanced across at her husband who raised his eyebrows slightly.

'Yeah, and as long as everyone hears *Pete's* opinion then he's happy,' Jo countered.

'Why wouldn't you want to live in a place like Roxton, Pete?' Emma asked.

'I told you, because it's like a fucking morgue,' Morton snapped. 'What is there to do? Go down the pub. Go for a walk. Go for a drive. That's fine for a holiday but not for fifty-two weeks of the year. Not for the rest of your fucking life!'

'What do *we* do in a city that's so different?' Tate wanted to know. 'We go to work, we come home. Sometimes we go out at night. That's it. It's not so different.'

'But we had prospects when we were younger. The kids who live in Roxton have got nothing to look forward to apart from stagnation. Just like their parents before them. And *their* kids will be the same. They'll settle for this way of life instead of going out and finding something better.'

'Not everyone's like you, Pete,' Tate said. 'Not everyone's as driven. We all want to make something of ourselves, but it's not an obsession with everyone the way it is with you.'

'Perhaps *you* should learn a lesson from me, Nick. You wouldn't be in the shit financially then, would you?' Morton said flatly. 'If you had a bit more ambition.'

Tate eyed him furiously for a moment then downed what was left in his glass. 'Maybe *you're* the one who needs the lesson, Pete,' he rasped. 'How about one on how to consider other people's feelings?'

'Meaning?'

'You don't give a fuck who you hurt to get what you want.'

'That's right. Do you think I should be ashamed of that?'

'It depends who you're hurting,' Emma interjected.

'So what are you telling me, Emma?' Morton said, turning to face her. 'That you've never hurt anyone's feelings before?'

'Not knowingly,' she told him. 'I wouldn't.'

'What if it was unavoidable?' Morton persisted.

'There's ways of doing and saying things, Pete. There's ways of getting what you want without hurting other people's feelings,' Tate protested.

'Well come on, Jo,' Morton said, looking at his wife. 'You must have a view on this.'

'You know what *I* think,' Jo told him, her voice low.

'No I don't. At least, not all the time, but you think I should. You expect me to be a fucking mind reader. You never tell me and then you moan and say I don't consider your feelings.'

'I gave up waiting for you to do *that* years ago, Pete,' Jo sneered.

'Don't play the martyr, Jo. It doesn't suit you.'

'Which part *would* you like me to play then, Pete? The loving wife? The understanding partner? Or the whore? That'd be your favourite, wouldn't it?'

'How about the drunk? You seem to have got *that* one down to a T.'

Jo shot him a withering gaze then reached for the wine bottle and refilled her glass.

'Why the hell don't you just stop?'

The furious outburst came from Emma.

'Both of you.' She looked at Morton and Jo in turn, the knot of muscles at the side of her jaw pulsating angrily.

Morton refilled his glass and took a swig before meeting her gaze. 'Stop what, Emma?' he demanded.

'You know bloody well what I mean, Pete. This . . .' she snarled through clenched teeth '. . . what you're doing. What you're saying to each other.'

'We're having a conversation,' Morton told her. 'You and Nick must talk to each other like this or is your marriage too perfect for that?'

'At least we're not at each other's throats all the time,' she told him. 'You two have been digging at each other ever since we left London. Can't you just let it go for *one* night? Haven't you both been through enough pain? Why keep dragging it up all the time?'

'So you think that by avoiding our problems they'll go away, is that it?' Morton said. 'If we don't talk about them then everything'll be rosy? Just like it is for you and Nick? Only it's not rosy, is it, Emma?'

'That's enough, Pete,' Tate said challengingly.

'Come on, we're all friends, aren't we? You're not supposed to keep secrets from your friends. You know all about Jo and I. What's happened to us. Why don't you tell us your own secrets? Get them off your chests. Clear the air.'

141

'You're drunk, Pete,' Tate told his friend.

'We're *all* fucking drunk, Nick. Drink makes you lose your inhibitions, doesn't it? Well come on, have another JD and tell us all your little secrets.' He poured whisky into Tate's glass. 'You told me a few things over a fucking *coffee* this afternoon. You should be pouring your guts out after so much wine and half a bottle of JD.'

'There's nothing to tell,' Tate insisted.

'Come on, we've had a beautiful meal cooked by our wonderful wives, we're all pissed. Let's *really* talk. All of us.' Morton downed more drink and sat back in his chair. 'Come on, who wants to go first?' He looked slowly around the table at the others.

'Just shut up, Pete,' snarled Tate. 'For once in your life.'

'And what if I don't?' Morton smiled. 'Come on, what is there to be scared of? All I'm asking for is the truth, or is that what really scares you, Nick – honesty?'

'You wouldn't know honesty if it kicked you in the teeth,' rasped Tate.

'Pot and kettle, Nick,' Morton chided, reaching for an empty wine bottle. As the others watched he put it down on the table and spun it, chuckling to himself.

'How about it?' he said, smiling crookedly. 'A little game of truth or dare?'

'Grow up,' Tate hissed.

'Coward,' Morton proclaimed coldly.

Emma saw the colour drain from her husband's face and recognised the fury in his eyes.

'Come on then,' Tate snarled. 'You want to play, so go on, spin the fucking thing.'

'Nick, this is stupid,' Emma protested.

'Everything about this is stupid,' Tate countered, his gaze never leaving Morton. 'Coming here was a stupid idea. Trying to pick up our friendship where we left off was stupid.'

'Now you're talking, Nick,' Morton smiled. 'A bit of honesty at last.'

'Spin it,' Tate insisted. 'You're right, Pete. Friends shouldn't keep things from each other, should they?'

Morton spun the bottle again, clapping his hands together when the empty receptacle came to a stop with the top pointing at Tate. 'Go on, Nick,' he said. 'Tell us a secret.'

43

'What do you want to know?' Tate asked evenly.

Morton shrugged then stroked his chin thoughtfully.

'Come on, Pete,' Tate urged. 'You wanted to play the fucking game. Think of something.'

'What will you do if your business goes under?' Morton said flatly.

'It won't,' Tate told him. 'I won't let it.'

'You said this afternoon you were scared it *would*.'

'Did you really, Nick?' Emma wanted to know.

'He's protecting you, Emma,' Morton breathed. 'He's being your knight in shining armour. He's as scared as you but he won't admit it.'

'Is that true?' Emma asked her husband.

Tate nodded.

'Why didn't you tell me?' she persisted.

'Because he had to be pissed first,' Morton chided. 'Dutch courage. It's not easy admitting something like that.'

'Was it easy for *you* admitting your affairs to Jo?' Emma asked, looking pointedly at Morton.

'Once she'd found out there was no point in lying, was there?'

Jo grabbed the bottle and slammed it down on the table.

'I don't need to spin it,' she said angrily, her gaze fixed on her husband. 'Question to you, Pete. Would you fuck Emma if you got the chance?' All eyes turned in Morton's direction. 'If you knew you could get away with it. If you were certain that I'd never find out.'

'Yes,' said Morton without hesitation.

Jo looked first at her husband and then at Emma who blinked hard and ran a hand through her hair.

'I'll take that as a compliment, shall I?' she said falteringly.

'Your turn, Nick,' Jo said. 'Ask a question.'

'All right, Jo, would *you* fuck *me* if you could get away with it? Without Pete ever knowing?'

'Yeah,' she murmured.

'What are we waiting for then?' laughed Morton, standing up and unzipping his trousers. 'Let's go, Emma. Let's leave these two alone.'

'Sit down, Pete,' Tate said quietly.

'I want to ask Pete a question,' Emma interjected. 'What's the worst day of your life?'

'Getting deep and meaningful now, are we?' smiled Morton. 'Had enough of the sexual questions? Scared it might lead somewhere we don't want to go?'

'Answer the question,' Emma insisted.

Morton paused for a moment. 'Worst day?' he mused. 'Finding out that Jo had lost our baby,' he said, tapping his index finger on the rim of his glass.

'What about you, Jo?' Emma continued. 'What was the worst day of your life?'

'Finding out I was pregnant,' Jo told her.

'You mean, losing the baby,' Morton corrected her.

'No, I mean the day I found out I was going to *have* a fucking baby,' Jo responded.

Morton looked puzzled. He rubbed his eyes, as if clearing his vision would somehow uncloud his mind too.

'I never wanted that baby, Pete,' Jo said. 'That's why I got rid of it.'

'You had a miscarriage.'

'No, I had an abortion. I didn't want the kid. I'd just found out about your affair. The last thing I wanted inside me was your child. Do you blame me?'

Morton looked blankly at her, as if he was having trouble understanding what she had said.

An impenetrable silence filled the room.

Morton seemed unable to speak. Jo was unwilling to add words to her last statement and Emma and Tate merely sat silently.

'Nick,' Jo said, finally. 'Worst day of your life?'

'No, fuck that!' Morton interrupted. 'You come out with a revelation like that and you just want to carry on playing the game?'

'You were the one who wanted to play, Pete,' Tate reminded him, something akin to triumph in his tone. 'You wanted to hear the truth. You just heard it. What's wrong? Can't you take it?'

Again the awful silence filled the room.

Morton had slumped back in his seat as if he'd just taken a blow to the chin.

'Nick,' Jo continued. 'What about you? Worst day?'

Tate looked down at the tablecloth for a moment, then he slowly raised his head, his gaze directed beyond those in the dining room towards the darkness outside. 'The day I killed my father,' he said flatly.

44

Around the table all eyes focused on Tate who merely took another drink and then refilled his glass.

'Your dad died of an overdose,' Emma said. 'The coroner said he took too many of the wrong tablets by mistake. Because of his Alzheimer's.'

'He couldn't remember which day of the fucking week it was, let alone what medication he should be taking,' Tate replied. 'Yeah, he took an overdose. I know because I gave him the pills to take.'

'Why, Nick?' Emma asked quietly.

'Because there was nothing left for him, Emma. That's what he wanted. You know what he was like when we used to go and visit him. He couldn't even remember who *we* were half the time.' Tate ran his index finger slowly around the rim of his glass. 'But every now and then he'd have these . . . I don't know what you'd call them . . . moments of clarity. He'd be like he used to be. Those spells didn't last long but when they came it was like everything came flooding back to him. And the worst thing was that he understood what he'd become. What the disease had done to him. That was what he hated. *That's* why he wanted to die and that was why I agreed to help him.'

'And the police never suspected you?' Jo murmured.

'Why should they?' Tate told her. 'Like I said, most of the time he didn't know what he was doing. He would have taken cyanide if someone had given it to him in the same jar as his tablets. He took whatever was put in his hand.' Tate swallowed more Jack Daniel's.

'So you got away with murder,' Jo said flatly.

Tate shot her a venomous glance. 'I did what he wanted me to do,' he said through clenched teeth. 'What would *you* have done? Let him suffer? I didn't want to watch him like that. Shambling about like some kind of . . . child. I did it because I loved him.'

'And you've kept that to yourself for nine years?' Emma said quietly. 'Why didn't you tell me?'

'It's not the sort of thing that just crops up in conversation, is it? "Oh, by the way, love, I helped my dad commit suicide. What sort of day have *you* had?"' He downed more liquor. '*And* after what had happened to *your* parents in that car crash? How the hell could I tell you?'

'I had a right to know,' Emma said angrily. 'Your dad could have lived for another ten or fifteen years, Nick. You could have had that time *with* him.'

'*What* time, Emma? Another ten or fifteen years of watching him get worse? Watching him deteriorate week by week? I couldn't have taken that and *he* didn't want it.'

'At least you had that option,' she rasped. 'You had the chance to spend more time with him and you didn't take it. I wasn't even given the *choice* when my mum and dad were killed. One day they were there, the next I was watching them being buried. I would have given anything to have had the choice you had, Nick.'

'What if they'd been paralysed or brain damaged in that accident instead of killed outright? Would you have wanted to sit and watch them every day until the doctors decided to switch off their life support?'

148

'I'd have wanted every single fucking second,' Emma snarled, tears welling up in her eyes.

Silence descended like a shroud. It was broken by Jo who sipped at her drink then looked again at Tate. 'I think what you did was very brave, Nick,' she said quietly. 'I would have been too scared. As much as I love my dad, I couldn't have done that for him.' She squeezed Tate's hand gently.

'Are we *all* going to congratulate Nick for what he did?' Emma chided. She wiped a tear from her cheek and reached for her drink. She raised the glass. 'Here, perhaps we should have a toast. To you, Nick. And what you did.'

Emma drank. This time she didn't bother to wipe the tears away.

45

'It's too early. This is only the second night they've been in that house.'

George Wilby shuffled uncomfortably in his seat, glancing around at the candles that lit the sitting room of Adam Wood's house. He looked around at his companions, waiting for one of them to make some comment.

'We knew this time would come,' Wood said. 'It always does.'

'But it doesn't always happen like this,' Wilby replied.

'We don't know enough about them yet, Adam,' Jack Howard offered. 'I agree with George. It might be a bit early. Give it a few more days. See what happens.'

Wood paced slowly back and forth in front of his large fireplace. 'We all know what happened last night,' he said. 'We know what's got to be done.'

Mark Jackson exhaled deeply. 'I agree,' he said.

'Christ Almighty, Mark, think about it,' Wilby protested.

'What's to think about, George?' Jackson told him.

'There's others, here in the village,' Wilby protested. 'Those four at the house can wait.'

Wood stroked his chin thoughtfully. 'Which ones in the village were you thinking of?' he mused.

'The Skelson boy for one,' Wilby said. 'Lisa McQuillan for another.'

'And your own son,' Wood added.

Wilby nodded.

'I think he's close,' he agreed.

'Samantha Ryan,' Wood said. 'I've seen it in her eyes.'

'So, what about the four at the house?' Jack Howard demanded. 'How long shall we leave them?'

'If we don't act quickly we'll lose control,' Wood insisted.

Jack Howard nodded. 'OK,' he said.

'There's someone we've forgotten,' Wood said, crossing to a darkened corner of the room. Almost invisible in the gloom there was an easel, the painting beneath it covered by a thin cloth. He took hold of a corner of the material and pulled.

The other three men looked on impassively at a painting of Catherine Pearce.

'The funeral's tomorrow,' Wilby said.

Wood studied the picture for a moment longer then replaced the material, hiding it from view once again.

'So, what do we do about those four at the house?' Mark Jackson asked. 'Do we go ahead?'

'Yes,' Wood said. He looked at each of his companions in turn.

'Tonight,' said Jackson.

'I'm not sure,' muttered Howard.

'We need an answer, Jack,' Wood insisted. 'It's getting stronger by the day.'

'All right then. Tonight,' Howard said.

'George?' Wood asked, looking at Wilby.

'Looks like I'm outvoted, doesn't it?' he breathed.

'Right then,' Wood stated. 'Come on, we'll take my car. Sooner we get there the better.'

'What if we *did* leave it?' Wilby added.

'And lost control?' Wood reminded him. 'Then we'd all better hope that there *is* a God. Because no bastard on this *earth* would be able to help us.'

46

Emma was the first to see the movement outside.

'What is it?' Jo asked.

She watched as Emma rose unsteadily to her feet and crossed slowly to the nearest window of the dining room, cupping her hands around her eyes to cut out the brightness within.

'Near the bottom of the garden,' she said quietly. 'I can see lights. There's someone out there.'

Tate joined his wife immediately, squinting into the gloom.

Both of them stood there, faces pressed to the window, searching the blackness.

'Perhaps you just thought—' Tate began.

'Thought what?' Emma snapped. 'Perhaps I imagined it? Maybe I'm just too drunk.'

Tate was about to speak again when he too caught sight of something. 'I can see it,' he said quickly. 'Looks like torches.'

Jo now joined them. She swayed uncertainly for a moment, putting out a hand to steady herself. '*Is* there someone out there?' she wanted to know.

'Who the hell is going to be out at this time on a night

like this?' Tate murmured. '*And* all the land at the back of the house is private. No one should be on it anyway.'

'Well, there's *someone* out there,' Emma insisted, again catching sight of the distant beams of light cutting through the gloom.

'Let's go and see who it is,' said Morton.

'Go out in *this*?' Tate grunted.

'I bet it's just some local kids fucking around,' Morton offered. 'They probably do this every time someone stays here. They're trying to scare us.'

Emma shook her head. 'I don't think it's kids,' she said quietly. 'The house is more than two miles from Roxton.'

'Then who is it?' Morton demanded. 'Come on. Let's go and find out.'

'Just leave it,' Jo snapped.

'They're trying to scare *us*,' Morton announced. 'Let's run out there and frighten the shit out of *them*.'

'If they wanted to scare us they'd have come closer to the house,' Jo said.

'Jo and I saw a path out there in the woods this afternoon,' Emma announced.

'Where does it lead?' Morton wanted to know.

'It was like a hiking trail or something,' Jo told him. 'It probably goes on for miles.'

'I'll look on my map,' Emma announced, suddenly energised by her idea. She hurried out of the room and upstairs to the bedroom she and Tate occupied.

'I think Emma's right,' Tate said. 'Why would kids come this far out just for a joke?'

'Instead of standing here we should go down there and see who it is,' Morton persisted.

'I'm not going outside in this bloody weather,' Jo said defiantly.

'They've gone,' Tate said, his face still pressed to the glass. 'I can't see the lights any more.'

154

The other two searched the blackness intently. Then, finally, Morton crossed to the French windows and twisted the key in the lock.

'Just leave it, Pete,' Jo protested, but it was too late. Morton pulled the windows open. A powerful gust of wind swept into the room, almost blowing him off his feet. A glass standing on the table was toppled by the force of the draught. He stepped out on to the patio, trying to catch sight of the lights in the darkness but saw nothing. He was actually heading for the flight of stone steps that led down to the lower level of the garden when Tate called to him.

'Come back inside,' he shouted, forced to raise his voice to make himself heard above the howling wind.

Morton hesitated a moment then retreated back to the warmth of the house, shutting the French windows behind him.

'Whoever they were they've gone,' he announced.

Emma walked back into the room holding the map. She spread it out on the table and traced one index finger over it. 'Here's the house,' she remarked, touching part of the map. 'But the trail isn't marked. I wonder why.'

'That's not an Ordnance Survey map,' Tate reminded her. 'The *main* features of the area are marked but—'

'I can see that,' Emma cut in. 'But that path we saw led out of the valley. If you followed it straight, in the direction those lights were moving, there's only one place it could take you.' Her voice dropped lower in volume as she traced her fingertip over the paper. 'To the mine.'

47

Jason Skelson cupped his testicles in one hand and squeezed them gently.

No lumps there.

He looked down at his groin.

No. The problem was not testicular cancer, it was something else. A growth that was eating away at the muscle of his thigh and groin.

He sat on his bed and glanced across at the clock on his bedside table. Before it lay the Stanley knife he'd taken from work that day.

Jason waited a moment, then reached across and grasped the tool. It certainly *looked* sharp enough.

The triangular blade glinted in the light. He pressed it gently against the pad of his thumb, testing its sharpness. He exerted more pressure. The blade split flesh with ease and blood welled from the cut.

Jason cursed and dropped the knife, sucking at his bleeding thumb, tasting the coppery flavour of the blood in his mouth.

Imagine what that would do to your thigh.

He looked down at his leg and tried to picture what his leg would look like after he'd hacked through the muscle to get to the growth he was convinced was swelling and spreading constantly.

If you cut too deep and slice through your femoral artery the spray will hit the ceiling.

He'd read that somewhere.

Jason got to his feet and walked across to his wardrobe. At the bottom of it there was a medical dictionary he'd bought on his day off from a shop in Derby. He returned to the bed and flicked through the book until he found the entry on cancer. There were photos of malignant tumours that had been removed from people's bodies. A mass of coagulated black cells that had been taken from one man's lung. The lump looked like a dollop of tar. Another illustrated ovarian cancer removed from a woman in her forties.

He wondered if the growth in his thigh looked the same. Would it be like that when he finally cut it free?

There was only one way to find out.

All night she'd been scratching her head. Raking at her scalp with her fingernails. At first distractedly but, as the night had worn on, with increasing ferocity.

Now Lisa McQuillan stood before the bathroom mirror, gazing at her own reflection. Again she tore at her head, anxious to relieve the maddening itches that tormented her. Just above her hairline it seemed to be worse and she gritted her teeth as she dug her nails savagely into her skin.

So great was her desire to stop the irritation that she closed her eyes and allowed her nails to rasp over her scalp like a file over metal.

When she looked into the mirror again she took a step back.

There was a thin ribbon of blood running down her temple.

Small fragments of skin and hair were visible beneath her nails. There was more blood on the tips of the digits. She'd scratched so hard she'd opened the cut on her head again. But at least the itching had stopped momentarily.

It was nits. It had to be nits. Just as she'd suspected in the beginning.

She scratched again.

From behind her she heard a low buzzing sound and, seconds later, the bloated fly she'd seen in the house earlier that day flew past her, bumping into the mirror.

Lisa looked at the corpulent insect for a second then snatched up a nearby towel and swung it wildly at the creature. She missed and knocked over some shampoo that was standing near the bath.

The fly buzzed around her head then flew away in the direction of the toilet. It landed on the seat and sat there, rubbing its front legs together.

Lisa struck at it again with the towel but even as swollen and large as it was, it moved too fast for her.

She heard it as it left the bathroom and flew out on to the landing.

Lisa washed her hands, scraping away the blood and fragments of skin, watching them disappear down the plughole. Then she carefully sponged the blood from her temple with a damp ball of cotton wool that she'd taken from a sealed bag. She used another piece to dab at the cut on her head, finally flushing it away when she'd finished.

She would wash her hair now, she told herself. Dry every inch of it carefully.

And she would find that filthy, disease-carrying fly and kill it.

The fly sat on the shade of her bedside lamp, wiping its front legs over its large compound eyes.

It finally took off and flew out towards the landing, its swollen, egg–laden body almost too heavy to be supported by its wings.

48

When she heard the ringing of her mobile, Samantha Ryan thought for a moment that it was the last vestige of a dream. She rolled over, one hand reaching blindly for the phone. As she picked it up she saw that the time showed 3.49 a.m.

'Hello,' she said croakily, rubbing her eyes, trying to clear her head.

'It's me,' said the voice at the other end of the line.

'What are you doing calling at this time in the morning?' she wanted to know.

'I just got in. I wanted to talk to you,' her boyfriend told her.

'You're drunk,' she said dismissively.

'We finished the job, so we went out for a few pints, went on to a club afterwards. I thought you'd be glad to know I'll be coming home in a few days.'

'A few days? Why not tomorrow?'

'We've got to go back to Leeds, finish off another job for a firm we did some stuff for a while back. The money's good.'

'I don't care about the fucking money. I just want you home. I need some help with Jack. I don't know how much more I can stand.'

'What are you talking about? He'll be fine. You can cope.'

'No, I can't. That's why I want you home.'

'In a few days.'

'Now,' she barked.

In the room next to her, she heard an all too familiar sound.

'Oh God, no, Jack's awake again,' she wailed.

'Well, go and see to him then.'

'I'm going,' she snarled.

The sound of the crying baby began to grow in volume.

'I'll ring you tomorrow,' her boyfriend told her.

'Don't bother unless it's to tell me when you're coming home,' she rasped, switching the phone off. She dropped it on to the bed and stumbled towards the makeshift nursery.

The crying was ringing in her ears by now. Grating on her nerves.

'Oh, Jack, please,' she murmured. 'Not now.'

She crossed to the cot and picked up the child, the odour of a soiled nappy filling her nostrils immediately.

Samantha looked deep into the child's puffy, red-rimmed eyes. 'You be a good boy for Mummy now,' she murmured.

The crying grew louder.

Adam Wilby paused at the bedroom door, head bowed almost reverentially.

He was naked despite the chill of the early morning air, but he felt nothing except the burning desire coursing through his veins like a drug. He glanced down at his erection, squeezing it firmly in one fist for a moment.

He sucked in several deep breaths before finally stepping into the room.

His wife was sleeping *(Sleeping, comatose – what was the difference?)* her chest rising and falling evenly.

Wilby moved to the side of the bed and looked down at her. He reached out a hand and touched her cheek. She turned her head towards him but her eyes remained closed. Her mouth was slightly open and saliva was running in a clear stream from between her lips.

Wilby leant forwards so that his face was close to hers then licked the saliva away with his tongue, tasting the secretion in his own mouth.

He climbed on to the bed beside her but still she didn't open her eyes.

He pushed back the covers, exposing her immobile form. Then he put his hand on her face again, pushing one index finger towards her mouth. He parted her lips gently and moved the digit inside the welcoming wetness. He felt her chew slightly on it and, at last, she opened her eyes.

There was no recognition in those blank orbs. She merely stared straight at him.

'Rachel,' he whispered as he parted her legs.

Wilby moistened his index and middle fingers with her saliva then rubbed the digits between her legs. He pushed the tip of his penis against her labia.

Could she feel him? Or was the paralysis so total that all nerve endings there were now dead?

She opened her mouth as if to say something but he knew no words would come forth.

Wilby spat on to his hand then massaged the saliva around the bulbous head of his penis. He tried to penetrate her but she wasn't slippery enough inside. He felt a dryness there that made him uncomfortable but he persisted, pushing a little harder, pressing another inch of his erection into her.

He took one of her hands and held it in his own, raising it to his face, drawing her fingers across his cheek as if he were a puppeteer. He closed his eyes and imagined that the gesture of affection was real, that she knew what she was doing.

That she wanted him.

His body was shaking slightly and he could feel the tears welling up in his eyes as he looked down at her.

She made a liquid gurgling sound in her throat and he pressed his lips to hers, stirring inside her mouth with his tongue to taste the mucus there.

And, as he did, he managed to penetrate her fully, thrusting deeply into her vagina, now lubricated slightly by his own fluids. He winced at the discomfort but persevered, working his hips into a rhythm as he began to thrust gently inside her.

His tears dripped on to her face as he remained above her but he kept up his urgent movements, seemingly mesmerised by her unblinking eyes.

Please see me.

He whispered her name again as he drew nearer to his climax. And when that release came he buried his face in the pillow next to her head as if he couldn't bring himself to look at her any longer.

Wilby recovered his breath then withdrew, looking down to see his oily white semen dribbling from her labial lips.

She moved her head slightly and he smiled down at her.

Next time, he told himself, it would be easier.

49

The wind that had buffeted the house the previous night had all but died away with the coming of morning.

Now Emma stood in the woods at the bottom of the garden looking back at the house. Dark clouds were scudding across the sky threatening more rain but, so far, it had held off.

Nick had slipped through the same gap in the hedge as his wife and was walking slowly back and forth, occasionally kicking at the fallen carpet of rotting leaves that covered the ridge.

'There *was* someone here last night,' Emma said, pointing at the path that cut through the woods. 'There are footprints on this path.'

'There's nothing sinister about that,' Nick told her, looking around him.

'I didn't say there was. I just think it's strange that people were using this path at that time of the night.'

Nick could only shrug. 'Jo's probably right,' he observed. 'It's a rambler's trail or something.'

'Who goes rambling after midnight, Nick? Besides, like you said, I thought this land was supposed to be private.'

'It might be a local custom,' he joked, but Emma didn't

smile. She walked a few yards up the slope, glancing alternately at the pathway and then up into the trees. 'Listen,' she said finally and stood still.

Nick did as she asked but then shook his head. 'I can't hear anything,' he told her.

'No. Neither can I. That's the whole point. There aren't even any birds in the trees.'

'Well, it is winter. Perhaps they've all flown south.'

'Very funny, Nick,' she said contemptuously.

'I'm sorry,' he shrugged, also looking up into the branches of the trees. 'Now you come to mention it, I can't hear any birds. I don't remember seeing any either.' His forehead creased. 'Actually, I haven't seen any animals of any description since we got to Roxton. No one walking their dogs. No cats prowling around the village. Nothing like that.'

Emma walked further up the incline. 'When Jo and I found this path yesterday I heard something moving about in these woods,' she said. 'I thought it might be a fox or a badger or something like that, but like you said, there aren't any animals.'

'It's just that we haven't seen them,' he told her. 'Don't badgers hibernate?'

'Dogs, cats and birds don't.'

'Anyway, there must be animals of *some* kind around here. Remember the night we arrived? Just before we reached Roxton, when Pete almost ran over something in the road? *That* must have been an animal.'

'How can you be sure? You said you didn't see it.'

'Then it was one of the locals out for a late night stroll,' he grinned. 'Just like last night on this path.'

Emma nodded slowly and headed back down the slope towards him. 'Nick, I want to go into Roxton,' she said. 'Have a look around.'

'When we've had some breakfast, the four of us—'

'We don't have to wait for Pete and Jo to get up,' she cut in. 'Anyway, after the amount *they* had to drink last night I doubt if we'll see them before lunchtime.'

'They weren't the only ones drinking, in case you've forgotten,' he murmured. 'It's just that we were the ones stupid enough to get up so early.'

'It's almost eleven now. Let them have a lie in,' Emma suggested. 'Come on. Let's get the car, Pete won't mind.'

'I wouldn't bet on it.'

Emma smiled and headed back in the direction of the small gap in the hedge where they'd first squeezed through. 'Well, by the time he finds out, it'll be too late, won't it?' she grinned.

50

Roxton's streets were more crowded than usual and Emma could see why.

'Market day,' she observed, noting the many coloured awnings that decorated the stalls. 'Let's go and have a look around.'

Her husband nodded and searched for a suitable parking space before finally swinging the car into a gap outside a bakery.

The clouds that had been threatening to unleash a downpour all morning were still clinging to their load as Emma climbed out of the Volvo. She glanced up at the mottled heavens and waited for Tate to lock the car.

They walked slowly up and down the picturesque streets of the village, taking their time browsing among the market stalls.

'Shall we get a coffee?' Tate suggested, nodding in the direction of a cafe across the street.

The bell over the door jingled as they entered and were met by the delicious aroma of freshly baked cakes. The cafe was fairly busy, populated by shoppers who had obviously decided they were also in need of refreshment before making their way home or adding to their purchases.

Emma sat down at a table near the window and glanced out, noticing that, from her vantage point, she could see the tall spire of the village church pointing accusingly at the cloud-filled sky.

Tate joined her a moment later and they shared a pot of coffee while enjoying some of the cakes they'd smelt upon entering.

'Do you reckon there's anyone in Roxton who *doesn't* know we're renting the house?' Tate asked. 'The woman behind the counter just asked me if we were enjoying our stay.'

'They're only being friendly, Nick.'

'Or nosey, as Pete would say.'

'Pete doesn't have a good word to say about anyone.'

She looked around the inside of the cafe and noticed a large painting hanging on one of its panelled walls. It depicted two weary-looking miners emerging from a metal cage that had obviously just been winched to the surface.

'Another of Mr Wood's creations by the look of it,' Tate said, seeing Emma's interest in the picture. 'The guy who runs the shop where I got your map.'

'Can we go in there before we head back?'

'If you like.'

'I want to have a look around the church as well,' she told him, nodding in the direction of the spire.

'Any particular reason why?' Tate smiled.

'It'll be interesting. That guidebook I was reading on the way up says it's been here since the fifteen hundreds. Besides, surely there'll be something for you to photograph, Nick.'

'Let's hope you're right,' he admitted. 'I thought you'd discovered religion and forgotten to mention it.'

She regarded him evenly over the rim of her cup. 'I wish I *did* believe,' she told him. 'I've tried. At least I did until . . .'

168

'Your mum and dad,' he said quietly, reaching across the table to touch her hand.

'Like the man said, "Would a God who is good invent something like death?"' She sipped at her drink. 'I don't think so.'

'You're blaming God again.'

'Who *should* I blame? Anyway, you're not exactly a big believer yourself.'

'Like the *other* man said, "I don't believe in God, but I am afraid of him."'

'I thought the only thing that scared you was failure, Nick. That's what you said last night anyway.'

'I said a *lot* of things last night. We *all* did.'

They finished their coffee and cake in silence.

'Where to first?' Tate asked finally.

'The church,' Emma told him.

51

The first spots of rain began to fall as they reached the wooden gateway that led into the churchyard. Emma looked up irritably at the sky but Tate ignored the specks and instead reached for his digital camera and began squeezing off shots of the imposing building.

As she walked along the path towards the main door of the church, Emma slowed her pace and glanced at the gravestones on either side of her. Those closest to the path bore more recent dates of their occupants' demise. There were flowers on two of them, some fresh, others rotting.

Further from the path there were stone crosses and other headstones that illustrated the length of time some had lain in the earth. She spotted one grave marked with the dates 1858–1903. Those who had once tended that spot would also be buried here now, she mused.

Another path led off to the right and Emma wandered along it, towards some willow trees whose branches hung over a number of older graves like decaying tentacles.

The graves here were even older, the stone markers themselves ravaged by age. She saw one close by and knelt to read the inscription:

FRANCIS HUTCHENS
SON OF JOHN AND MARGARET HUTCHENS
BORN 17TH SEPTEMBER 1782
DIED 15TH JULY 1812
MARRIED IN THIS PARISH

The rest had been worn away by the passage of time and the ravages of the weather.

'He probably lived here all his life.'

Emma heard Tate's voice behind her as she continued to look at the gravestone.

'Probably never travelled more than five miles from Roxton in all that time,' he continued.

'People still stick close to the town.'

Both of them looked round as they heard the words.

'Sorry if I disturbed you,' the newcomer said.

The man was in his mid-forties. Around his neck his priest's collar was almost radiant in its whiteness.

'My name's James Lawrence,' he told them. 'I'll be conducting the ceremony later. May I ask if you're friends of the deceased?'

Both Emma and Tate seemed momentarily lost for words.

'We're just visiting,' Emma said. 'We're not from Roxton. We're renting a house a couple of miles away with some friends.'

'I didn't think you looked familiar,' Lawrence told them. 'I know most of my flock on sight by now.' He smiled and there was tremendous warmth in the gesture.

'I think you're the only one in the town who doesn't know we're tourists,' Tate told him.

'Not much escapes them,' Lawrence smiled. 'I think I've been accepted now, but it's taken me four years.'

'You're not from the village then?' Emma stated. 'I mean, you don't sound as if you are.'

'No. I was in a parish in Windsor. They like to move us

171

around. This position was offered to me when the previous incumbent died, so I took it. They say a change is as good as a rest, don't they?'

'You said there was a funeral this afternoon?' Emma queried. 'We can leave now—'

'No, no,' Lawrence cut in. 'It isn't for another two hours.' The rain was beginning to fall more quickly.

'Can we have a look inside the church?' Emma asked. 'Would that be all right?'

'By all means.' He smiled that infectious smile once again and they followed him inside the building.

'Have you visited this part of the country before?' Lawrence asked as they entered the church.

'No. As a matter of fact it's our first holiday for years,' Emma confessed. 'We just felt we needed a break.'

'I get time off for good behaviour occasionally,' Lawrence smiled. 'My curate looks after things when I'm away.'

'Where do priests go for their holidays?' Tate wanted to know, reaching for his camera.

'Anywhere they can afford,' Lawrence told him.

As they walked slowly through the nave, Tate glanced at the stained-glass windows on either side of the church.

'You don't mind if I take some pictures, do you?' he asked, brandishing his camera.

'Of course not,' Lawrence told him. 'Be my guest.'

Tate thanked him and snapped away at the windows, marvelling at the craftsmanship. Even with the dull light from outside the brilliance of their colours was not diminished.

'The windows were used as teaching aids in medieval times,' Lawrence offered. 'With fewer people being able to read in those days it was easier to instruct them using the illustrations depicted in the windows. Like the Ten Commandments.' He pointed to a window that bore several different panels, each depicting separate acts. 'Thou shalt not covet thy neighbour's house,' he mused pointing at one of the scenes showing soldiers besieging a castle. He pointed to the next one. 'Honour thy father and mother.'

Emma looked at the tableau, her face expressionless.

'Thou shalt not kill,' Lawrence continued, pointing at a window showing a small figure kneeling before a bearded man.

Tate swallowed hard and snapped the scene.

'That doesn't look very instructive,' Emma noted, pointing at a window showing a man being held down and whipped.

'The representation of the law,' Lawrence informed her. 'A reminder of what would happen to people if they transgressed against man's laws, not just God's.'

'And *that* one?' Tate wanted to know.

The window showed Christ being pulled from the Cross by several people who all bore enraged expressions.

Tate took several pictures of it.

'It's new,' the vicar continued. 'Twenty or thirty years old at most. A lot of the panels in this part of the church are recent. Apparently there was some vandalism, some of the older windows were broken. The people who lived in Roxton chose the designs of the new ones.'

Emma looked up in bewilderment at another window close to the pulpit that depicted a screaming man surrounded by a variety of demons. At the bottom of the window the figure of Christ was hunched in a foetal position, eyes closed.

'Who *made* the new windows?' Tate asked, taking more pictures.

'They were designed by Mr Wood, the gentleman who runs the art gallery in the village,' said Lawrence.

'I was in there yesterday,' Tate remarked, eyeing the windows inquisitively.

They finally reached the chancel and both Emma and Tate stopped walking and looked down, Tate reaching again for his camera.

'Impressive, isn't it?' Lawrence said quietly.

52

The plaque was set into the stone floor of the church just in front of the altar. It was made of polished black marble which gleamed as the dull light fell across it. There were names engraved on it, etched in gold to make them more visible against the black surface.

'It's a memorial,' Lawrence told them. 'I don't know if you've heard but there was an accident at the mine, an explosion.'

'We were told,' Emma said quietly. 'The night we arrived we went into the pub. We were talking to Mr Wilby. He told us about it.'

'George,' Lawrence smiled. 'Yes, he works *here* now. Helps to keep the churchyard tidy. Tends to the older graves. That kind of thing.' They all looked more closely at the black marble rectangle. 'Twenty-three names. That's all that's left, I'm afraid. The bodies were never recovered as far as I know. The explosion did too much damage. There was no way of removing them from the mine.'

Emma crouched and read some of the names. 'These men must still have family in the town,' she mused.

'There's a service held every year on the anniversary of the disaster to honour those who were killed.'

'What does the inscription mean?' Tate said, pointing to the words at the top and bottom of the plaque. 'That's not Latin, is it?'

'Most of it is,' Lawrence commented.

Tate looked puzzled. '*Most* of it?' he queried.

'As far as I can gather, the rest is old English. Pre-Norman conquest, possibly even further back in history than that.'

'Do you know what it says?' Emma wanted to know.

'The basic meaning of the inscription at the bottom is *From pain to fear released*,' the priest explained. 'And before you ask me, no, I have no idea what that is supposed to mean.'

'What about the one at the top?' Emma persisted.

'As far as I've been able to work out it translates as *Beyond the reach of death*. Perhaps Mr Wilby could explain it to you. After all, he was one of the four men who survived the accident.'

'He told us,' Emma said, standing up. 'We were going to call in at the antiques shop too. Someone told us that Mr Wood was a bit of a local historian and *he* survived the accident too, didn't he? He might tell us something about the stained-glass windows he designed. He might even explain what they mean.'

'If he tells you, let me know, will you?' Lawrence said, lowering his voice conspiratorially.

'We'd better go,' Tate interjected. 'We've taken up enough of your time.' He extended his hand which Lawrence shook warmly.

'It's a pleasure to have people in the church. Perhaps we might see you on Sunday.'

They both nodded sharply and attempted conciliatory expressions.

'I won't hold my breath then,' Lawrence smiled.

He walked them to the door and watched as they headed back down the path between the gravestones.

For long moments he stood there motionless, before finally turning and heading back down the nave towards the altar. He looked up at the large wooden cross that hung there, the life-size figure of Christ hanging from it. Lawrence allowed his gaze to travel over the figure, pausing at the serene features of its face.

As he had done many times before, Lawrence noted that the head was turned slightly to the left, as if the beautifully carved image could not bear to look upon the interior of the church.

53

'It's only a car, Pete.'

Jo Morton took another drag on her cigarette and pushed one hand into the pocket of her fleece as she stood waiting for the kettle to boil. Her bare feet were just visible beneath the hem of the jogging bottoms she wore and she flexed her toes on the tiles of the kitchen floor.

'He should have asked before he took it,' her husband said irritably. 'Besides, he's not insured.'

'He's supposed to be your friend. Don't friends share things?'

'What's that supposed to mean?' Morton wanted to know, catching the edge in her voice.

'Well, you said last night that you'd fuck Emma if you could get away with it. If you'd use his wife, what's wrong with Nick using your car?'

'And didn't you say something about sleeping with Nick? Don't start this shit now, Jo.'

'You wanted to play the bloody game, Pete. You were the one who wanted to hear everyone's . . . confessions.' She shot him a contemptuous glance then reached for the kettle and poured boiling water on to the instant coffee in the mug before her.

'No one had to say anything if they didn't want to,' he countered. 'Obviously everyone felt like unburdening themselves of their secrets, didn't they? You certainly fucking did. Why did you never tell me about the baby? Why didn't you *tell* me you'd had it aborted?'

'Like you've always told *me* the truth about everything?' She sipped her coffee. 'Have you ever tried it on with Emma?'

'For Christ's sake, Jo. Leave it, will you?'

'Why? Are confessions just for drunken dinner parties? Tell me now. Have you?'

'Of course I haven't.'

Jo nodded.

'I'm telling you the truth,' he rasped. 'And anyway, I think you getting an abortion without consulting me is a little more important, don't you?'

'Or did you try it and she told you to fuck off? Is that it? More afraid of admitting a blow to your ego than another possible infidelity?'

'Listen, if you want to think I've fucked Emma, tried to fuck Emma or got knocked back by Emma, then do it. Make your own choice, because whatever I say you won't believe me. Why don't you ask her when she gets back? See what she says. Perhaps you'll believe *her*. And that isn't what I wanted to talk about. I asked about this abortion.'

'I know what you asked about, Pete, but we're talking about what I want to talk about. If anything happened between you and Emma then she's not going to tell *me*, is she?'

'Listen to yourself, Jo. You're paranoid.'

'If I am then *you've* made me that way, Pete.'

'If I've made your life such a misery, why haven't you left me?'

'Nowhere else to go,' she said flatly. 'Perhaps I was hoping that things *might* improve.'

'If you hadn't killed our kid perhaps they would have.' There was something close to hatred in his eyes as he looked at her.

Jo stood there for a moment longer then ambled towards the kitchen door. 'I'm going to have a bath,' she said flatly. 'Why don't you stand at the front door so you can see when Emma and Nick get back with your precious car. Then you can stop worrying.'

Morton heard her footfalls on the stairs. He drank the Alka-Seltzer in two gulps, wincing as he drained the glass. He banged the empty receptacle down on the worktop so hard a crack spread across the bottom of it. He looked at his reflection in the glass, distorted and twisted by the crack.

'Fucking bitch,' he muttered under his breath.

54

Adam Wood smiled broadly as Emma and her husband entered his shop. 'Back again?' he grinned, nodding at Tate. 'Not come to complain, I hope.'

Tate shook his head. 'This is my wife,' he said. 'This is who I bought the map for.'

'Nice to meet you,' said Wood. 'Are you the real collector? The one who's dragged him back in, looking for bargains?'

'Will I find some?' Emma asked.

'That depends what you're looking for,' the older man told her.

'I'm actually looking for information,' Emma confessed. 'The man who runs The George and Dragon *and* the vicar both told us you were a bit of a local historian. That you might be able to help.'

'Have you been talking to Reverend Lawrence?' Wood enquired, his smile fading slightly.

'We had a look around the church today,' Emma informed him. 'We saw the stained-glass windows you designed. They're very unusual.'

'What did the Reverend have to say about them?' The smile had now completely disappeared.

'He said that they were put into the church about twenty or thirty years ago.'

'He's right. What else did he say about them?'

'We were just saying that the designs were unusual and he agreed.'

'Is that why you came in here? To ask me about those windows?'

'No. It's just that your paintings seem to be all over the town. We saw the one you did that's in The George and Dragon and then the windows in the church. You're obviously a talented man.'

'You're very kind.'

'Even if some of your subjects are a bit . . . unusual.'

'Unusual by whose standards? Yours?'

Emma caught a slight edge in his voice. He looked at her unblinkingly for a moment then his tone softened considerably. 'You're renting Springbank, aren't you?' he said. 'How are you settling in?'

'Fine,' Emma told him. 'It's a beautiful house. I found a path at the bottom of the garden, in the woods, that looks like some kind of hiking trail. I was just wondering if you knew where it led, because when we checked on the map it looks as if it leads straight to the mine.'

'That's right. It does.'

'We were thinking of visiting it. Just out of curiosity and as it has played such a big part in Roxton's history.'

'So, you're interested in our art *and* our history, are you?' Wood breathed and Emma was aware that his tone had darkened once more.

'With all due respect, Mr Wood,' Tate interjected, 'there's not *that* much to do around here except see the sights and try to learn something. Is there anything so wrong with that?'

'What do you want to know about the mine? Twenty-three men died down there. When it closed it ripped the heart out of this village and its community. What more do you want to know?'

'Other people who stay at the house must show an interest in Roxton and its surroundings,' Emma protested.

Wood sucked in a deep breath. 'I apologise,' he said quietly. 'If you've been to the church today then you probably know what's happening this afternoon. About the funeral of Catherine Pearce.'

'The vicar mentioned it,' Emma admitted.

'She'd lived here all her life,' Wood continued. 'Like most folk in Roxton. It's a close community. When someone from the town dies, it's like losing a member of your family. You can only understand that if you live somewhere like this.'

Emma nodded.

The silence that had descended was broken as Samantha Ryan emerged from behind the black curtains at the back of the shop. She looked at Tate then nodded politely in Emma's direction before reaching for a duster and going to work on the glass counter near the till.

'So, what will we see if we go up to the mine?' Tate asked.

'Some old buildings,' Wood told them. 'Nothing more. Not enough to interest you, I wouldn't have thought.'

Emma nodded and turned towards Tate. They both took a step towards the door of the shop.

'Not going to look for bargains?' Wood smiled.

'We're here for two weeks,' Emma told him. 'We'll be back in.'

They walked out, the bell over the door jingling behind them.

Wood watched them head across the street, back in the direction of the market square.

'What did they want to know about the mine for, Mr Wood?' Sam asked tentatively.

'It *interests* them,' Wood said sarcastically, still watching from the window. 'Sam, you look after the shop. I've got to go out for a while.'

He was already heading for the door.

55

Jo closed her eyes and slid deeper into the warm bath water, allowing it to lap around her neck and chin. The scent of the bubble bath was strong in her nostrils. She raised one shapely leg into the air and watched as the water ran down her calf and thigh.

Outside, she could hear the wind beginning to gather momentum once more and she wondered if the house would be battered by the same kind of venomous gusts that had been visited upon it the previous night.

The slow dripping of one of the taps was the only sound that echoed around the large marble bathroom.

She reached for the glass of wine she'd brought up with her and sipped it, luxuriating in the warmth of the water.

The tap continued to drip.

Jo pushed one toe into it, smiling to herself as the water ran down over her foot. She lowered the leg back into the bubbles and exhaled contentedly.

She felt something soft and slippery beneath her heel and kicked gently at it.

The soap.

Jo took another sip of her wine then replaced the glass

on the side of the large bath, feeling the pliant touch of the soap against the sole of her foot now.

She frowned.

The soap was on its metal dish beside her. Not in the bath.

Jo sat up; the tap was still dripping. The sound reverberated inside the room.

Whatever she had initially felt beneath her heel she now felt against her ankle. She lifted her leg out of the water to inspect it but there was nothing there.

Jo filled both hands with water and splashed her face gently.

That same feeling of a slippery, almost oily, substance she now felt on her cheeks and fingers. It was as if she had immersed her hands in mucus and smoothed it over her visage. Puzzled, she looked at her hands but saw nothing on the slightly pruning skin of her fingertips.

She dropped both hands into the water and felt the warmth against her skin again. Closing her eyes once more, she sank back into the water as far as her nose.

Water filled her ears momentarily and she remained in that position, the roaring of her own blood loud inside her head.

She felt something move beneath her left hand and jolted upright suddenly; it felt as if her fingers had closed around the body of a long, bloated worm.

It was all she could do to stifle a scream.

She raised her hand from the bath, clear of the bubbles and, with her eyes bulging in their sockets, she gaped at what she held.

There could be no mistaking it. No matter how insane, irrespective of how impossible the vision before her was, she could see it in her fist like some foul trophy.

It hung there like a replete, corpulent leech, bloodied tendrils of flesh hanging from both ends. There were several thick blue veins pulsing along its length, more vivid because of the rust colouring of the slippery object itself.

She was holding a length of umbilical cord.

56

For what seemed like an eternity, Jo could only gape in horror at the length of pulsating flesh she held. She finally dropped it back into the water, scraping her heels against the bottom of the bath, desperate to be out of it. Away from this monstrous intrusion. But she slipped and fell back with a splash.

The scream she was so desperate to release was trapped deep inside her. It was as if her throat had spasmed and was refusing to open up and allow the ululation free.

She felt a tightness in her chest and realised that she was having trouble breathing.

At the bottom of the bath she saw a small dark shape rise to the surface of water that was now rapidly darkening in colour until it was the same hue as wet bricks.

Jo watched the shape, trying to make out what it was.

No larger than her hand, it seemed to be fashioned from the same tissue as the umbilicus that now floated beside her. She could see something black gleaming on the shape as it bobbed to the surface and she finally managed to make out what it was.

The foetus floated like excrement that refused to be flushed.

Jo opened her mouth to scream but still no sound would come. She wondered when this nightmare would end. When she would sit bolt upright in the bath, woken from this dream because, she reasoned, that was what this must be. Some foul, twisted product of her unconscious. She wasn't awake. She *couldn't* be.

She saw more matter begin to ooze from the taps. Thick and, for the most part, clear but for some streaks of crimson that coloured it like bloodied snot from a broken nose.

The first reeking mess welled at the mouth of the taps, formed large thick globules, then dropped into the dark water with loud splashes that reminded Jo of fecal voiding into a lavatory bowl.

Wake up. Wake up.

And, all the time, the water level rose – driven upwards by the addition of the mucoid discharge now pumping from the taps.

She tried to force herself out of the bath, away from this succession of monstrous images. But she was paralysed with fear, unable to move any part of her body other than her eyelids which she blinked frantically as if wishing the rapid movements would wipe the scene from view.

The foetus floated towards her, turning slightly so that she could clearly see its disproportionately large black eyes.

It was in the advanced stages of decomposition, pieces of flesh peeling away from it like blistered paint, and now Jo became aware of the stench emanating from the tiny body.

The stink of putrescence was powerful enough to finally force a reaction from her body.

Her stomach contracted and it was the signal for all her other muscles to suddenly begin working. She screamed as she dragged herself out of the bath. Jo hit the marble floor with a thud that knocked the wind from her.

Naked, she crawled towards the bathroom door and tugged at the handle.

It was locked.

She screamed again and tugged violently at the handle but it wouldn't give.

Jo began hammering on it with her wet hands, tears now pouring down her cheeks.

She turned and looked at the bath. The water level had risen to the rim by now, the dark fluid that filled it was ready to spill over on to the pristine tiles beneath.

The rotting foetus was still floating on the surface.

Then the water could rise no further.

A waterfall of bloodied filth spilt over the sides of the bath and spread across the bathroom floor, the rancid stench filling the room.

Jo felt it lapping at her feet as she continued banging on the door.

There was something warm between her legs and she realised that she'd wet herself with fright, but mingled with the yellow urine that dribbled down her thighs there was something darker.

Blood was trickling from her vagina, small red spots of it hitting the already filthy tiles beneath her.

Jo clapped her hands to her labia for a second then pulled them away crimson, one hand sliding across the white door to leave a red smear.

On her other palm there was something black and gleaming. Something that looked uncomfortably like the eye of the foetus she'd seen floating in the bath.

She fainted.

57

Peter Morton chopped the cocaine, pushed it into two lines and paused for a moment before snorting the first one.

He sat back, wiping the side of one nostril then sniffed up the second line.

He crouched at the bedside table for a moment then finally got to his feet.

It was still quiet inside the bathroom where Jo was bathing. He'd heard nothing when he'd ascended the stairs and now, ten minutes later, there was still only the sound of a dripping tap emanating from the room.

Morton crossed to the door of the en suite and tapped gently. 'Jo,' he called.

No answer.

'Jo,' he said again, raising his voice slightly.

Still nothing.

'Fair enough. You want to play the fucking martyr then that's your business. If you want to be sulking when Nick and Emma get back then get on with it.'

He leant close to the door and heard the dripping tap once again.

'For fuck's sake,' he rasped.

He tried the handle and pushed against it, prepared to walk in. The door struck something heavy and Morton frowned. He pushed harder and managed to force his way far enough into the room to see that what was blocking his entrance was Jo herself.

She was lying face down on the bathroom floor.

Morton squeezed through the gap and knelt beside her, feeling how cold her skin was. He pulled her bathrobe from the hook on the back of the door and wrapped it around her, cradling her in his arms.

'Jo,' he said, a note of urgency in his voice.

Her eyes snapped open and she looked at him with an expression of pure terror on her face.

She struggled to escape his grasp, looked back at the bath, then staggered into the bedroom.

'What happened?' Morton asked, following her into the bedroom where she was now sitting shivering on the edge of the bed, her wet hair hanging around her face like reptilian tails.

'Didn't you hear me?' she gasped. 'I screamed.'

He shook his head. 'Why did you scream?'

I had a nightmare. I saw the child I had aborted floating in a bath of blood and discharge.

'What happened? What were you doing on the floor?' he demanded. 'Did you slip or something?'

Tell him what you saw.

Jo got to her feet and walked to the door of the bathroom. She looked inside.

The marble room was as sparklingly pristine as it had been when they'd first arrived at the house. No blood. No bloated lengths of umbilical cord. No rotting foetus.

Tell him what you saw.

'Where *were* you?' she wanted to know.

'Downstairs. Where the hell did you *think* I was? I went outside for a breath of fresh air, that was all. Why?'

She pulled the robe more tightly around herself. 'I want to leave here,' she told him flatly. 'I want to go home. I didn't want to come in the first place.'

'Why do you want to go? Jo, tell me what the fuck happened, will you?'

'I don't *know* what happened!' she exclaimed, unable to look at him any longer.

'Well, when you work it out, let me know, will you? But I'll tell you one thing now – we're not leaving this house. Why should we? Besides, the two weeks here are paid for. If we leave we lose the money.'

She had no answer for him.

Outside, they both heard the sound of a car engine. Wheels crunching on the gravel drive.

'About fucking time,' Morton said under his breath. He turned towards the bedroom door then hesitated. 'Are you sure you're all right?'

'Don't worry about me, Pete,' she murmured sardonically. 'You go and check that Nick's brought your car back in one piece.'

Morton opened his mouth to say something then merely shook his head and walked briskly out of the room.

Jo waited until she heard his footsteps on the stairs, then she got to her feet and padded back across to the en suite and opened the door wider.

The floor, the tiles and the bath were all gleaming. Even her glass of wine was still standing, half empty, on the edge of the bath.

Jo studied the room for a second longer, the sound of the dripping tap filling her ears.

She slammed the bathroom door shut.

58

The wind that had been building gradually during the afternoon died to little more than a chill whisper with the onset of night. The icy air also dispelled the threat of rain and, for that at least, Emma was grateful.

She glanced out of the dining-room window and noticed that there were some thin veils of mist across the garden, but apart from that, the night was still.

'Perhaps we can get out and about tomorrow if it stays dry,' she said hopefully, sipping her wine.

'Where do you want to go?' Morton asked.

'I thought we could drive out a bit further. See what we can find,' she said.

'Wasn't your trip into Roxton riveting enough for you this afternoon?' Morton wanted to know.

'It was very interesting, actually,' Emma said, aware of the sarcasm in Morton's voice. 'Shall we have a look at the pictures?'

'I'll go and get the camera and the laptop,' said Tate. 'We can go through them.' He got to his feet and headed for the dining-room door.

'I can't wait,' Morton said, smiling uninterestedly.

Emma shook her head and looked at Jo who was gazing

down distractedly at her plate, occasionally sipping her wine. 'You're quiet, Jo,' Emma said. 'Are you all right?'

Jo nodded. 'I've got a bit of a headache, that's all,' she said without looking up.

Morton eyed her across the table. 'A couple more glasses of wine and she'll be fine, won't you, sweetheart?' he chided.

Jo was about to say something when Tate re-entered the room. He set his laptop on the dining-room table and attached it to the digital camera with a small lead.

Emma and the others moved around to look at the screen as the first images came into view.

'What are you going to do with these when we get back then, Nick?' asked Morton. 'Make a calendar and sell it? That'd bring in a few quid, wouldn't it?'

Tate shot him an irritable glance then returned his attention to the screen. There were some pictures that had been taken on the way into Roxton. Some more of the market.

Tate scrolled through to the first shots of the church. There was one of Reverend Lawrence and Emma silhouetted in the doorway of the main entrance.

'Don't tell me, *he* used to be a miner before the bloody thing closed down,' sneered Morton. 'Another one with a hidden talent. One of them becomes a restaurant owner, another takes over a pub. One's a painter and the other one just dosses around the village talking to people. They must have the best careers reassignment manager in the country here.'

'Reverend Lawrence came here from down south,' Emma explained.

'Anyway, what's so strange about people starting new careers, Pete?' Tate wanted to know. 'They had to do something after the mine closed.'

'It's just a bit hard to accept that a guy who'd dug coal all his life would suddenly want to start working in the catering business, isn't it?' Morton insisted.

'Why?' Tate said. 'He said his wife had experience.'

'Mr Wood who owns the art gallery obviously just has a natural gift when it comes to painting and stuff like that,' Emma added.

Morton nodded. 'But the vicar's always *been* a vicar?' he asked wearily.

'Yes,' Emma told him.

There were a series of pictures of the stained-glass windows.

'They're beautiful, aren't they?' Emma said, gazing raptly at the images. 'Reverend Lawrence told us all about them.'

'Did he tell you what *that* was?' enquired Morton, pointing at something on one of the pictures.

'I can't see anything,' Emma said.

'There,' Morton repeated. 'At the top of that window panel. There's a mark. Perhaps there's something wrong with your camera, Nick.'

'I'll zoom in on it,' Tate murmured, bringing the picture into sharper focus. He then enlarged the top right-hand corner of the shot.

'I didn't see that this afternoon,' he said quietly.

The image was still a little blurred but it was now possible to make out a shape. It looked like a small figure, hands drawn up beneath its chin, its head disproportionately large for the size of its body.

'It looks like one of those things they have *outside* churches,' Emma offered. 'Gargoyles. There's a face there.'

'Could you accidentally have got some kind of reflection in the shot, Nick?' Morton asked, suddenly more interested in what was before him.

'Check the other pictures, Nick,' Emma urged.

Tate scrolled through them.

'It's on *that* one too,' Emma said.

'And it's the same figure,' Tate murmured.

'It reminds me of something,' Emma offered.

196

'A gargoyle, like you said,' Tate added.

Emma shook her head.

'It looks like a foetus,' Jo said, her voice barely more than a whisper.

59

All four of them studied the enlarged image for a moment longer.

'Jesus,' muttered Tate. 'It *does* look like a foetus. The way they look in ultrasound pictures.'

'That's crazy,' Emma interjected. 'That window's more than four hundred years old. No one alive then would have even known what a foetus looked like and, even if they did, why put the image of one on a stained-glass window? Reverend Lawrence said the windows were used as teaching aids. What would *that* teach?'

'They *would* have known what they looked like,' Tate argued. 'Women were more prone to still-births all those years ago. I'm sure they must have known what a foetus would look like.'

'If the kid was still-born it would be fully formed though,' Morton offered. 'It'd look like a proper baby. A foetus doesn't, does it? It's got that weird big head, like the one in these pictures.'

'There'd have been miscarriages,' Emma said. 'They would have known. I didn't think of that at first.'

Jo got to her feet and walked to the other end of the table where she poured herself some more red wine.

'You say the vicar told you the windows were used as teaching aids?' Morton echoed. 'Perhaps it was something to do with not having abortions.'

He looked at Jo. 'Perhaps he was telling them it was a sin,' Morton continued.

'One of the windows was about the Ten Commandments,' Emma remembered. 'It might have been something to do with "Thou shalt not kill".'

'Thou shalt not kill your own kid,' Morton said acidly, his gaze still fixed on Jo.

Her hand was shaking as she raised the glass to her lips.

'Check the other pictures, Nick,' Emma urged.

The next two or three showed the panels that had been put there hundreds of years ago.

'The following ones are newer windows,' Emma explained.

They looked at the first, depicting Christ being pulled from the Cross.

'There,' said Tate, zooming in on one of the panels.

It was a small image of two goats, one being mounted by the other. The ram had unmistakably human features.

'Perhaps that's something to do with adultery,' Jo hissed, glowering at her husband.

Tate scrolled to the next shot. The figure of Christ had been removed from the Cross and was lying curled up near the bottom of the window.

'Nick, go back a minute,' said Emma. 'To the shots of the older windows.'

Tate did as she asked. 'What are you looking for?' he wanted to know.

Emma inspected each of the shots with a quizzical eye. She nodded slowly to herself as if a question was being answered. 'In all of the older windows showing the crucifixion, when Christ was on the Cross didn't the Romans put some kind of plaque over his head?' she said.

'Something that said King of the Jews? As a way to humiliate him.'

'What are you getting at?' Tate wanted to know.

'The plaques are in the panels of the *older* windows but not the new ones. In *those* there's a scroll or something where Christ's head should be,' Emma continued, 'but it doesn't say King of the Jews.'

'How the hell do *you* know what it says?' chuckled Morton. 'Are you some kind of religious authority since you visited the fucking church?'

'In all the pictures of the crucifixion that you see, the words on that plaque say Rex something or other on them, Rex was Latin for King. The scroll in *this* window doesn't say that.' She tried to pick out the words individually. 'They even *look* different. You can see that.'

Morton nodded slowly.

'*Ille video*,' Tate said falteringly, his eyes fixed on the screen. '*Quid consilium maneo*.'

'*Occultus*,' Emma said, picking out the last word for him. '*Ille video quid consilium maneo occultus*.'

'Well, that's a big help, isn't it?' Morton said scornfully.

'I wonder what it means?' Emma pondered.

'It probably doesn't mean anything,' Morton grunted dismissively. 'Nothing important anyway.'

'*Occultus*,' Emma murmured. 'Is that where the word "occult" came from, I wonder?'

'*Video* it says there,' Morton laughed. 'Perhaps that's the origin of VCR.'

'It's pronounced vee-day-oh,' Emma corrected him.

'Oh, sorry, an expert,' Morton snorted. 'Why not just ask your friend the vicar what the fuck it all means?'

'We can find out ourselves,' Emma said. 'Nick, go online. Find a website that can translate Latin into English. There must be one somewhere that does that.'

'Why are you doing this?' Morton asked, pouring

himself another drink. 'What do you think you're going to find?'

'I'm just curious,' Emma said.

'You know what curiosity does – it kills cats.' Morton downed what was left in his glass, refilled it and moved closer to the screen. 'Go on then, I'm almost drunk enough. Let's see what little secrets you can find.'

60

'There's ten pages of the bloody things,' said Tate exasperatedly, gazing at the results of his search inquiry. 'There must be hundreds of sites.'

'Try that one,' Emma urged, pointing to one marked *Translation Unlimited*.

'They want you to pay for the translation,' said Tate, trying another site. 'Same on that one.'

'A lot of them look like Latin lessons or study courses,' Morton interjected.

'*Latin to English Dictionary*,' Emma spotted.

Tate brought up the site. 'Oh, shit,' he muttered as the screen was filled with a huge list of alphabetically arranged Latin words.

'Click on one of them,' Emma suggested. 'Something we already know.'

'What about *Rex?*' Tate smiled. 'We *know* that means King.' He scrolled down then moved the cursor on to the relevant word and tapped.

Emma nodded as the screen displayed the translation.

Rex, regis m. king.

'Check each word in the pictures you took,' Emma urged. 'Jo, can you get a piece of paper and a pen, please?'

Jo hurried off, returning a moment later with her handbag. She pulled out a small notepad and a pencil and handed them to Emma.

'*Ille*,' Emma said, then she spelt it out, watching intently while Tate found it on the list and clicked on it.

'That, he, she, it,' he read. 'Great. It means four different fucking things.'

Emma wrote them all down.

'*Video*,' she continued, again spelling the word aloud.

Tate found it. 'To see,' he told her. 'Also, perceive, understand, consider, take care, see to it.'

'*Quid*,' she continued.

'What or why,' Tate announced.

She gave him the next three words and he found their meanings as defined by the site.

'So, what does that give us?' Tate wanted to know.

'*Consilium*, according to that, means plan, deliberation, policy, advice, assembly or wisdom. It doesn't make sense.'

'What about the last two words?' Tate questioned.

'To stay, remain. That's the meaning of *maneo*,' Emma told him. 'And *occultus* means hidden or secret.'

She considered the words written on the pad. 'If we just had *one* translation for each of the words on the window it would make things easier,' she muttered.

'Try them one at a time,' Tate suggested.

'That to see what plan stay hidden,' Emma began.

Tate shook his head.

'He perceive why deliberation remain secret,' Emma read again, shrugging her shoulders.

'The words might not be *literal* translations,' Tate said hopefully. 'We might have to adapt them until they make sense in modern English. Try it again.'

'He,' Emma began, writing slowly. 'Understands. What. Advice. Remain. What if it's *will* remain? Hidden.'

'That sounds more like something,' Tate said, nodding.

'You could be here all night doing this and still never figure out what the fuck it means,' Morton said, scanning the night-shrouded garden beyond the windows.

'I'm going up to bed if no one minds,' Jo interjected. 'I don't feel too great.'

'I might join you,' Morton said, draining his glass.

He paused for a moment longer, his eyes drawn to something beyond the glass of the French windows.

Morton put his glass down then cupped his hands around his eyes and pressed his face to the pane. 'Hey, come and look at this,' he said quietly.

The others hesitated.

'You want a mystery to solve, Emma?' Morton continued. 'I've got another one for you. You know those lights you saw on that hiker's trail in the woods last night?'

Emma nodded and finally got to her feet, crossing to the window to stand alongside Morton. A moment later, Tate joined her.

'Unless I'm more pissed than I think I am, you might have been right,' Morton said. 'It looks like they're back.'

Emma squinted into the gloom that, every now and then, was broken by the jagged light of a torch beam. 'There's someone out there,' she breathed.

61

'Kids mucking about, same as before,' Morton told her.

Emma shook her head. 'Not at this time of night,' she insisted.

'Somebody pissing around,' Morton continued. 'Having a laugh.'

'So what are we supposed to do?' Tate challenged.

'See who it is,' Emma told him. 'See where they're going.'

'Why, for Christ's sake?' Morton snapped. 'Whatever the fuck they're doing, just leave them to it. They're not hurting *us*. We don't own this house, Emma. We don't belong in this town.'

'I want to know what's going on,' Emma said flatly.

'Why?' Morton rasped. 'So you've got another mystery to solve? Fed up with your church windows?'

Emma watched as the torch beam cut through the blackness once again. 'Whoever it is seems to be following the same path,' she murmured. 'Up towards the mine.'

She turned and looked at Tate. 'I want to see, Nick,' she said. 'If we take the car we can get there before them.'

'You can't be sure that's where they're going,' Tate insisted.

'Then let's find out where they *are* going,' Emma pressed.

205

Morton shook his head. 'I don't believe I'm hearing this,' he said, grinning.

'Look at it as an adventure.' Emma smiled. 'You can't tell me you're not curious, Pete. And last night *you* were the one who wanted to go out there and follow them.'

'It's probably someone taking their fucking dog for a walk. I really couldn't give a flying fuck who's out there *or* what they're doing,' Morton told her.

Emma and Morton locked stares for a moment longer.

'All right,' he said finally.

'This is crazy,' Jo offered. 'Nick, are you going to go along with this?'

'It can't hurt,' Tate shrugged.

'Come on, Jo,' Morton said. 'It'll be a laugh. Christ knows we need some fucking laughs.'

Jo stood still, looking at each of her companions in turn. 'I'm not going,' she said defiantly.

'Then stay here on your own,' Morton hissed. 'Finish off the wine. I'm going to get my coat. It looks cold out there.'

'Come with us, Jo,' Emma said quietly, placing one hand on her friend's arm.

For a fleeting second the image of a blood-filled bath and its aborted contents swam into Jo's mind and she visibly paled.

Want to be in the house alone with those thoughts?

'You go,' she said finally.

Emma hesitated a second longer.

'Go,' Jo insisted.

'If we take the car we'll get to the mine before whoever's on the path,' Morton said, returning in his coat. 'But, like Nick said, what if whoever it is isn't heading for the mine?'

'What else are we supposed to do? Follow them along the path?' Tate asked.

'Take the car,' Emma insisted. 'If they're going to the mine then we'll be there before them and we'll see what they're doing there. If not . . .' She shrugged, allowing the sentence to trail off.

Morton hurried out, car keys gripped in his fist. Tate was close behind him.

Emma looked at Jo one last time but Jo merely shook her head and crossed to the French windows. In the darkness beyond the bottom of the large garden she could still make out the light on the pathway that cut through the woods.

When she turned around she heard Emma slam the front door behind her and then the crunch of gravel as the car pulled away.

Jo hesitated a moment, her eyes drawn towards the laptop that still sat on the dining-room table.

She crossed to it, glanced at the screen and sat down.

62

Even with the Volvo's heater on full blast it was cold inside the car. Here and there thin veils of mist drifted across the hillsides, blown by gusts of wind. Tate drove slowly in case there was any ice on the narrow country roads.

'We're not even sure we're going the right way, are we?' Morton said, peering out into the gloom.

'The mine has to be this way,' Emma remarked. 'Look, there's a road leading off to the left. Take that turning, Nick.'

Tate did as he was instructed and found that the Volvo was labouring a little as it negotiated an increasingly steep incline.

Trees rose thickly on either side of a road that gradually seemed to break up until the car was travelling over little more than lumps of rough stone. It was as if the road had merely disintegrated now that it wasn't used any more.

The headlights picked out a high, wire-mesh fence topped with rusted barbed wire. Beyond it were several stone buildings and something they all recognised. It rose into the night air like a sentinel.

'Isn't that the winch they used to hoist the men up and

down?' Tate mused, eyes fixed on the massive structure with its two distinctive wheels at the top.

He brought the car to a halt outside the gate and clambered out. 'The gate's padlocked,' he said, pulling at a rusty chain that secured the entrance.

Emma was also out of the car, prowling up and down the fence like a caged animal. 'Over here,' she called.

The two men scurried across to where she stood.

'There's a gap in the fence,' she said. 'We can get through here.'

'This is fucking mad,' Morton laughed.

'Sshhh,' Emma snapped, slapping him across the shoulder.

'I feel like one of the Famous Five,' Morton grunted.

'Just get through, Pete,' Emma urged, following him. 'Nick, you'd better turn the car headlights off. We don't want anyone to see us or know we're here.'

Tate nodded and hurried back to the car where he switched off the engine and the lights. The darkness flooded in around them.

Morton snagged his coat on a piece of twisted metal. 'For fuck's sake,' he hissed. 'This coat cost me a fucking fortune.'

Emma pushed him gently on, trying to ignore his complaints about the rip in his sleeve.

Tate followed them through into the area that led towards the winding shed. The winch tower rose high above them and Emma could hear the dull clang of metal on metal from somewhere nearby.

A path, now long overgrown, led between two small brick sheds up towards the winch tower.

'Let's see if we can get inside one of those,' Tate suggested, gesturing towards the nearest of the constructions. 'We can wait there. We should be able to see if anyone comes.'

'It looks as if the path up from the woods comes out over there,' Emma said, pointing in the direction of some trees over to the right. 'If whoever's coming this way is on the path, we should see them when they arrive.'

'Fucking door's locked,' Morton hissed, putting his weight against the wooden partition of the nearest brick building. He glanced around and picked up a large stone that lay on the ground nearby.

'What are you doing, Pete?' Emma asked, seeing him heft the stone before him.

She'd barely finished the sentence when he struck the handle of the door three times. It came off and he pushed the door open.

'Come on, get inside,' he urged.

The air was thick with dust, damp and mildew. Emma coughed and put a hand to her mouth, trying to mask the stench of thirty years of neglect.

There were coat hooks on the blackened walls. Beyond them were cracked and broken tiles. She could just make out some rusted shower heads.

'This must be where the miners got changed after they'd been down to the coalface,' she mused.

The dust was several inches thick on the floor and each step sent the noxious detritus into the air where it swirled and clogged their noses.

Morton dug in the pocket of his coat for his lighter. He struck it and held the sickly yellow flame up to illuminate the inside of the building. 'What's that?' he wanted to know.

There was a dark shape in one corner of the room, close to the showers.

Emma crossed slowly to it, realising it was an overcoat still hanging on a clothes hook.

'Perhaps it belonged to one of the men who was killed in the explosion,' she murmured.

Beneath it, almost submerged in the thick dust, was a yellowed and curled-up black and white photo. Emma

210

crouched down and pulled it free, brushing the grime from the picture and inspecting it.

It was a woman and a young baby.

She wondered if it had fallen from the overcoat, if it had belonged to the owner of the garment. Had that been his family? Had he indeed been one of the men who had died below ground on that fateful day they'd already heard so much about? Almost reverentially, she pushed the picture back inside the coat pocket then stepped away.

The building was plunged into darkness again as Morton flicked off his lighter, the metal having grown hot in his hand.

Tate was trying to rub away the thick dust and filth from the small windows of the building so that he could see out.

He paused when he saw a beam of light lance across the ground close to the brick construction. 'Someone's coming,' he hissed.

'I told you,' Emma said quietly, moving slowly to join her husband.

'What are we supposed to do?' Morton asked. 'Jump out on them and demand to know what they're doing here?'

Emma waved her hand exasperatedly, in a gesture designed to silence him.

The torchlights were coming nearer.

'What if they're coming in here?' Tate asked, his voice catching.

Emma had no answer. She still had her hand over her nose and mouth in an effort to keep out the choking dust and stifle any possible cough or sneeze.

Peering through the filthy panes of glass, hidden from view of the newcomers, Emma, Tate and Morton saw four figures pass close by the building.

The leading two both carried torches and one of them turned to glance at his companions. As he did, the cold white light picked out their features.

Emma let out a gasp of surprise.

63

Tate and Morton also looked on with bemused expressions.

'So much for kids mucking about,' Tate murmured, his gaze fixed on the four figures. He studied their faces intently.

Adam Wood led the way, a torch gripped in his fist. Close to him, also carrying a torch, was Mark Jackson. Not far behind them were Jack Howard and George Wilby.

'Why would they be here now?' Emma mused, the question not directed at anyone in particular.

She and her two companions watched as the four men picked their way over the uneven ground. George Wilby moved off towards the small, bunker-like stone building next to the tower and Emma saw him fumbling in his pocket. He produced a key and let himself in.

There was a moment's silence then a low, ominous rumble that grew in volume.

'Look,' Emma said, glancing skyward.

The two large wheels that controlled the winch were turning slowly, metal grinding against metal.

The other three men had walked towards the mine entrance. There was a sliding metal door and, beyond it, another partition that looked like a huge grille.

Adam Wood slid the door to one side and he and his companions stepped into the cramped, dark space that was the cage.

Emma heard him shout something to Wilby and the wheels of the winch began moving more quickly.

'What the fuck are they doing?' Morton murmured.

'The mine's still working,' Emma said, her eyes on the small building next to the tower.

'But why?' Tate mused.

The rumbling of the winch filled the cold night air and the ground shook slightly.

'How far down do you think it goes?' Morton asked.

'Two or three hundred feet,' Tate guessed. 'Probably more.'

'I don't understand this,' Morton grunted. 'And don't tell me they're here to pay their respects to their dead mates.'

Emma could only shake her head.

'I think we should get back to the house,' Tate said. 'We obviously shouldn't be here. If they wanted visitors they wouldn't have the gate padlocked, would they?'

'Didn't Wilby say something about the buildings having been left alone for a reason?' Emma asked. 'You know, the first night we arrived, when we met him in the pub and he told us about the explosion in the mine. I'm sure he said something about all the machinery and buildings having been left intact as some kind of memorial.'

'He didn't say they still went down there though, did he?' Morton offered, an edge to his voice. 'Especially not in the middle of the fucking night!'

'Let's just go,' Tate insisted.

'We can't,' Emma told him. 'We'll never get back to the car without Wilby spotting us.'

'What the fuck's he going to do if he does see us?' Morton wanted to know.

'We're probably trespassing, Pete,' Tate said by way of an answer.

'So what do we do?' Morton demanded. 'Stand in here freezing our arses off all night until the four of them go back to Roxton? Fuck that. He'll never see us in the dark. We can get back to the car and be away before he even knows we were here.'

They looked at each other, as if testing the validity of the idea.

'All right,' Emma said finally.

Tate eased the door open a fraction and glanced out.

The building they were hiding in was a good hundred yards from the winding shed. A hundred yards of pitch darkness.

'Pete, you go first,' Tate said. 'Go.'

Morton slipped through the door and ran hell for leather in the direction of the gap in the fence where they'd slipped through. He kept low to the ground, looking back once in the direction of the winding shed.

The rumble of machinery was still loud in the night air. Emma guessed that the cage hadn't reached the bottom of the shaft yet. The noise would mask their passage over the hard ground.

She slipped past Tate and out into the night, running as fast as she could, her feet pounding.

She'd gone fifty yards when the grinding of the winch stopped.

Deathly silence descended.

64

For interminable seconds, Emma froze, looking fearfully over her shoulder in the direction of the winding shed, expecting Wilby to emerge any second.

And what if he does? What have you done wrong?

She nodded to herself, her breathing gradually slowing. Her heart continued to pound against her ribs so hard she feared the sound would travel through the darkness and alert not just Wilby but the whole of Roxton.

She remained ducked low to the ground, aware of a terrible chill running through her. It was as if it was seeping upwards from the frozen earth, permeating the soles of her boots then creeping inexorably up through her veins until it clutched her heart. As she exhaled, her breath clouded before her.

A hazy curtain of fog was moving slowly across the open ground between Emma and the fence. She began to edge slowly towards it, walking as if she was reluctant to put too much pressure on the cold ground for fear of making a noise. She shivered as the mist enveloped her but moved on at a steady pace, seeing the fence ahead. It was only a vague outline in the cloying darkness, but if she could reach it undetected she could slip through the gap in the fence.

There would be no need for Wilby, Jackson, Howard or Wood to know that she or anybody else had been here.

Fifty yards.

Again she glanced over her shoulder and still Wilby hadn't emerged from the winding shed.

Or at least she couldn't *see* him.

Forty yards.

Keep going. Don't look back.

She was less than twenty yards from the fence when she felt the hand grip her arm.

Emma screamed.

'Come on,' rasped Tate in her ear, the hand he'd clasped around her arm tugging at her, urging her to sprint the last few yards with him towards the gap in the fence and the car that waited beyond it.

George Wilby heard the scream echo through the night and he bolted from the winding shed, eyes narrowed in an effort to see through the blackness. He ran back inside and snatched up the torch that lay beside the control panel.

He strode back out and aimed the beam in the direction of the scream. The powerful light caught the outline of two figures pulling at the wire fence. He saw them heading for a car then frowned as he saw the car reverse, heading backwards up the narrow road that led to the main gate of the mine workings.

'Hey,' Wilby shouted, advancing towards the fleeing car, his torch waving wildly. 'What the bloody hell do you think you're doing?'

But the vehicle had already disappeared into the enveloping night, hurtling away with its tyres squealing. He caught a glimpse of the headlights as they flashed on, then there was only blackness once more.

He stood there for a moment longer then turned and headed back into the winding shed, wondering who had been so close to the mine.

'Think you can run, do you?' he murmured to himself. 'Well, you'll see that you can't. There's nowhere to run. You'll realise that soon enough.' He would raise the cage again when he heard the signal. A bell would be rung inside it, notifying him that the occupants were ready to be brought back to the surface.

And when they came back up from the subterranean depths he would tell them what he'd seen.

65

'And what the hell were you expecting him to do if he *had* seen us?' chuckled Morton, looking into the back seat where Emma sat.

'We were trespassing, like Nick said,' she answered.

'Yeah, but what would they have done to us?' Morton persisted. 'Moaned a bit, called us interfering southern bastards and that would have been it. Yet we were all creeping around as if we'd just discovered they were fucking Satanists or something.'

Emma also laughed. A combination of alcohol, adrenalin and relief.

Relief at what? The fact that you didn't have to explain yourself to Wilby and his friends?

As they pulled into the driveway of the house it did all seem just a little bit ridiculous. After all, there was probably a very good reason for the four men being at the mine, even at such an ungodly hour.

'I just wouldn't have wanted them to think that we were snooping,' Emma declared.

'What kind of fucking word is that?' laughed Morton. 'You make us sound like extras from *Scooby-Doo*.'

Emma and Tate both smiled.

'If they're going to be pissing about in the woods near the house we're renting during the early hours of the morning then they've got to expect people to be curious,' Morton continued. 'Especially if they were on private property. Just because they live in the town doesn't give them a right to wander about wherever they bloody well like, does it?'

'I agree,' Tate said. 'But we'd still have looked pretty stupid if they'd caught us.'

'And what would they have done?' Morton wanted to know. 'Barred us from the local? Stopped us eating at The George and Dragon? Not let you buy any more of Adam Wood's charming paintings?' He grunted. 'Give me a fucking break.'

He hauled himself out of the Volvo as Tate brought it to a halt and switched off the engine.

'Wait until we tell Jo what happened,' Emma said.

'She'll be in bed if she's got any sense,' Tate remarked. 'And I don't blame her.' He looked at the house. There was a light burning on the landing.

'I need a drink,' Morton said. As he pushed open the front door he pulled off his coat, shaking his head as he glanced at the tear in the material of the arm. 'Look at that. Shit.' He hung the coat on the stand in the hallway and headed for the kitchen, blundering through the door noisily.

'Pete,' Emma hissed. 'Jo might be asleep.'

Morton shrugged, slapped on the lights in the room and retrieved a clean glass from a cupboard. 'Come to Daddy,' he murmured, picking up a bottle of Jack Daniel's from the worktop beneath.

As he wandered past the bottom of the stairs he looked up towards the landing. 'Honey, I'm home,' he called, laughing.

Tate looked at Emma and shook his head. All three of them headed back into the dining room.

Jo was sitting at the end of the dining-room table, her face pale, her eyes heavy-lidded.

'I thought you'd be in bed,' Morton told her.

The others joined him.

'Are you all right, Jo?' Emma wanted to know.

'Have fun on your little adventure?' Jo enquired flatly.

'They're off their heads,' Morton said, downing a large measure of JD. 'The whole lot of them. Roxton is inhabited by nutters. Wandering about in the middle of the night, pissing around down disused coal mines. Inbred nutters.' He raised his glass in salute.

'He sees what will remain hidden,' Jo said quietly.

Emma frowned and moved closer to her friend.

'The inscription on the first of the windows,' Jo continued. 'That's what it means. I worked it out using that dictionary.'

'How can you be sure?' Emma wanted to know.

'It makes sense, doesn't it?' Jo challenged. 'I worked through all the possible meanings of each word then cross-referenced them until I figured out whether or not they were verbs, nouns, present tenses, conjugations or whatever else.'

Emma saw the scribblings on the pad beside the laptop, the image of the window still displayed on the screen.

Jo scrolled to the image of another of the windows. 'The inscription on *that* one means, Let fear be consumed,' she explained before clicking on the third.

'And that?' Tate enquired, looking at a window showing the Cross where Christ had been crucified being hacked down by men with axes.

'Beneath us he gives life,' Jo told him.

'Beneath us,' Emma murmured.

'There was only one word I couldn't work out,' Jo said. 'But it appears on *every* window. Sometimes only in the tiniest writing, sometimes even written backwards, but it's there on every one of the new windows.'

'Lorican,' Emma said, looking at the pad where Jo had scribbled the word.

'And it wasn't in the Latin dictionary?' Tate echoed.

'It isn't a Latin *word*,' Jo informed him. 'The closest thing to it is *lorica* and that means breastplate. As far as I can see, it doesn't mean anything in Latin.'

'Then what is it?' Emma wanted to know. 'Another language?'

Jo zoomed in on one of the window panels bearing the word. 'I think it's a name,' she said softly. 'I did a search of the Web but there were so many references to it. Everything from a chord progression in music to some kind of games console chat room. There were too many mentions and none that sounded anything remotely like what we're looking for. It's too difficult to filter the name out.'

'So we're no closer,' Emma said quietly.

Jo shook her head.

66

'Whatever the fuck it is, let's leave it until the morning.'

Morton's words seemed to echo around the inside of the dining room. He looked at each of his companions in turn.

Jo and Emma were still gazing at the screen. Only Tate nodded.

'I agree,' he said. 'I'm exhausted, apart from anything else. We'll get a good night's sleep. Clear our heads. Enough's happened tonight already.' He put his arm around Emma's waist and pulled her to him.

'I think we should go up to the mine tomorrow,' Emma suggested. 'Have a look around in the daylight.'

'Fuck the mine,' Morton said. 'Fuck the secret puzzles and fuck everyone in Roxton. We came here for a holiday, not to get mixed up in what those idiots do in their spare time. It's none of our business and it never has been. I think we're all making far too much of it.'

'You saw what happened tonight, Pete. How can you say that?' Emma snapped.

'*You* tell *me* what I saw, Emma,' he rasped. 'I saw some torchlights on the path at the bottom of the garden. I saw an abandoned mine. I saw four local blokes arrive at that mine, blokes who'd worked down there and lost friends down there. I saw three of them go underground. That was *it*.'

'Don't you think it's weird?' Emma persisted.

'Maybe it is, but it's none of our fucking business,' he repeated.

'What do *you* think, Nick?' Emma demanded, turning towards her husband.

'It is weird,' he said quietly. 'I'll give you that. But perhaps we *are* making too much of it. We've all been drinking. And the business with the inscriptions on the church windows, it probably means nothing.'

'You didn't say that before,' she barked at him.

'What do you want me to say?' he snapped. 'What do *you* think is going on? What do you think is the significance of the windows and the mine and everything else?'

Emma pulled angrily away from him.

'We need to get away from here,' Tate continued. 'Forget about all these so-called secrets that we think we've discovered. Let's drive into Derby tomorrow, have a meal, do some shopping. Forget about Roxton for a while.'

'Why don't we just pack our cases and go home?' Jo interjected. 'There's nothing keeping us here.'

'Why the hell should we go home?' Morton demanded. 'So some of the locals are a bit fucking touched.' He tapped his temple. 'That's not our problem. They haven't tried to hurt us. They haven't even bothered us. They couldn't give a shit about us.' He drained what was left in his glass. 'Let's go to bed.'

He stumbled towards the door, pausing a moment to look back at the others. 'I'll see you all in the morning,' he called. 'Unless some mad Roxton devil-worshippers come and get me in the night.'

They heard him laughing to himself as he blundered up the stairs.

Jo sat at the laptop for a moment longer then slowly got to her feet.

Emma reached out and squeezed her arm, wanting to say something but not sure what it was. Instead she merely watched as Jo padded out of the room and made her way upstairs.

'Come on, Emma,' Tate said quietly. 'Let's go to bed.'

'Is that what you really think?' she began irritably. 'That all this means nothing?'

He sucked in a weary breath. 'I think we might be over-reacting,' he told her.

'Then what the hell was going on up at the mine tonight?'

'I don't know.'

'Like you said, we shouldn't have been there. We were trespassing.' She clicked on to a photo of the church.

'Leave it, Emma,' Tate murmured.

'You go to bed,' she told him without looking up. 'I won't be long.'

'What are you looking for? More secrets? More mysteries that aren't even there?'

She ignored him.

He paused for a moment longer then made his way towards the stairs.

Emma clicked on to another photo. Then another. She rubbed her eyes, exhaustion draping itself around her like a blanket. She yawned and sat back on the chair, rolling her head gently from left to right as she felt the stiffness growing in her neck and shoulders.

She looked back at the screen.

The faces of her mother and father peered out at her.

Emma blinked hard, expecting the image to disappear.

She looked closely at it. There seemed to be no background to the picture. Only her dead parents in the foreground with nothing more than a blur behind them.

She clicked on to the next photo.

It was the graveyard of Roxton church. There were two coffins lying on the wet earth, one containing her mother, the other her father. Dressed in the clothes they had died in, the injuries that had killed them still vivid.

Emma looked at the next picture.

She herself was in that one. Kneeling naked between the two coffins. As she always was in her nightmares.

As she looked at the picture she felt a tightness in her chest. It was as if an iron vice had been fastened around her sternum and was quickly being closed. Her breath was coming in short gasps. The crushing pain was spreading across her chest, down her left arm and up her neck into her jaw.

She struggled to her feet, wanting help, wanting someone to stop this terrible pain.

Her vision swam.

As she reached the dining-room door, her legs buckled beneath her.

The pain was almost intolerable now. She dragged herself along the carpet to the bottom of the stairs and tried to call her husband's name.

She knew what was happening and she wanted to see his face one last time before she died.

Not here. Not now.

Emma was aware of movement on the stairs, of someone making their way back down towards her but moving slowly and sedately with no semblance of urgency.

She looked up and saw that there were two figures.

White stars danced behind her eyelids.

The two figures were kneeling over her now.

She looked up into the dead faces of her mother and father and, in that final second before darkness overcame her, she found the breath to scream.

67

Nick Tate could hear movement and talking in the other main guest room as he reached the top of the stairs.

Another row?

He was beginning to wonder how the hell Jo and Pete had managed to stay together and, more to the point, how much longer they would remain that way. Before his eyes he had seen their relationship deteriorate in the last few days. Perhaps it was because of what had been said. Too much drink. And yet he'd known the seeds of that self-destruction had been there long before they'd reached the house.

Tate passed through his own room and into the bathroom where he spun the taps and filled the sink, turning to urinate while he waited for the water level to rise.

He flushed the toilet when he was finished and turned back to the sink, spinning the taps to turn them off.

For a moment he studied his reflection in the mirror. A quick shave and then he would clamber gratefully into bed. Hopefully, by that time, Emma would have joined him.

He coated his cheeks and chin with shaving foam and reached for his razor, pausing a moment.

Remember when you used to shave your father? Used to hold his head and use that old cut-throat of his to remove his whiskers?

He cursed under his breath as he nicked himself on the left cheek.

How many times did you want to draw that blade across his throat? Just finish it, there and then. Just as you knew he wanted you to.

A single drop of blood dripped into the water with a loud plink.

Tate cut himself again while shaving his top lip.

There was more blood this time and it mingled with the white foam of the shaving cream.

But you didn't need the cut-throat in the end, did you? Giving him the pills was better. Not as messy. Not as suspicious.

Another cut appeared on his left cheek. A larger one on his right.

Fuck this. He'd do it in the morning. He was obviously more tired than he thought.

He bent down to wash the remnants of blood-flecked shaving cream from his face. The cuts stung.

Tate straightened up to inspect his reflection, to see how bad the cuts were.

He *had* no reflection.

The only thing he could see was the bathroom behind and around him.

Something made him turn, then look back again into the mirror.

He still couldn't see himself.

What was this madness?

With one shaking hand he reached out and touched the glass, spreading his fingers until his whole hand was pressing against the mirror.

He shook his head but there was still no image before him.

228

Get a fucking grip.

Tate took a step back, his fear mingling with anger and disbelief.

Where am I?

He almost laughed, nearly spoke the words aloud.

You can't lose a reflection, you fucking idiot.

His breath was coming in short gasps now. His mouth was dry.

You're cracking up.

Tate snarled something and let the blood-stained water out of the sink, watching it swirl around the plughole.

When he looked into the mirror again there *was* an image there. But it was standing behind him. To the rear of where his own reflection should have been.

Twisted. Angry. Glaring at him.

His father.

Tate felt the touch of the cut-throat razor against his flesh then the coldness of the blade as it was drawn across his throat, hacking effortlessly through his larynx and carotid arteries.

Blood exploded from the severed vessels, hitting the mirror with incredible force.

Tate tried to scream but he merely dropped to his knees, his eyes rolling upwards in their sockets, his grip on consciousness fading quickly.

Two more savage cuts, one to each side of his neck, lacerated his jugular veins and then pressure on the top of his skull. His hair was being tugged. He felt a knee in his back, pushing him against the front of the marble sink that was now swimming with blood.

His head was coming free, only held in place by his spinal cord. He felt his father's hands trying to snap it. Trying to tear his head off.

And, finally, he saw it all in the mirror before him.

68

When she touched him, it was with a tenderness so long absent he'd forgotten it.

Morton smiled and lifted Jo's head slightly, gently holding her soft hair between his fingers. She smiled at him and kissed him on the lips, her perfectly manicured nails trailing slowly around his testicles and the base of his penis.

He felt the swell of her breasts as she pressed more tightly against him and the wind that was now blowing strongly around the house seemed a million miles away from the warmth inside the room where he and his wife writhed in the throes of their passion.

She straddled his thighs, looking down at his erection, cradling it in one hand. With her free hand she reached back between her legs and rubbed gently for a second.

Morton closed his eyes as he felt the liquid warmth being smeared over the bulbous head of his penis. He drew in a breath, excited and surprised by the extent of her arousal. The warmth on his stiff shaft was growing more intense.

He looked down.

Even in the darkness of the room he could see that his penis and testicles were glistening with dark fluid.

There was a pungent odour in his nostrils now which he recognised as blood.

He saw Jo reach back between her legs then hold up her hand, crimson dripping from it.

Using the blood as a lubricant she massaged his shaft and, for precious seconds, he remained immobile beneath her. Torn between his revulsion and the sheer pleasure that was enveloping him.

He spoke her name, wondering if she herself hadn't realised that she was bleeding.

She merely looked down at him, but this time he saw the tears in her eyes.

When her hand came from between her legs the next time she had slivers of slippery skin beneath her nails, hanging like translucent webbing.

She moved her hand with incredible speed, pushing the nail of her index finger into his urethra, boring deeper until she was as deep as the pad of her finger.

Morton tried to scream as fresh blood now poured over his stomach and thighs while Jo held his softening erection upright. She lowered her blood-drenched vagina on to it with one expert movement and, despite the pain, Morton thrust upwards to meet her.

He felt the top of his lacerated penis butt against something soft.

It took him only a second to realise that it was the bulbous head of his dead child. His penis penetrated the barely formed bones and drove into the brain of the foetus.

Again he screamed, and this time Jo joined him in that explosion of sound.

She raised herself up and the tiny body of the foetus seemed to drag itself free of her vagina, little fingers gripping at her bloodied labial lips to gain purchase as it tore its way from between her thighs.

Jo was shaking uncontrollably now, looking down at the

foetus and the riven remains of Morton's penis. His now flaccid organ flopped to one side and she gripped his scrotum with both hands, pulling hard, until the skin ruptured and one swollen testicle came free.

How many women had he betrayed her with? How many others had touched him there? she wondered, her mind spinning as she looked at the pulsating sphere in the palm of her hand. And she listened to his screams and added her own as the foetus continued to pull itself from her vagina, forced out by the discharge that followed it. The umbilical cord that still joined her to it was twisting and turning like a maddened snake.

Morton's body was bucking uncontrollably now, his eyes wide with pain and horror.

Jo reached for the foetus and pressed down on its large head with the flat of her hand.

The head seemed to swell for a second then it burst like an overripe melon.

More screams.

69

They woke together. As if some huge alarm had been tripped.

A switch thrown that had catapulted all four of them from their nightmares simultaneously.

But, as they woke, the nightmares didn't fade, they remained etched into their brains. Vivid and glowing like fresh weals from some savage beating. Burns from a glowing-hot poker that had been seared into their minds.

Emma stumbled out of bed, clutching at her chest, wondering where the pain was.

She looked across at her husband who was sitting bolt upright, both hands gripping his throat, his eyes wide and staring.

They regarded each other for long seconds then Emma reached out towards him.

'I had a nightmare,' she gasped as he pulled her closer.

'Me too,' he answered.

'It was my mum and dad again.'

'The same as usual?'

'No. They were here. I saw myself at their grave side but I was the one who died.'

He stroked her hair.

'I saw my father too,' Tate confessed.

There was a knock on the bedroom door and, when Emma called for the newcomer to enter, she looked up to see Jo standing pale and wan in the doorway.

'Are you all right?' Emma asked.

'We had nightmares,' she said. 'Both of us. We heard screaming coming from your room too when we woke up.'

'Same here,' Emma told her.

Morton joined her, running a hand through his hair. 'I've never known a nightmare so vivid,' he said, clearing his throat. There was still dread in his eyes. 'Never.'

'I saw the baby again,' Jo said, looking down. 'The baby I had aborted.'

'*Again*?' Emma said. 'You said you saw it *again*. Have you had that nightmare before?'

Jo sat down on the edge of the bed, her hands clasped together. 'When I was in the bath yesterday,' she began, 'I saw something . . . imagined something. I might even have been dreaming *then*. I saw a foetus. The bath was full of blood.' She lowered her head.

'Why didn't you say something?' Emma insisted.

'So your nightmare was about the child you had aborted?' Tate asked.

Jo nodded.

'What about you, Pete?' Tate continued. 'What was yours about?'

'I saw the aborted child in *my* dream too,' Morton murmured. 'But it was Jo who was . . . mutilating me. Ripping my fucking balls off. Literally.'

'I saw that in my dream,' Jo echoed. 'I wanted revenge for what you'd done. For your cheating.'

'Yours involved your parents,' Tate said to Emma. 'But also your worst fear. Sudden death. A heart attack.'

'How do you know that?'

'Your nightmares always involve your parents.'

'But they don't always involve me having a heart attack. You knew about that too.'

Tate swallowed hard.

'So what was your nightmare, Nick?' Morton wanted to know.

'My father. I saw my father. He killed me.'

'Like you killed him,' Morton observed. 'All four of us, simultaneously, had nightmares about our worst fears. Jo and I even shared the same images in the fucking dream. And you knew what Emma was dreaming about.'

'Let fear be consumed,' Emma said quietly.

'What did you say?' Tate asked.

'Let fear be consumed,' she repeated. 'It was the inscription on one of the church windows.'

Her words hung in the air like a rotten smell.

70

Samantha Ryan waited for as long as she could endure before glancing at the bedside clock. She shook her head wearily.

2.13 a.m.

Her baby son had been crying for well over an hour now.

Sam had thought that if she left him long enough he would tire himself out and simply fall asleep again but that had not happened. Her fear of what neighbours might say had also prevented her from continuing with this particular strategy.

She had lain in bed listening to his strident shrieks, her fists clenched, her eyes screwed closed in the hope that the noise would cease.

Just one night's rest. Please.

She stumbled as she got out of bed, pulling her dressing gown around her.

Her son continued to cry.

'All right, Jack,' she called, advancing unsteadily towards his room. 'Mummy's coming.'

When she reached the threshold of the child's room she paused, leaning against the frame of the door for a moment to support herself.

She could see him in his cot. So small. So frail. It was hard to comprehend that a figure so small could produce such deafening sounds. Sounds that Sam could bear no longer.

'Jack,' she whispered, almost sorrowfully. 'Please.'

He still cried.

However, as she leant over him, the little boy momentarily stopped. Sam rejoiced in the precious seconds of silence.

'Good boy,' she said, her voice cracking. 'You be quiet for Mummy, now.'

He looked at her with his large, watery eyes for a second longer then began crying again.

Sam shook her head, her own tears welling up. 'No, Jack,' she said.

She reached in and lifted him up, gazing directly into his face.

'No,' she repeated. This time the word was spoken with a reproachful rather than soothing tone. 'Shut up,' she rasped.

He struggled in her arms, his exhortations now louder.

'Stop it,' she snapped, shaking him once.

His head snapped back and the sudden movement seemed to stun him momentarily into silence.

Again Sam welcomed that fleeting second of peace like a thirsty man welcomes a drop of liquid. But it passed all too quickly.

Jack began to cry more loudly.

She shook him again. Harder this time and for longer.

Even when blood began to run from both his nostrils, some of it spraying onto her face and neck, she still shook his tiny form vigorously.

He vomited, but it was as if she had settled into a rhythm and she could not stop.

By the time she slammed his small head against the side

of the cot for the third time he was making no sound at all.

Sam dropped to her knees, a smile on her face.

The silence was exquisite.

She was breathing heavily from her exertions but Jack had stopped crying. That was all that mattered to her.

Sam stroked his head with one hand, not even noticing the blood that coated her palm.

All she was aware of was the glorious silence.

'Good boy,' she whispered.

71

Despite the grey sky that darkened the morning, Emma was grateful that they'd at least been spared the rain. She stood at the bedroom window gazing alternately up at the cloudy heavens and out across the valley in the direction of Roxton.

'Come with us,' Tate said, emerging from the bathroom.

'I don't feel like a trip into Derby, Nick,' she told him. 'I've already told you that.'

'So you're going to leave *me* to act as referee once Pete and Jo start?'

'Everything'll be fine,' she said turning to face him.

There was a long silence, broken by Tate. 'Are you going to be all right here on your own?' he asked. 'After what happened last night.'

'After a nightmare?' she smiled, the gesture looking strained. 'Why shouldn't I be?'

There was a knock on the bedroom door and Jo peered into the room. 'I just wondered if you were ready?' she asked. 'Pete's already outside in the car. Impatient sod.'

'I'm coming,' Tate told her, picking up his wallet from the bedside table. 'And before you ask, no, Emma isn't going to change her mind. I've already tried persuading her.'

Emma smiled at them both.

'Go and enjoy yourself, Jo,' she grinned. 'You always used to say you fancied having two blokes at the same time. Now you can have one on each arm.'

'That wasn't what I used to mean,' Jo said, raising her eyebrows.

They all made their way down the stairs where Emma kissed Tate and said her goodbyes, watching as the Volvo pulled away. After a few moments she wandered into the kitchen.

There was a small notice board beside the phone on the far wall. Tacked to it were several business cards bearing the numbers of taxi firms.

She dialled the number of the first one she came to.

'Hello,' Emma said. 'I'd like a taxi into Roxton please. Yes, as soon as you can.' She gave them the address of the house.

The taxi, the voice at the other end of the line assured her, would be with her in ten minutes.

Emma hung up and hurried upstairs to change.

She got the driver to drop her close to the market square. The church was a short walk away.

She reached it in less than five minutes, pausing for a moment at the wooden archway that spanned the path leading up to the imposing building.

Her boots crunched on the gravel as she walked and she slowed down again as she reached the grave of Catherine Pearce.

There were a number of wreaths and other floral arrangements on the freshly turned earth, the cellophane wrapping around them crackling with each gust of wind.

Emma noticed that someone was placing a small bouquet on one of the graves away to her right. She glanced at the other visitor for a moment then made her way towards the church door and entered the building.

Right, now you're here, what exactly are you going to do?

She paused beside the font, noticed that there was no one inside the church and made her way down the nave, her heels clicking on the stone floor.

Emma looked to her right and left, at the stained-glass windows old and new and, more particularly, at the previously unknown words that decorated them.

He sees what will remain hidden.

She glanced at the pulpit, as if expecting Reverend Lawrence to be standing there.

Beneath us he gives life.

She reached the memorial to the dead miners and lowered her head reverentially as she studied it for a moment before moving on towards the chancel.

Let fear be consumed.

It was obvious to Emma by the time she was facing the altar that Lawrence was not inside the church. She wondered where he might be and decided to try the vicarage. She stood gazing up at the large figure of Christ that hung above the altar, then turned and made her way back briskly through the church.

She almost collided with George Wilby as she left the building.

Emma jumped back, letting out a gasp of surprise.

'Hello, there,' Wilby said good naturedly.

'Hello,' she said, regaining her composure.

Had he seen her the previous night? Was this all some elaborate game?

'Looking for the vicar?' he asked.

Tell him the truth.

'It's not important if he's busy,' she said.

'No, he's around. He's always around. Where's your husband and your friends?'

'They've gone into Derby for the day.'

'But you didn't fancy it, eh? Big towns; too much hustle

and bustle. You're better off here. It's quiet and no one's in a hurry.' He regarded her evenly. 'Although you look as if *you* are.'

'I've got a few things to do before I go back to the house.'

'I'll let you go then.' He stepped to one side and she hurried back on to the path leading away from the church.

Emma was sure she could feel his eyes on her as she headed for the street.

She turned.

Wilby was nowhere to be seen.

Imagination running away with you again? Or did he see you last night?

She swallowed hard then walked off in the direction of the vicarage.

72

The gate creaked slightly as Emma opened it and made her way up the short path to the ivy-covered façade that formed the front of the vicarage.

The houses on either side of it looked very similar and, for brief moments, Emma wondered if she was being watched. If curtains were twitching.

She sucked in a deep breath.

Get a bloody grip, for Christ's sake. You're getting paranoid.

She banged three times on the front door and waited.

Lawrence answered almost immediately.

'Hello,' he said, smiling.

'I'm sorry to disturb you,' she told him. 'But I wondered if you had a minute to spare?'

'By all means,' Lawrence grinned, ushering her inside. 'I've just made a cup of tea, if you'd like one.'

She accepted his offer, allowing him to show her through into the small and immaculately kept sitting room.

'Have a seat, please,' he urged. 'I'd like to take some credit for the way the place looks but I'm afraid that's down to Mrs Alsop who cleans for me. It's one of the perks.' He wandered off into the kitchen.

Emma looked around the room. At the open fireplace,

the shelves of books and the TV and DVD player. She smiled as she noticed several CDs and DVDs lying near the machine.

As Lawrence re-entered the room he saw her gazing at the various titles.

'I know "Britney Spears' Greatest Hits" might not seem church prescribed,' he mused, 'but I always maintain that I shouldn't have to give spiritual guidance in a cultural vacuum.' He laughed and poured Emma's tea.

She nodded.

Tell him why you're here.

'Sugar?' he asked, tongs hovering over the bowl.

Again Emma nodded and he dropped a lump into her cup.

'Do people still visit the mine?' she asked.

There. It's said.

Lawrence looked puzzled.

'Is it used in any way, shape or form these days?' she continued.

'It closed over twenty years ago.'

'I didn't mean as a workplace.'

'I'm not with you.'

'The memorial to the men killed in the accident that happened down the mine is in the church. You showed my husband and me yesterday. But is there anything inside the mine itself? Do people still go down there?'

'Why would they?'

Emma could only shake her head.

Tell him.

'For the last two nights we've seen torches on the path at the back of the house we're renting. The path that leads to the mine. Last night we drove there. My husband, one of our friends and I. We saw some men there. Mr Wood who runs the antiques shop. Mr Howard who owns The Snipe and Mr Jackson from The George and Dragon. They

244

went *down* the mine. Mr Wilby was with them. I wondered if you knew why.'

'And you saw this?'

Emma nodded.

'I have no idea why they'd want to go down there,' Lawrence told her. 'Why don't you ask them? I'm sure they'd be happy to explain—'

'I'd rather not,' Emma cut in. 'They might think we were interfering.'

'With what?'

'That's what I'd like to know.'

'What do *you* think they were doing down there?'

Emma shook her head gently then took a sip of her tea. When she looked up, Lawrence had his gaze fixed on her. She shifted uncomfortably.

'Does the word Lorican mean anything to you?' she asked.

73

Lawrence repeated the word then shook his head. 'Should it?' he asked, attempting a smile that never touched his eyes.

'It's on the windows in your church,' she explained. 'In large letters, small letters. Sometimes written backwards. But it's there. It's even more prominent on the newer windows.'

'How do you know?'

'We looked at the photos my husband took inside the church yesterday. We worked out the meanings of the Latin inscriptions on the stained-glass windows. They're not exactly . . . biblical.'

'I see your point, but *He sees what will remain hidden*, for instance. The "He" could refer to God,' Lawrence told her. '*Beyond the reach of death* is one of the inscriptions on the memorial to the dead of the mine disaster. Those who are with God *are* beyond the reach of Death.'

'What about *Let fear be consumed?*'

'All fears are consumed by God, any earthly worries are removed by him.'

Emma nodded.

'There's nothing strange about the inscriptions,' Lawrence told her.

'I thought you didn't understand them,' she said, challengingly. 'You told us yesterday that you didn't.'

'No. I said I wasn't sure what the new stained-glass windows *represented*, not that I didn't understand the inscriptions on them.'

'*Beneath us he gives life*,' Emma offered. '*Beneath* us? Isn't God meant to be in heaven?' She pointed a finger skyward. 'What's *that* supposed to mean? What's beneath us that gives life?'

Lawrence got to his feet and walked across to the fireplace, warming his hands before the dancing flames.

'The inscriptions aren't always literal,' he said without looking at her. 'Different interpretations can be put on them.'

'So what interpretation would *you* put on something like that?'

'Life comes from the earth. The earth is beneath our feet. God created the earth. God gives us life.'

Emma looked mildly disappointed for a moment as Lawrence turned back to face her. 'That still doesn't explain the meaning of Lorican,' she persisted.

Lawrence shrugged. 'I told you yesterday that some of the words in the church were old English,' he explained. 'Medieval. Lorican might be one of those words.'

'It must mean something important if it's so prominent.'

'May I ask you something? I don't mean to pry, but what exactly are you trying to find in my church?'

'I wasn't trying to find *anything*, Reverend Lawrence. It's just that it's getting more and more difficult to ignore it.'

'Ignore *what*?' he snapped.

'What's going on in Roxton,' she blurted out.

'And what do you *think* is going on? What's so terrible about this town and the people who live here? They're normal people just like you and your husband and your friends. I had the same kind of mentality when *I* first came here. I expected it to be a closed community that didn't welcome strangers. I was wrong.'

'I'm not talking about people's hospitality, Reverend. I've never questioned that. I came here today hoping you could help me. All I'm asking you to do is consider what I've told you.'

'That's the whole point. You haven't told me *anything*.'

Emma got to her feet. 'Why are men still visiting the mine?' she demanded. 'The only four men, I might add, who survived a disaster that almost destroyed this town. One of those men designed the windows in your church. Windows that show the *weakness* of God and His son, not His strength.'

Lawrence lowered his head slightly.

'The mine's the key to all this,' Emma insisted. 'It always *has* been. I'm right, aren't I?'

She was already on her way to the front door. Lawrence hurried after her, grabbing her arm. She tried to shake loose but he gripped her tightly.

'Look in the town library,' he said, his voice little more than a whisper. 'You'll find your answers there.'

She paused, looking questioningly at him, but he had the front door open now.

'Thank you for calling,' he said, his voice rising in volume once more.

Emma stepped out on to the path, looking back at the priest. He held her gaze for a moment longer then shut the front door.

Inside the house, Lawrence leant against the wooden partition, his forehead pressed to the heavy oak, his breath coming in short gasps.

He finally turned and headed back into the sitting room.

'What did she want?'

George Wilby was standing close to the kitchen door, looking at the priest.

Lawrence froze.

'How long have you been here?' the priest wanted to know.

'The back door was open,' Wilby told him. 'I came in. Heard voices. I recognised hers.'

'I didn't tell her anything.'

'I heard *some* of what was said. She'll come back, you know. She won't let it drop. She's a determined woman. She won't stop until she's found her answers.' He fixed Lawrence in an unblinking stare. 'You'd better hope she doesn't find them from *you*, Reverend.'

74

Roxton library was a large grey stone building that looked as if it had been hewn from one massive lump of granite instead of built brick by brick.

Emma hesitated for a moment on the bottom step of the five stone stairs that led up to its black-painted main doors. Her mind was spinning with the conversation she'd just had with Reverend Lawrence. She could still see the look on his face as he'd shut the door.

Had someone been watching them?

Emma tried to shake herself free from the grip of paranoia that had closed around her. She made her way up the remaining steps and into the library itself.

The interior looked more modern than she'd expected. There was a large desk straight ahead, behind which stood a young woman who smiled welcomingly at her before resuming her work at a computer.

Another member of staff was pushing a trolley around the shelves, checking the numbers on the spines of books and replacing them in their appointed places.

To her left was a brightly decorated area with bean bags, small tables and chairs and paintings of cartoon characters which she realised was where the children's books were housed.

Ahead of her, beyond the main desk and slightly to the left, was the fiction section, a reference area and what she took to be the equivalent of a reading room.

There were just three customers as far as Emma could see. A man in his twenties was walking slowly back and forth along the rows of fiction. Another man was skimming through a book he'd taken from the MILITARY HISTORY section and there was a woman in her forties heading for the main desk to check out the armful of books she was carrying.

Emma passed her and headed on into the reference section.

Where to start?

She looked at the vast array of volumes before her as if expecting one to leap out and offer up the information she sought.

Emma moved over to the encyclopedias, running one index finger over the spines of *Britannica*. She stopped at the volume that might contain what she wanted (an explanation of the meaning of Lorican) and wondered about pulling it out. Instead, she moved slowly around the reference section, occasionally glancing in the direction of the two men.

Were they watching her?

Paranoia again? Get a fucking grip.

There were history books, volumes about the geographical area. About Roxton itself. About everything.

Where do I start?

Emma turned and saw that the woman at the desk had finished checking out her books and was making her way towards the exit.

The young woman working at the computer looked over at Emma and smiled again before continuing with what she was doing.

Emma returned the gesture and looked back at the endless rows of books again.

Look in the town library. You'll find your answers there.
Lawrence's words came flooding back into her mind.

But where? Think.

The word she sought was old English, that much she knew. Old English. Historical. Medieval.

Find books that cover that period.

She picked out three, including one about stained-glass windows in England. Another was a study of English history from 1400 to 1600. The third was about churches.

Emma flicked through the contents pages, then the indexes of all three. Nothing. No mention of the word Lorican.

If Jo couldn't find it on the Web search then how the hell do you hope to find it now?

She chose more. The volume of *Britannica* that she hoped would contain the entry. A book about monasteries. Another concerning historical figures that had lived in medieval times.

Again nothing.

Help me.

She slammed the last book shut, noticing that the young woman behind the desk was looking at her.

Watching her?

Emma replaced the books she'd already viewed and wondered where to look next. She wondered if it might be worth consulting books about ancient languages. It seemed safe to assume that the word Lorican was archaic. And yet, if it was, why had it appeared in stained-glass windows only thirty years old? Nevertheless, she moved on to the next section and took down two dictionaries of medieval language.

Not a mention of Lorican.

Emma let out a long and tortured sigh. *This was impossible.*

There was only one thing to do. She would have to go

back to Lawrence, find out more information from him. Get him to either *tell* her or *show* her where to look. It was the only way. She moved slowly on, around the shelves that towered above her, passing through the labyrinth of reference material. Up one aisle and down another, looking to the left and right, her mind spinning.

She looked towards the main desk and the young woman tapping away at her computer keyboard.

Emma smiled to herself.

Perhaps there *was* another way to find what she sought.

75

'Sorry to be so vague,' Emma said apologetically. 'But that's all I've got.'

'No title or author?' asked the young woman behind the desk.

'Sorry. Just that one word.'

'Well, I'll try and find it for you, but our cataloguing system will only show anything with that word in if it's in the *title* of a book *and* if we've got it in stock. The central system's updated quite regularly though. There might even be a copy in another library if *we* haven't got it.'

'That's fine,' Emma said. 'If you wouldn't mind trying it for me, please. This is how you spell it.'

She pushed a piece of paper towards the young woman who nodded and carefully typed the letters L O R I C A N into the system.

'Let's see what comes up,' she said, smiling that efficient smile.

Out of the woman's view, Emma crossed her fingers.

'It's not showing anything, I'm afraid,' the young woman said finally, glancing at the screen. She scrolled down.

Emma felt her heart sink.

'Wait a minute, there *is* one record with that word in

the title, *The Lorican and other Legends.*' She tutted. 'It looks as if it's out of print though. It's old. The last edition was printed in 1926. I'm sorry.'

Why the hell hadn't the Web search come up with that reference?

'You said there might be a copy in another library. Could you check that for me, please?'

The young woman did as she was asked.

'It's showing that there aren't any copies, I'm afraid,' she told Emma.

'Is there an author's name with it?'

'J.S. Kramer.'

'What about a category? Is it fiction or non-fiction?'

'According to this it's showing up as a reference book.'

'Which section?'

'Myths and Legends. It's also listed under The Occult.'

Emma frowned and leant over the desk to look at the computer screen.

'Thanks for your help,' she said, smiling wanly. 'You haven't got a piece of paper I could scribble on, have you, please?'

The young woman handed her a couple of lined sheets and Emma thanked her, then turned and made her way back into the reference section, scanning the shelves once more.

The Occult.

Emma paused before a shelf bearing the label: WITCH-CRAFT.

She hesitated, scanning the titles: *An Encyclopedia Of Witchcraft And Demonology*; *The Necromancer*; *The Satanic Mass*; *The Book Of Demons*; *A Dictionary Of Devils And Demons.*

Her mouth was dry, her breathing low and rapid. She took two encyclopedias and a dictionary from the shelves and retreated to a nearby desk.

There was no mention in either of The Lorican.

Emma moved back to the shelves and spotted a slim, yellowed volume called *Haunted England*.

Emma went straight to the index, running her finger down the contents. It was there.

Lorican, the, Habitat 96 Origins 71–2

Emma flicked quickly to the pages she wanted and began reading, the fusty smell of the old paper strong in her nostrils. As she read she pulled the pieces of scrap paper closer to her, scribbling notes. She was halfway down the page when she stopped, her mouth moving silently like a fish dragged from water.

'Oh, my God,' she breathed.

76

Emma had no idea how long she'd been in the library. Only that it had been daylight when she'd entered and now, as she ran towards the vicarage, the early dusk that winter brings had blanketed the land.

The air was much colder too and her breath clouded before her as she hurried back across the village, glancing briefly in the direction of the church. It looked strangely menacing in the growing blackness. A large stone monolith, it towered above the gravestones that surrounded it like some all-powerful monarch over its subjects.

Emma reached the tree-lined road that led towards the vicarage and slowed her pace a little, trying to catch her breath. There were lights on in the houses. Islands of illumination in a sea of ever-deepening blackness.

The vicarage, however, was unlit.

She made her way through the creaky gate and up the short path to the front door where she knocked loudly and waited.

There was no answer.

She wondered if Lawrence might be in the church. He might even have gone into the town itself to do some shopping, she reasoned. His vocation didn't limit him merely to dwellings of a clerical origin after all.

She knocked again.

Still no answer.

She took a couple of steps back and looked up at the windows of the first floor. There was no sign of movement up there either.

Almost against her better judgement, Emma stepped off the path on to the small patch of lawn in front of the living-room window. She moved across it, cursing as her heels began sinking into the wet earth.

She cupped her hands around her eyes and pressed her face to the glass of the window.

The television was on inside the living room but, apart from the dull, flickering light cast by the moving images from the screen, there was no other illumination. There was also no sign of Reverend Lawrence.

For a second, Emma wondered exactly what she was going to say to the cleric if he did actually appear. Should she thank him for his help (as apparently reluctant as it had been), or share with him the information she'd gathered during her time in the library?

For one fleeting moment she wondered if her best course of action would be to scream insanely at him for allowing her to acquire the knowledge she'd gained in the course of her research.

It seemed a redundant question anyway; Lawrence showed no signs of answering his door. She moved back on to the path, took one last look up at the house and turned away, pausing again at the gate to look once more.

Perhaps she would phone him when she returned to the house. Possibly even visit him again the following day.

She glanced at her watch, realising that her husband, Jo and Morton would probably be home by now. She needed to get back and speak to them. To share what she'd discovered.

Again she looked at the vicarage and, this time, she felt the hairs on the back of her neck rise.

Fear?

She tried to fight the emotion.

Had she known who was watching her from the bedroom window of the vicarage, she might not have found that so easy.

77

They moved unhurriedly within the dark confines of the vicarage. Unworried by the possibility of intruders or visitors.

The lateness of the hour helped.

Inside the sitting room, the television was still on. They could hear laughter from the audience of the comedy show that was on the screen. It was curiously incongruous in what was otherwise undisturbed silence.

'What about his belongings?' George Wilby asked, stopping to glance at the television screen as he passed through the sitting room.

'Don't touch anything,' Adam Wood said.

'People will want to know where he's gone. People in Roxton.'

'They'll be curious, yes. But does anyone *really* care?'

Wilby considered the question for a moment then walked back out into the hallway of the vicarage, the laughter from the television show echoing behind him in the other room.

'What do you think he told her?' Wood mused, standing beside his companion, hands planted on his hips.

'Not much,' Wilby said quietly. 'Not enough.'

'Well, that's something we'll find out in time, George. I'm sure we can handle it, *whatever* he told her.'

Wilby nodded, his gaze still fixed ahead.

'We'd best get on,' Wood offered, running a hand through his hair.

He too looked forwards, his gaze appraising.

The body of Reverend James Lawrence hung from a thick rope that had been tied to the balustrade on the landing.

His eyes were open, bulging wide in their sockets. The blood vessels there had ruptured in a number of places. His blackened tongue was protruding from one corner of his mouth, dried spittle on it and also around his lips. There was a dark stain on the front of his trousers and the air was coloured with the odour of urine.

Lawrence's face was the colour of dark grapes and there was yellowish-black bruising around his neck and beneath his chin. In places, the flesh had been rubbed raw by the rope and there was dried blood on the heavy hemp.

His body hung perfectly still, his feet a yard or so off the ground. One shoe lay beneath him, dislodged by the impact when his body had reached the end of the rope.

Rigor mortis had already set in and his fingers were fixed in a claw-like pose as if to grab the two onlookers.

Wilby and Wood gazed at him for a moment longer then Wood merely shrugged.

'Come on, George,' said Wood, disinterestedly. 'We can't stand here looking at him all night. Let's cut him down. Get him out of here.'

Wilby nodded.

Both men stepped towards the body.

From the sitting room, another chorus of laughter accompanied their movements.

78

'It all adds up.'

Emma sat on one of the stools in the kitchen and looked at each of her three companions in turn.

Tate stood nearby, arms folded across his chest.

Jo was seated opposite her, a cup of coffee cradled in her hands.

Morton was leaning against a worktop close to his wife, alternately glancing down at the notes Emma had scribbled and then at Emma herself.

It was he who burst out laughing.

'What the fuck are you on, Emma?' he guffawed.

'You heard what I just said,' she snapped angrily. 'What I just told you. You can see for yourself what I copied out of that book.'

'It's bollocks,' grunted Morton.

'I suppose I should have expected a reaction like that from you, Pete,' Emma sneered.

'From any reasonable person,' he countered. 'It's insane.'

'So, does everyone think I'm crazy?' Emma asked.

'Let's just think about it,' Tate said, attempting to inject some reason into the discussion. 'Read that again, Emma.'

'Oh, come on, Nick, what for?' Morton protested.

'Read it, Emma,' Tate repeated.

She looked at her scribblings. 'The Lorican was believed, as far back as Roman times, to be a powerful spirit,' Emma began. 'It was worshipped by some ancient tribes, including the Iceni – Boudicca's tribe. The Druids offered sacrifices to it.' She looked at her three companions briefly then continued. 'It lived beneath the ground. It fed on fear. Over the years, many places thought to be haunted could possibly have been built over the dwelling places of a Lorican. It never maintained the same shape or form. It always took on the appearance of its victim's worst and darkest fear.'

'And how does *that* make sense?' Morton asked. 'What has *any* of that got to do with us, or with Roxton?'

'It explains some of the inscriptions inside the church,' Emma said. '*Let fear be consumed*. The Lorican fed on fear. People's worst nightmares nourished it. One of the inscriptions on the memorial to the men killed in the mine disaster said, *From pain to fear released*. One of the windows had the inscription, *Beneath us he gives life. Beneath*. It lives below the town.'

'In the mine?' Jo mused.

'So what were Wood and the others going down there for the other night?' Morton asked. 'If there's some kind of fucking *monster* down there then what the hell were they doing? Visiting the bloody thing?'

'It was worshipped thousands of years ago,' Emma told him. 'Treated like a god.'

'So you think the people of Roxton are worshipping some thousand-year-old creature that eats fear and lives in the mine?' Morton snorted. 'Give me a break.'

'Not worshipping it, no. But I think that there are a few who are aware of it,' Emma told him. 'Adam Wood, George Wilby, Jack Howard and Mark Jackson for a start. I think Reverend Lawrence knows about it too. If he didn't want me to find out about it, why would he send me to the library to discover this information?'

'And you say that you haven't spoken to him since you found out about the Lorican?' Tate asked.

Emma shook her head.

'Do you think this . . . thing caused those nightmares we had?' Jo asked.

'Oh, don't *you* start, Jo,' Morton said irritably.

'It's possible,' Emma said, ignoring him.

'But *you'd* been having bad dreams for weeks before we arrived here,' Tate reminded her.

'The rest of us hadn't,' she said. 'We've had shared nightmares since we've been here. That kind of thing just doesn't happen. Not without a cause. A reason.'

'So what did it do before *we* arrived?' Jo enquired. 'Whose fear did it feed on?'

'The people in Roxton,' Emma said with an air of assurance. 'Possibly the other people who rented this house before us. Everyone's got something they're afraid of. The Lorican obviously has the power to find out exactly what that fear is.'

'I still don't understand why Wood and the others were going down into the mine if that's where this thing lives,' Tate said.

'That book said that the Lorican could bestow a great treasure on those who protected it,' Emma announced. 'Perhaps that's what Wood and the others are doing. They're protecting it in return for something.'

'So what do we do now?' Morton chided. 'Arm ourselves with burning torches and storm the mine? That's what they do in horror films, isn't it?' He shook his head. 'Emma, have you really stopped to think how fucking ridiculous this whole story sounds?'

'Yes I have. It's not easy for me to believe either, Pete. That's why I want to go to the mine tonight.'

'And do what?' Tate asked, the colour draining from his face.

'I want to see what's down there,' Emma told him.

79

'Now I *know* you're mad,' Morton said flatly. 'If what you've just told us *is* true and there's some kind of fucking demon, or whatever the hell you want to call it, living in the mine, then we should pack our bags and get out of here now. Not go looking for the bloody thing.'

'I want to prove I'm right,' Emma announced.

'Not that way,' Morton snapped.

'There is no other way,' Emma rasped.

Morton held up his hands. 'Great,' he muttered. 'Right then, you go off and find your monster, I'm going back to London. If you're right then there's no fucking way I'm staying here anyway, and if you're wrong then I'm not sure I want to spend another week in a house with you. Sorry.'

'Wait a minute,' Tate said. He looked at Emma and saw the determination in her eyes. 'There are other things to consider. An explosion down that mine killed twenty-three men. The bloody thing is obviously unsafe. Even if we manage to get down there in the first place, it could collapse on us. We haven't got the knowledge or the equipment to go down there safely.'

'What about Wood and the others?' Emma protested. 'They went down. The mine didn't collapse on them.'

'They worked down there all their lives,' Tate reminded her. 'They know what they're doing. We don't.'

'I'll do it with or without your help, Nick,' she told him. 'You can all go back and leave me here, but I'm going to find out the truth. One way or another.'

'I'm not leaving you to do this alone,' Tate said quietly.

'Jo, what about you?' Emma asked. 'Are you leaving or staying?'

Jo exhaled wearily and shook her head. 'I don't know,' she said.

'Yesterday *you* were the one who wanted to go home,' Morton reminded his wife.

'Pete?' Emma continued. 'Are you leaving or not?'

He eyed her warily, his anger barely concealed. *Or was it fear?*

'What good is it going to do?' he wanted to know, his tone softening a little.

'I need to know the truth, and if it involves confronting my worst fears then I accept that,' Emma informed him.

'You need to know the truth,' Morton rasped. 'You need to know whether the Lorican exists.'

'That's right,' said Emma.

Morton ran a hand through his hair. 'I can't even believe we're having this fucking conversation,' he grunted. 'If anyone could hear us they'd think we were mad. They'd lock all four of us up and throw away the key.'

'So, what's your answer?' Emma persisted.

'You want to go to the mine and try and find this thing?' Morton repeated. '*If* it exists?'

Emma nodded.

'Why don't we just call the police?' Morton insisted.

'And tell them the story I told you?' Emma smiled. 'What will they think, Pete? Are you going to tell them? They'll react the same way *you* did.'

267

'Do you blame them?' Morton wanted to know.

'So, are you in or out?' Emma continued.

'All right,' Morton murmured. 'But if there's nothing down there then we pack tonight, we leave here and we never talk about this again.'

'Agreed,' Tate told him.

'And what if we find something?' Emma asked.

'We might not be alive long enough to worry about it,' Morton said. 'How big is this thing supposed to be?'

'I don't know,' Emma confessed. 'All I know is what I've read. What I've told the three of you.'

'What was the name of the book?' Morton asked.

'*Haunted England*,' Emma told him.

'So this thing's a ghost?' Morton persisted.

'It's been blamed for hauntings. For causing the manifestation of people's worst fears. But it isn't a ghost itself. Not according to the book.'

'The book,' Morton nodded resignedly.

A deep and almost impenetrable silence descended, closing around them like a vice.

It was broken by Tate. He walked across to the knife block on the worktop and pulled out a large kitchen knife, hefting it before him. The fluorescent light from the ceiling sparkled on the razor-sharp blade.

'I'm not sure this'll be enough if there *is* something down there,' he said, his voice catching.

'Give me one of those,' Morton added, taking another of the knives from Tate.

'We'll need torches too,' Jo said.

'There's a couple in the car,' Morton reminded her.

'So how do we kill this thing?' Tate enquired. 'What did it say in that book?'

'It didn't say anything about killing it,' Emma admitted. 'If the Lorican exists it could be hundreds, even thousands of years old. It's survived this long and you want to go in

there and fight it with nothing more than a kitchen knife?
Jesus Christ.'

'What do you suggest we do?' sneered Morton. 'Shoot
it with a fucking silver bullet? Or drive a stake through its
heart or some shit like that?'

'We'll have to make do with these,' Tate said, brandishing
the kitchen knife before him.

'And why are we talking about killing it?' Emma insisted.
'What gives us that right?'

'Let's see if it even exists first, before we figure out how
to kill it,' Morton said. 'I've got a feeling this is all going
to turn out to be bullshit.'

'Let's hope you're right,' Tate echoed.

Emma got to her feet. 'There's only one way to find
out,' she offered.

80

They drove in silence to the mine. Following the same route they'd taken the previous night. Only this time they weren't fortified by too much alcohol, and in the chilly night everything around them seemed to be visible with greater and more menacing clarity, despite the blackness that closed in around the car like an incoming tide around a stranded bather.

Morton brought the Volvo to a halt twenty yards from the padlocked gate that led into the area before the winding tower. The two huge wheels that formed a pulley creaked in the growing wind and Emma glanced up at them warily as she hauled herself from the car.

Moving with caution over the wet and slippery ground, they made their way through the gap in the fence, Emma leading the procession. She flicked on her torch, the beam lancing through the blackness, illuminating the winding shed and other buildings.

'That's where Wilby was last night,' Emma said, waving the torch in the direction of the winding shed.

Tate tried the door and wasn't surprised to find that it was locked.

'Break it down,' Morton insisted. 'If Emma's right

about what's down there in that fucking mine it won't matter anyway, will it?' He took a kick at the door. The impact reverberated over the hillside, amplified by the night.

He kicked at it again but still the wood held firm. Tate joined him, aiming for the lock.

There was a groan of splintering wood and the handle came away along with a piece of the door. The partition swung back on its hinges and slammed against the wall.

Morton and Tate aimed their torches at the inside of the building, the beams picking out several pieces of machinery close to them. The largest had several dials, buttons and switches on it. Beside it were two levers that reminded Tate of something out of the cab of a steam train.

One of the buttons was marked: CAGE. There was another that proclaimed: POWER. Emma reached forwards and pressed it.

'What the fuck are you doing?' snarled Morton as the night air was filled with the sound of grinding machinery. It was as if some massive robotic leviathan had woken and was stretching, building up its strength. 'They'll hear that all the way to Roxton.'

'How else are we supposed to get down into the mine?' Emma rasped, turning quickly on him. 'This is what they did last night.'

'You don't know that for sure,' Morton protested. 'Or did they have a book in the fucking library called *Mining for Beginners*? We don't know what we're doing here. If we hit the wrong button . . .' He allowed the sentence to trail off.

'There's got to be a way of opening the cage,' Tate said, his eyes fixed on the button that bore that word.

'Do it,' Emma urged.

Tate hit the button.

Closer to them there was a sound of metal on metal.

Emma stepped outside the winding shed and looked up at the two huge wheels at the top of the tower. They were turning slowly.

'Press it again, Nick,' she called.

Tate did as he was told and Emma heard another grinding of metal as the wheels stopped.

'That's it,' she said, stepping back inside the shed. 'It looks as if that button opens and closes the cage and lowers and raises it too.'

'There must be more to it than that,' Tate protested. 'These levers are used for something.'

'Well, pull one of the fucking things and see what happens,' Morton said.

Tate grabbed the one closest to him and pulled it towards him. A red light on the control panel glowed like a luminous blood blister.

The two wheels that formed the winch began to turn again, grinding loudly in the stillness of the night.

'Someone's got to stay here and work the winch,' Tate said. 'Only three of us can go down into the mine. Otherwise there's no way of getting back up again.'

'I'll go down with Emma,' Morton said flatly. 'You and Jo stay here. Work the machinery.'

Tate looked at his wife and hesitated for a moment, then he nodded. 'Once the cage reaches the bottom of the shaft I'll give you forty-five minutes. That should be long enough to have a look around.' He glanced at his watch. 'It'll take a good ten minutes to reach the bottom of the shaft.'

'We can't be sure of that, Nick,' Emma protested. 'What if it takes longer?'

'I'm bringing the cage back up at twelve forty-five,' Tate told her. 'No later.'

Emma nodded and checked her own watch. She and

Morton moved towards the door of the winding shed, torches in hand.

'You watch yourselves down there,' Tate warned.

81

The cage was fifteen feet square, suspended on thick metal cable like a mobile cell. It rocked very slightly from side to side as they stepped into it, torches flashing around the gloomy interior.

The floor of the construction was covered with dark muck that Emma thought might be an accumulation of mud and coal dust. She could see footprints in the filth. Made, she guessed, by the feet of the men who had entered it the previous night.

The cage lurched slightly as it began to descend.

Emma coughed; the smell that reached her nostrils was of damp earth, dust and oil. The noise grew louder as the cage slid deeper into the shaft.

Morton looked around him, his face pale, his jaw clenched. 'I hope this fucking thing's safe,' he said, forced to raise his voice over the grinding of the mechanism that was lowering them ever deeper into the bowels of the earth.

Emma didn't answer. She was too busy shining her torch around the inside of the cage, picking out handprints on the walls here and there. Someone had scratched their name on the metal close to the grille door.

'I wonder if he was one of the men who died in the disaster?' she mused.

'Perhaps your monster got him,' Morton chided.

The cage continued to descend.

'How will you know when they're at the bottom of the shaft?' Jo asked, watching the control panel.

'The winch will stop,' Tate told her. 'At least, I assume it will. Once the cable's reached its limit, logically the cage'll *have* to stop.'

'Logic? Nothing that's happened since we left London has been logical.'

Tate looked at her wan features and tried a comforting smile.

'Do you believe what Emma said, Nick?' she queried. 'About this . . . thing? The Lorican?'

'I don't know what to believe any more, Jo. I *know* I had a bad dream the other night that was unlike anything I've ever experienced before. But whether it was caused by some mythical creature living below the ground . . .' He allowed the sentence to trail off. 'Christ, it sounds even crazier when you say it out loud.' He sucked in a weary breath.

'What if they find the Lorican, Nick?' she insisted. 'What if it *is* down there?'

Tate wished he had an answer. He kept his eyes on the control panel, the hairs on the back of his neck rising.

The air was becoming mustier. Emma found it harder to breathe. She could visualise dust clotting in her nostrils and she tried to breathe through her mouth.

'Can you feel that?' she asked, looking at Morton. 'It's getting colder.'

He shook his head. 'Feels the same to me,' he told her. 'We must be close to the bottom of the shaft by now.'

She shone the torch beam on to the face of her watch and checked the time.

As if in answer to her query there was a heavy thud as the cage shuddered to a halt so abruptly that both of them almost overbalanced.

Emma crossed to the grille door and shone the torch through the slats.

The beam illuminated a long tunnel, supported on both sides and across the ceiling by concrete struts. It seemed to slope downwards, even deeper into the earth.

'The end of the line,' Morton said quietly.

Emma hesitated a moment longer then slid the grille open and stepped out into the area at the bottom of the shaft. Morton followed her, aiming his torch at the walls.

They both looked at their watches.

'We've got enough time to have a look around and get back here,' Emma said.

'Let's go and find your monster,' Morton said, grinning crookedly. He slid his hand inside his jacket and pulled out the large carving knife he'd taken from the house.

'I thought you didn't believe, Pete,' Emma said, nodding towards the blade.

Morton said nothing.

They set off down the tunnel.

82

The chill that Emma had felt as the cage descended had all but disappeared. Inside the tunnel itself the air was still cool but it was also cleaner. She found that she could breathe more easily. It still had a fusty odour to it, but apart from that it was tolerable.

Walking side by side with Morton, both of them shining their torches ahead, she occasionally reached out and touched the concrete-braced walls.

'How far do we go?' Morton whispered, his voice bouncing off the walls of the tunnel. 'This tunnel could go on for miles.'

His breathing was low and rapid now. He shifted the knife and torch from one hand to the other. Despite the chill in the air he was sweating, the beads of moisture glistening on his forehead.

He cursed as he felt his hair brush against one of the overhead supports. 'Wait a minute,' he snapped, flashing the torch above him. 'The tunnel's getting narrower. The ceiling's lower here than it was twenty yards further back.'

At first Emma wasn't sure, but the further they progressed the more she became convinced that Morton was right. Another hundred yards and they were both forced to stoop.

The walls on either side were also closing in. It was impossible for Emma and Morton to still walk alongside each other.

Emma took the lead, now almost bent double as she moved deeper. 'We must be near the coalface,' she whispered.

'Why's the tunnel narrower then?' Morton snapped. 'They'd have wanted as much room as possible when they were working down here.'

Emma shone her torch ahead. 'We can't go much further,' she observed, squinting at what lay before them.

The tunnel telescoped down to a gap in the rock that was barely four feet square.

'Perhaps there's another tunnel leading off from this one,' Emma said quietly. 'Perhaps we missed it. Or maybe it was where the cage stopped. We'll have to go back and look.'

Morton glanced at his watch. 'There isn't time,' he said. 'We've got less than fifteen minutes before we have to be back at the cage.'

'Nick's not going to bring it back up without us.'

'He won't know whether we're in it or not, will he? We said twelve forty-five.'

'So what do we do?'

Morton swallowed hard and kept his torch fixed on the hole.

'Do you reckon that hole's big enough to crawl through?' he asked.

Emma nodded. 'You stay here,' she told him. 'I'll go through.'

'Help yourself,' Morton exclaimed, stepping back slightly.

Emma slipped into the narrow opening. 'Keep your light pointed inside,' she muttered over her shoulder, her own torch bumping against the soft earth floor of the passage as she crawled. 'Pass the knife through when I tell you.'

What had been a tunnel was now little more than a

culvert, no wider than a storm drain and, Emma realised with horror, the further she crawled, the narrower it was becoming.

Her heart was thudding hard against her ribs and her mouth was dry.

She bumped the torch against the wall of the passage and it went out.

She was plunged into impenetrable darkness for a second and she couldn't contain her gasp of fright.

'Are you all right?' Morton called, his voice sounding a million miles away. 'Emma?'

She tapped the torch and it burst into life once more. 'Yeah, I'm all right,' she called back, not even sure if he could hear her.

Why the hell did you do this in the first place?

Emma was gasping, trying to suck in some air as she crawled.

What possessed you to come down here?

She crawled on, aware that there was another small opening ahead of her. So constricted had the space become by now that she was forced to lie on her belly, the ceiling of the subterranean passage only inches above her head. She tried to control her breathing, claustrophobia gnawing at her like some carrion creature. She couldn't turn around in the passage. Her only way out was to inch backwards the way she'd come.

This realisation sent waves of panic rushing through her and she closed her eyes tightly for a second, trying to regain control of her senses.

What if the passage collapsed?

She forced the thought to the back of her mind, but it wouldn't disappear.

You'll be buried alive beneath thousands of tons of rock and earth.

'You've got less than ten minutes,' Morton called.

Emma opened her eyes slowly.

Crawl on? Or go back?

She was about to move forwards when she felt the ground shake beneath her. Fragments of earth fell from the roof of the passage and showered her.

The rumbling grew in intensity. More earth spattered her.

Emma wanted to scream.

Instead she pushed herself backwards, dropping her torch in the cloying blackness, concerned only with getting out of this long narrow cylinder that was threatening to become her tomb.

More earth fell on to her and, with a conviction that almost stopped her heart, she realised the passage was about to collapse.

83

From somewhere behind her she felt hands close around her ankles. Felt someone pulling her out from inside the hole.

She lay sprawled on the floor of the tunnel and looked up to see Morton.

'Come on,' he said, helping her to her feet. 'Let's get out of here. The whole fucking lot's coming down.' A lump of debris the size of a football dropped from the ceiling and missed his head by inches. A second piece, as big as his fist, struck him just above the left ear and split his scalp. Blood ran freely from the cut and Morton reeled momentarily.

The earth was shaking beneath them. But also above them and on both sides. It was as if some giant hand had seized the tunnel and was crushing it, determined to trap them below ground.

'We've got to get back to the cage,' Morton hissed as they ran, grateful that they were in the wider part of the tunnel now.

He aimed his torch back the way they'd first come, in the direction of the fifteen feet square construction that would take them back to the surface and to safety.

The rumbling stopped as abruptly as it had started.

For precious seconds they continued to run, both unaware in their flight that silence had flooded back into the subterranean area. It was Emma who slowed her pace first.

'Wait,' she gasped, grabbing Morton's arm.

'What the fuck are you doing?' he snarled, trying to pull free. 'We're going to be buried down here. Come on!'

Still she gripped his jacket.

'It's stopped,' she snapped.

He didn't understand her. In his panic, her words may as well have been spoken in some foreign language.

'Pete,' she shouted, her voice echoing inside the tunnel. 'Stand still!'

Despite himself, Morton did as she told him.

The silence was total. The earth no longer moved beneath their feet. No debris fell from the ceiling of the passageway.

'It's stopped,' Emma whispered, looking around.

'But the whole fucking place was caving in,' he protested, shining his torch upwards towards the roof.

'*Let fear be consumed*,' Emma said quietly.

Morton looked blankly at her.

'It didn't happen,' she said flatly. 'The tunnel wasn't collapsing.'

He raised his hand to the place above his left ear where the stone had struck him. 'Then what about this?' he demanded, pressing his fingers to the cut above his ear.

When he drew his hand away there was no blood on his fingers. No trickles of the crimson fluid on his face. He touched the area tentatively again.

No pain. No gash.

'Something hit me,' he protested. 'I felt it. It cut me.'

'The Lorican *wanted* us to think the tunnel was collapsing,' Emma said. 'It wanted to frighten us.'

'The fucking roof was coming in,' he snarled. 'You felt it too.'

'I felt what it wanted me to feel,' Emma muttered. 'It feeds on fear, Pete. If we don't believe what it tells us, it has no power over us.'

Morton tried to slow his breathing. He glanced at his watch. 'Let's get to the cage,' he said. 'Nick'll be taking it back up in a couple of minutes. I want to get out of here.'

They hurried the last few yards along the tunnel towards the shaft, the torch beam waving before them.

Ten yards away, Morton stopped running, the breath catching in his throat.

Behind him, Emma also froze as she saw what his torch beam had illuminated.

84

Jo and Tate were standing in the cage, hands by their sides.

Behind them, Adam Wood, George Wilby and Mark Jackson stood shoulder to shoulder.

Emma saw something long and metallic glinting in the torch light and she realised instantly that Wood was carrying a shotgun.

The twin barrels yawned, aimed at Jo and Tate.

'Did you find what you were looking for?' Wood asked, nudging the shotgun first into Tate's back to force him from the cage, then into Jo's as she stepped out to join him.

Tate moved closer to Emma and snaked an arm around her waist. Jo hurried to join Morton.

'I'd put that knife down if I were you,' Wood said, swinging the shotgun up to his shoulder and squinting down the sight at Morton.

He hesitated a moment.

Wood thumbed back the twin hammers, the click echoing around the inside of the mine.

Morton dropped the blade.

Wood lowered the gun but kept it pointed in the direction of the two couples.

'What did you expect us to find down here?' Emma asked.

'Answers,' Wood told her.

'Or did you get those from Reverend Lawrence?' Wilby offered.

'That's my business,' Emma said with as much bravado as she could muster.

'That's where you're wrong,' Wood told her. 'It's the business of everyone in this village. It's never been anything to do with you though. None of it.'

'Are you going to kill us?' Morton wanted to know.

'Why would you think that?' Wood asked.

'Because you're pointing a fucking shotgun at us,' Morton reminded him. 'It's a fair assumption.'

'Not unless you give us reason to,' Wood told him. 'But even if we did, what difference would it make? No one would ever find your bodies, would they? Not buried down here. Who's going to come looking for you? The police?'

'People know we're staying at the house,' Morton protested. 'Our families know. Our friends back in London.'

'And what happens when you don't go back?' Wood insisted. 'The house would be emptied of your clothes. The police would ask people in the town when they last saw you. No one would know if you just decided to leave during the night. Why should they suspect us?'

'It sounds as if you've got it all worked out,' Tate interjected.

Wood lowered the shotgun slightly. 'We're just protecting our own interests,' he explained.

'And the Lorican,' Emma cut in. 'You're protecting that too.'

Wood nodded. 'For more than twenty years now,' he confessed. 'Ever since we found it down here.'

'One morning,' Wilby added, 'we were working at the coalface. The four of us. Me, Adam, Mark and Jack. Part of the seam caved in. We thought we were going to be buried alive, thought the whole bloody mine was coming down on us. But there was a chamber – I don't know what else to call it – something beyond the coalface.'

'We went through,' Mark Jackson continued. 'All four of us. We didn't know what we'd found. The chamber was big. Forty or fifty feet from top to bottom.'

'The Lorican was inside,' Wood said. 'We were terrified. We didn't know what the hell it was. George tried to get out, go for help, but he couldn't move. None of us could. Then it spoke to us. In here.' He tapped his temple. 'It asked for our protection. It told us what it could give us in return. Told us it had something we wanted. All we had to do was make sure no one hurt it.'

'By that time, some of the other men who were working down here with us had found the entrance to the chamber,' Jackson cut in. 'They panicked. I don't really blame them. Two of them ran, tried to get back to the cage. We had no choice but to kill them.'

Emma gripped Tate's arm more tightly as she listened intently.

'We knew that if any of the others reached the chamber the Lorican would be found,' Wilby told them. 'We knew they'd try to kill it. We didn't want that. We didn't want it destroyed.'

'Why not?' Emma wanted to know.

'Because what it offered us was too valuable to ignore,' Wood told her.

'I went back to the surface,' Wilby announced. 'Got some explosives and brought them back down here. When the four of us were safely out we brought the mine down on the other men. Buried them down here under thousands of tons of rock.'

'You murdered twenty-three of your friends to save that thing?' Emma said. 'What did it give you that was so

286

valuable? What's important enough to kill twenty-three people for?'

'Are you afraid of death?' Wood asked her.

Emma nodded slowly.

'Show me any person who says they aren't and I'll show you a liar,' Wood persisted. 'I'm afraid of dying. Every person in this world is frightened of something. The Lorican took away our fear. Just like it has done for dozens of others these past twenty years. The lives of twenty-three men is a small price to pay for that.'

'The Lorican feeds on fear,' Emma breathed. 'Why would it take yours away?'

'There are plenty of others it can feed from,' Wood told her. 'You four have found that out.'

'That's the treasure it guards,' Jackson announced. 'The power to remove fear. That's what it did for *us*.'

85

'But there's a price to pay,' Wood continued, seeing the looks of disbelief and confusion on the faces of the four people facing him. 'There's always a price. It still has to feed. On everyone's darkest fear. The thing that they try to hide the most. Like I said, everyone in this town is frightened of something. Everyone in this *world* is scared of feelings they have. Emotions they can't control. Situations they're put in. They try to hide them. They bottle that fear up until it eats away at them like a disease. The Lorican finds out what that fear is and uses it.'

'And you help it?' Emma murmured.

'It doesn't need our help,' Wilby snapped. 'Just our protection. And if it dies, so do we.'

'No more fear for the rest of your lives?' Morton sneered. 'That thing told you that and you fucking believed it, you dozy cunts.'

'You haven't got a clue, have you?' rasped Wilby. 'As Adam said, there's a price to pay. Everyone it gives the gift to is bound to it for the rest of their lives. They can never leave Roxton. Catherine Pearce found that out. The Lorican gave her the gift but she still tried to run from it. Why do you think she died in a car crash?'

'The woman who was in that accident the day we arrived here,' Emma stated.

Wood nodded.

'But you said the Lorican was protected by you,' Emma continued. 'How did *she* find out about it?'

'Like I said,' Wood continued. 'It gets in here.' Again he tapped his temple. 'She came because she wanted to. Others have done the same over the years and more will as time goes on. All they have to give in return is a little of themselves.' He smiled crookedly. 'Their fear.'

'Is that what you gave?' Emma wanted to know.

'All of us,' Wilby confirmed.

'You've got the same choice,' Wood told them, his voice even.

'You expect us to believe that?' snapped Morton. 'I don't even think it exists. If it does, where is it? Why haven't we seen it?'

'You want to see it?' Wood snarled, taking a step towards Morton. 'Look behind you. All of you.'

Morton turned to look back down the tunnel but he could see nothing except darkness. When he glanced back at Wood the older man had lowered the shotgun completely and was standing motionless, looking beyond Morton and his companions. It was as if he could see something in the gloom that they couldn't.

Wilby and Jackson were also staring off into the blackness of the tunnel.

Waiting.

Emma was the first to see movement.

'There,' she whispered, tugging on Tate's jacket with her hand and pointing with one quivering finger.

The figure that emerged slowly from the gloom was a woman. Her hair was dark but streaked with blonde highlights. She walked gracefully on her bare feet over the rough floor of the tunnel, moving closer to those who watched.

Her head was lowered. She seemed to be gazing at the ground as she walked, unaware of their staring eyes. As she drew closer they could all see that she was naked.

Another few steps and she raised her head.

The figure was identical to Jo except for one thing.

The eyes were missing.

86

Where the shining orbs should have been there were just empty sockets. Blood was dribbling down the cheeks like crimson tears.

Jo had to use all her self-control to suppress a scream as she stared, as if mesmerised, at the image of herself.

As she and the others watched, the figure's belly began to swell and undulate. The skin rippling around the navel.

Behind her came another figure, also naked. Unmistakably male, it sported a large erection which it cradled in one hand.

'What the fuck is this?' said Morton, gazing at the figure that was a mirror image of himself.

Wood and the others said nothing but merely watched impassively.

Morton watched his image (his clone, his doppelgänger, his double, or whatever the fuck it was) as it walked close to the eyeless copy of Jo, its hand now sliding briskly up and down its erection.

Jo was shaking uncontrollably as she watched the two figures.

Emma clung tightly to Tate's arm as she saw two more figures making their way up the tunnel towards herself and the others. She let out a moan of distress as she saw that the newest figures were her mother and father.

Both bore the injuries that had killed them. She could see her father's ribcage clearly through the gaping rent in his chest. Portions of her mother's intestines trailed around her feet as she walked, the torn ends occasionally brushing the cold earth beneath.

Tate saw an image of his father lumber into view, sputum and vomit bubbling over his lips. It was carrying a bottle of pills in one hand. White capsules that he recognised only too well. They were the pills he had fed his father when he'd helped him kill himself.

All five figures were within twenty feet by now, clearly visible to those who gazed at them. Jo's double put its hand to its belly and smoothed the skin down, as if trying to brush the creases from a piece of material. As its fingers touched flesh, its sharp nails gouged in. They tore at the flesh slowly and deliberately. No frenzied ripping, just the measured movements of someone unfastening a parcel whose contents they have no desire to see.

A strip of flesh came away easily. Then another.

Morton's double moved its hand more feverishly on its penis, its face contorting in a look that appeared to be more pain than pleasure.

It ejaculated with a loud grunt and, as it did, its clawing hand tore the erection in half. The figure ripped the top three inches of its shaft away, brandishing them momentarily in one fist.

But what spewed from the end of the severed, putrescent penis shaft was not the oily, white semen they had all expected. It was a foul-smelling mixture of blood, pus and mucus that sprayed into the air in three or four large and noxious gouts – one of which spattered the belly of Jo's double.

It seemed to act like a trigger.

The flesh covering the double's belly split wide open and Jo's double plunged its hand deep inside.

Jo screamed as she saw that it was tugging something free.

It finally held the foetus in one hand, holding it by the throat, the remains of the umbilicus dangling from its belly. Another tentacle-like section was hanging from the stomach of the double itself.

Emma took a step back as she watched the figures of her mother and father sink to their knees, both of them pointing accusing fingers at her.

Her mother was crying, trying to hold her intestines in. Coiling the pulsating lengths of viscera around her hands.

Tate felt her sobbing against him but his own attention was on the figure of his father.

'Murderer,' it rasped, spraying vomit and mucus into the air. 'Murderer.'

'They're not real,' Emma said through clenched teeth.

'They're the Lorican,' Wood told her. 'They're what you fear most. It knows.'

'They're not real,' Emma repeated more loudly, turning to look at the apparitions

Are they real? Are you so sure they're not?

'You're not real,' she bellowed at the top of her voice, tears staining her cheeks.

She took a step towards the figures but Tate grabbed her and held her to him.

'They're not real, Nick,' she snarled, trying to pull free. 'They're what it *wants* us to see.' And this time she succeeded in pulling away from him.

'Emma, keep away from them,' Tate shouted.

She moved briskly towards the apparitions, the breath frozen in her throat. She could feel pain in the centre of her chest. A crushing force that grew more intense as she got closer to the five figures.

293

'You're not real,' she said again, but she winced as the vice-like grip around her heart tightened. She could feel pain flowing along her left arm now.

The five figures were standing motionless, merely looking at her.

Emma stumbled. Her neck hurt. It was creeping into the left side of her jaw and, all the time, the agonising pain in the middle of her chest grew worse.

'Oh, God, no,' she whispered, her legs buckling beneath her. White stars danced behind her eyelids. Her head was spinning.

'Emma,' Tate roared as he saw her fall to the ground.

He ran towards her, cradling her head in his lap as he knelt beside her.

Her lips were blue. They fluttered soundlessly. She managed to put one hand to the centre of her chest. 'My heart,' she gasped, her eyes screwed up in agony. A single tear rolled from the corner of one of them. 'I don't want to die, Nick. Not now. Not like this. Please.' She gritted her teeth against the pain and shuddered in his arms. He held her to him in desperation.

'She's having a heart attack,' he shouted frantically. 'Help me. Get a fucking ambulance.' Tears were now filling his own eyes.

He looked back down at Emma's face. It was as if all the blood had drained from her cheeks. Her flesh was as white as milk and when he held her hand she felt unbearably cold.

'Nick, please help me,' she said, her eyes bulging in their sockets with a mixture of agony, fear and desperation. She tried to squeeze his hand but there was no strength left in her grip.

Jo and Morton looked on helplessly.

Wilby, Jackson and Wood watched as Emma's life slipped slowly away from her.

Even the five apparitions stood motionless, gazing down at her impassively.

'Don't leave me,' Tate sobbed, close to her face. 'Hang on. Please.'

She tried to speak but the pain was too much. She opened her mouth but all that escaped was a low wheezing sound. Emma shook her head, her expression one of terrified helplessness.

'Don't die,' Tate cried, his tears falling on to her face. He dug his fingers almost savagely against the pulse on the left side of her neck.

It was barely detectable.

Still no one moved.

'Help her,' Tate whimpered, his body jerking uncontrollably as he held his dying wife, helpless realisation spreading through him more strongly by the second.

Another thirty seconds and she would be dead.

87

'We've got to help her,' Jo said, pulling away from Morton.

'There's nothing we can do,' he told her, his voice low.

'Get her out of here,' Jo snarled at Wood and his companions. 'Before it's too late. You're letting her die. You might as well put that shotgun to her head.'

'*Beneath us he gives life,*' said Wood quietly, his eyes on Emma whose own eyes were now closed.

'Just help her,' screamed Jo.

'*We* can't do anything,' Wilby told her. 'But the Lorican can.'

'What are you talking about?' Tate demanded, tears still staining his cheeks.

'*Beneath us he gives life,*' Wood repeated. 'She doesn't have to die.'

'Then tell me what to do,' Tate rasped, clinging tightly to Emma who barely moved beneath his grip.

'Do you want her to live?' Wilby said.

'Of course I do,' Tate shouted. 'Help her.'

He felt movement close to him and he recoiled as he remembered that the visions of Emma's mother and father were still standing watching.

The figure of her mother moved towards him, the intestines still trailing from the rent in her stomach.

He watched as the figure leant forwards and knelt beside Emma, placing one bloodied hand on her forehead.

Tate looked into the face of the apparition. It bore deep cuts and yellowing bruises all over it. He looked directly into the rheumy eyes but they seemed to gaze straight through him. He waited for the smell of decay to assail his nostrils or the stench of death to fill his head, but there was no odour.

Still holding Emma's body, he watched as the figure of her mother leant closer and planted one soft kiss on her lips. Then the figure struggled to its feet and moved back to stand with the others.

Emma still felt icy cold in his arms but, as he clung to her, he felt her body jerk slightly. He heard a rasping sound in the back of her throat. He realised that she was taking a breath, filling her lungs. And, once she had done so, her face remained serene. If she'd been in pain before she didn't appear to be now.

He saw colour flooding back into her cheeks. 'Emma,' he whispered, not daring to believe what was happening. Not even *understanding* what was going on before him.

She opened her eyes and looked at him.

'Thank God,' he murmured.

'God had nothing to do with it,' Wilby told him.

Tate looked at the older man and his companions. They turned as one and headed back towards the cage.

'We'll send it back down for you,' Wood told him, pulling the metal grille across.

There was a loud clanking of machinery and it began to rise slowly.

Jo was now kneeling on the other side of Emma, holding her hand, stroking her face.

Morton remained motionless, watching as the five

apparitions moved slowly back into the darkness of the tunnel. He watched until they had disappeared into the gloom.

'What happened?' Emma murmured, drawing in another deep breath.

Tate wished he had an answer for her.

'What can you remember?' Jo asked.

'I had a terrible nightmare about dying,' Emma said. 'I saw my parents. Then . . .' She seemed to simply run out of words. She tried to sit up.

'Just stay there for a minute,' Tate told her, brushing the hair from her face, wiping his own face with the back of one hand.

She reached up and touched his cheek. 'There's no need to cry, Nick,' she told him, smiling. 'Not any more.'

88

Time appeared to have lost its meaning. Minutes had stretched into hours, hours into days it seemed.

Emma could remember nothing of their journey from the house to the mine. Only the silence that accompanied the ride back seemed to stay with her. Barely a dozen words had been exchanged between them from the time they had wandered into the cage and been hauled up the shaft from the mine till the time they arrived back at the house.

Tate had scarcely let go of her, his arm had remained around her like a father protecting his child in a crowded shopping centre.

Now, as she sat in the sitting room of the house, she was aware of nothing except her surroundings. Every colour seemed to glow with renewed brilliance. Each smell was richer and stronger in her nostrils. She was more aware of the texture of everything she touched.

Tate, Morton and Jo looked drained. Their faces pale. They looked as if they hadn't slept for days. Their hands and faces were grimy with mud and coal dust, their clothes dirty.

Emma noticed that there were dirty footprints on the thick pile carpet in the sitting room.

'Are you sure you're going to be all right, Emma?' Jo asked, squeezing her hand and leaning forwards to kiss her.

She nodded.

'I'll stay with her,' Tate said. 'Don't worry.'

'I won't be long,' Jo announced. 'You can come and help me, Pete.'

Morton moved mutely out of the room and Emma heard his footfalls on the stairs as he followed Jo.

'Where are they going?' she wanted to know.

'To pack,' Tate smiled. 'The sooner we get out of here the better.'

'Get out of where?' Emma asked, a look of concern on her face.

'Out of this house. Out of Roxton.'

'Why?'

'We can't stay here, Emma. Not after . . .' He allowed the words to trail off.

Emma sat forwards in her seat. 'Why do we have to leave?' she asked. 'I don't want to go, Nick.'

'We've got to get back to London.'

'I'm not leaving here. I can't.'

There was a strength in her voice that took Tate by surprise.

'Emma, we've got no choice. Not now,' he told her.

She got to her feet, shaking her head.

'You can't remember what happened when we were down in the mine,' Tate persisted. 'You didn't see what the rest of us saw. We can't stay here.'

'I *know* what happened, Nick, and that's one of the reasons I'm not leaving,' Emma announced. 'And I don't just mean when the holiday's over. I mean *ever*. There's nothing for us back in London, you know that. If we stay in Roxton we've got the chance to start again. A new life. Away from all our worries. If we sell our house down south we'll be able to buy somewhere here for a fraction of the

300

price. You can start your business again *here*. I can find work easily enough. We won't have any money worries again. We won't have any more worries about *anything*.' She smiled. 'No more fear.'

Morton wandered back into the sitting room.

'The packing won't take long now,' he said. 'We can be back on the motorway in less than an hour.'

'I'm not leaving, Pete,' Emma told him. 'I've just told Nick the same thing. I'm not leaving this house and I won't leave Roxton.'

Morton regarded her impassively for a moment. 'Fine,' he said. 'You stay, but me and Jo are getting out and if you've got any sense, Nick, you'll come with us.' He looked at Tate.

Morton hesitated a moment longer then headed back upstairs.

'Let them go,' Emma said venomously. 'We don't need them here.'

Tate took a step towards her, arms outstretched.

'I mean it, Nick,' she rasped. 'I'm *not* leaving.'

'I thought I'd lost you once. I'm not going to lose you again,' Tate snapped.

'What are you going to do? Drag me out of here?'

She heard more footsteps on the stairs. Morton carried the first of the suitcases out to the waiting Volvo and placed it in the boot.

'Come on, Nick,' he called as he headed upstairs for the next case. 'Let's get going.'

'Emma, we *can't* stay here,' Tate protested. 'Not in this house. Not in Roxton. Our lives are back in London.'

'Not any more,' she told him defiantly.

Morton returned with the second case, Jo close behind him.

'There's something wrong with this place,' Tate insisted.

'Then you go,' Emma said calmly. 'Go with Pete and Jo. Go now. Leave me.'

'I told you,' Tate said through gritted teeth. 'I won't lose you again.'

'Then stay with me,' she countered.

'Come on,' Morton shouted, hurrying out to the car. Those inside the house heard the Volvo engine burst to life.

Jo hesitated in the doorway, looking imploringly first at Tate, then at Emma.

'Jo, come on!' Morton roared.

'Emma, please,' Jo implored.

'You go,' Emma told her without looking at her.

'Nick?' Jo said, glancing at her friend.

Tate shook his head slowly. 'I can't leave either,' he murmured. 'Not without Emma. You go.'

Jo waited a moment longer, then hurried out of the front door to join her husband.

Inside the house, Tate and Emma heard the Volvo pull away.

302

89

'It looks like it's just the two of us,' Emma said, a faint smile playing on her lips.

'What the hell's wrong with you, Emma? Why are you acting like this? What did that thing do to you when we were in the mine?'

'It saved my life, Nick,' she rasped. 'You know that.'

'It changed you.'

'It made me see what my life could be like. What *our* lives could be like. I don't know why you can't understand that. There's more for us in Roxton than there is in London.'

Tate shook his head.

'Pete and Jo will tell people what happened here. What happened in the mine,' Emma protested.

'And who's going to believe them?'

'Someone will. Someone will come to Roxton. They'll find out what's going on. They'll find the Lorican. Destroy it.'

'Listen to yourself, Emma. You sound like Wilby, Jackson and the others. You sound as if you don't *want* it to be found.'

'Why should I? Like I said, it saved my life, Nick.'

'I don't believe that. *Some*thing saved your life, but it wasn't any myth, legend or superstition.'

'Then what was it?' she demanded, her features contorted with fury. 'Some miracle sent by God?' She laughed and the sound raised the hairs on the back of Tate's neck. 'What did *you* see down in that mine, Nick? Tell me the truth.'

'I saw you having a heart attack,' he said quietly. 'I saw you dying.'

'What else did you see?'

'I saw something that wasn't there,' he said flatly. 'I *imagined* that I saw something.'

'My father and mother. *Your* father. Doubles of Jo and Pete. *That's* what you saw. That's what we *all* saw. We saw the Lorican but, like Wood said, we all saw it in the form it *wanted* us to see it in.'

Tate shook his head.

'Admit that's what you saw, Nick,' Emma demanded. 'And admit that you saw it save my life.'

He couldn't speak. Couldn't force the words out. It was as if to speak them, to acknowledge what he'd seen as real, would be taking the first step on a path that led to madness.

'Yes, I saw you dying,' he finally breathed. 'I saw you having a heart attack. Then I saw you come out of it. And I thanked a god I didn't believe in for that.'

'The Lorican saved me,' she said evenly. 'You know that. And I won't let it be destroyed.'

'You haven't got any choice. As soon as Pete and Jo get back to London . . .'

'If they don't make it back they can't tell the police or anyone else what happened here.'

'They don't even have to get as far as London. They can stop at the first services. Use their mobiles. Ring the police. Tell them what happened. Tell them what Wilby and the others said.'

'No one will believe them.'

'Someone might. Eventually, people will come here, Emma. They'll go to the mine. They'll find the Lorican.'

'Then that can't be allowed to happen, Nick.'

90

'Slow down a bit, Pete.'

Jo's words were lost as Morton pressed down even harder on the accelerator and sent the Volvo roaring into a sharp bend. The road was flanked on both sides by tall trees that loomed over them ominously in the darkness.

'I just want to get away from this fucking place as quickly as possible,' Morton rasped, glancing down at the dashboard clock which showed 3.18 a.m.

'Why wouldn't Emma and Nick come with us?' Jo queried.

'I don't know and I don't care. What they do now is *their* business.'

The car skidded a little as Morton took another corner at speed which forced him to ease the pressure on the accelerator slightly. There was ice on the road in places: he could see it glistening in the powerful headlights.

'Down in the mine—' Jo began, but Morton cut her short.

'Forget it, Jo,' he snapped. 'I don't want to talk about it.'

'What *were* those things?' she insisted.

'I *said* forget it. We'll deal with it when we're away from here. This whole fucking place is crazy.'

'I know what I saw, Pete. Does that make me crazy too?'

He glanced briefly at her and their eyes locked for precious seconds.

When he looked back at the road there were two figures illuminated by the headlamps. For interminable seconds it was as if everything had slipped into slow motion.

Jo opened her mouth to scream as she saw the figures. Morton stamped hard on the brake, wrestling with the wheel.

It was his own image and that of Jo that the lights had picked out.

Naked, dripping blood on to the icy road. They stood motionless as the car sped towards them.

Morton twisted the wheel sharply, feeling the back wheels of the Volvo beginning to swing around. He realised with horror that the vehicle was fishtailing. The front wheels also failed to grip as he slammed on the brakes again.

The car left the road doing sixty, hurtling across the grass verge towards a dry-stone wall.

It hit the wall and demolished it, pieces of debris spinning in all directions.

What about the fucking air bags? Why weren't they working? Why?

The windscreen exploded inwards as a lump of flying stone struck it. Jo and Morton were showered with glass and Jo felt a fragment pierce her eye. She shrieked and clutched at the shard, feeling warm blood spewing on to her fingers.

The car careered onwards, hit a slight rise in the earth beyond the wall and actually left the ground. It rose several feet into the air, lights still blazing, and in the dazzling beams Morton saw the thickly planted trees that the Volvo was heading towards.

The air bags . . .

As if fired from a cannon, it flew through the air before slamming into a large oak with incredible force.

The impact sent the steering column backwards at devastating speed. It pulverised Morton's sternum and he felt a moment of incredible pain as several broken ribs tore through his lungs. The fleshy sacs burst and he felt his mouth filling with blood.

Beside him, her eye still speared by the piece of windscreen, Jo was hurled forwards. She slammed into the dashboard, her face powering into the glove compartment so hard that the left side of her skull and most of her forehead was obliterated.

The car rolled over once and, just before he lost consciousness, Morton smelt the pungent odour of petrol and realised in his final moments that the fuel tank had ruptured.

Where the spark that ignited it came from, he never had the chance to wonder.

The Volvo exploded, a shrieking ball of red and yellow flames illuminating everything for a hundred yards in all directions before a noxious black mushroom cloud of smoke settled over the blazing wreck like a shroud.

Pieces of twisted metal rained down like shrapnel.

Inside what was left of the Volvo, the crushed and lifeless bodies of Peter and Jo Morton burnt.

91

'Emma, listen to yourself,' Tate said imploringly as he moved towards the door of the sitting room. 'This has got to stop.'

'What's got to stop?' Emma demanded, following him. 'What are you doing, Nick?'

'If it was the Lorican that saved your life then, like I said, it did something to you as well.'

'You just said it,' she snapped. 'It saved my life. Shouldn't you be grateful for that?'

'What was it Wood said? "There's always a price to pay." What price are you going to have to pay, Emma? What are you going to have to give it to appease it?'

'I don't care what I have to give it, Nick.'

He spun round angrily. 'Well *I* do,' he rasped.

She watched as he snatched a carving knife from the block on the worktop.

'I'm going to kill it,' he snarled.

'You can't,' she said, her voice losing its hard edge. She walked across to him, her face full of pleading instead of the fury he'd seen moments earlier. 'If it saved me then you should be grateful. I won't live in fear any more. It saved my life then it saved my sanity, Nick. What has it done that's so wrong? Would you rather it had let me die?'

He looked into her eyes, his own filling with tears.

'Let it give *you* that gift too,' she whispered. 'We'll be together for ever. No more fear. We'll never be apart.'

'I can't,' he gasped.

Emma reached towards the hand that held the knife but Tate pulled away.

'I love you, Nick,' she told him. 'I never want to be without you. If you let the Lorican give you what it gave me then we can have what we've got for the rest of our lives.'

Again she reached for the knife and, this time, he loosened his grip on it slightly.

Emma slid her fingers among his, grasped the handle of the blade and eased it free.

'Tell me what's so awful about being together for ever?' she said, kissing him on the cheek.

He shook his head. Tried to speak.

'I love you so much,' she whispered.

'People will come. One day, someone will find the Lorican.'

'No one will ever find it, Nick. We'll be here to help protect it, just like Wilby and the rest of them. If that's the price we have to pay, then what's so terrible about that?'

She kissed him on the lips.

'No,' he said, pulling back slightly. 'This isn't right. I can't.'

Again she kissed him on the lips. 'But I *can*,' she murmured.

Tate felt as if he'd been punched in the stomach with a cold fist.

At first he felt no pain at all. Just the realisation of what she'd done.

He stepped back slightly, looking down at the wound in his stomach where Emma had stabbed him.

Blood was pouring down the front of his jeans, spattering the tiles of the kitchen.

She advanced upon him and drove the knife into him again. And again.

He looked at her imploringly and dropped to his knees.

'I love you,' she said, her face expressionless.

His body convulsed. He felt cold.

'But I can't let you kill it, Nick,' Emma told him, looking down at him.

He was clutching his punctured stomach with both hands, trying to hold his riven intestines in, portions of them bulging through his fingers like corpulent, slippery worms.

He tried to speak her name but the only sound that came forth was of the blood that surged up his windpipe and ran over his lips.

Emma looked into his eyes one last time then ran the blade across his throat.

The cut was deep. From ear to ear. The gash opened wide and blood erupted from the severed arteries, some of it spraying Emma who merely stepped back and watched her husband fall forwards at her feet. A crimson pool spread out swiftly around him.

His body jerked convulsively once then was still. She knew he was dead.

She calmly put the knife down on the worktop then turned towards the phone on the wall nearby.

She'd ring Jack Howard. He'd help her. Or, if not him, then Wood or Jackson or Wilby. Probably all four of them. They'd know what to do.

Emma looked down at her husband's body then she picked up the receiver and dialled.

Howard told her he'd be with her in twenty minutes.
She thanked him then sat and waited.
After all, time was one thing she had plenty of.

92

The pain was worse. Jason Skelson was *sure* of it. He couldn't wait any longer. Even now the cancer might be eating away at him. Spreading to other parts of his body.

He sat naked on his bed looking down at his groin, the Stanley knife gripped firmly in one hand.

Don't think about it. Just do it.

He made the first cut to the side of his right testicle, surprised at how little blood there was.

The second cut was a little deeper and ran parallel with his hamstring.

Don't cut too deep and cut through that.

He sucked in a deep breath, trying to concentrate on the relief that this was going to bring him instead of the blood that was now staining his sheets, soaking through into his mattress.

The third and fourth cuts he made with lightning speed, opening an almost perfectly square laceration in his thigh. He sat there for a moment, noting with satisfaction that the blood was pumping rather than spouting from the wound.

Missed the femoral artery. Good.

He dropped the bloodied Stanley knife and dug the first two fingers of his right hand into the wound, probing around inside it like a surgeon with tweezers. He felt the warmth of his own blood pouring over the digits as he searched for the place where he *knew* the growth to be.

Find it and remove it as quickly as you can.

He felt the slippery threads of veins, like crimson spaghetti beneath his fingertips as he pushed and pulled. He even felt the throb of muscle.

A bump.

No. More than a bump. Something bulbous. About the size of the end of his thumb.

He looked down and saw it amidst the blood. The lump was black. Like a long-dried-up prune.

Jason retrieved the Stanley knife and cut into the base of the lump, tearing at it with his fingers until it began to come free. There was just one small tendril of flesh holding it in place now and he sliced effortlessly through that before pulling the lump free. He held it before him, his vision beginning to swim.

He heard banging on his bedroom door. Heard a voice somewhere off in the distance that he recognised as his mother. She was calling his name.

She would see the growth when she got inside the room. *She* would show the doctor, then everyone would know he'd been right. They'd all know he had cancer.

That was his last thought before he passed out.

The wheels of the winch that carried the cage down to the bottom of the shaft and up again quivered slightly in the breeze. The thick steel cables that lifted the contraption clanked against their housing. But, above ground, everything was silent.

It was below ground, three hundred feet or more that there was activity.

Anyone walking above the mine would have felt the ground tremble slightly.

93

When Emma heard the knock on the front door she didn't hesitate. She walked across the kitchen, past the body of her dead husband, and out through the hallway to open the door.

She looked at the two men who stood there, but if she was surprised it didn't register on her face.

'I spoke to Jack Howard,' she said. 'He told me he'd be coming to help me.'

George Wilby nodded. 'There was a change of plan,' he told her. 'That's why we're here instead.' He motioned to the other, younger, man with him. 'This is my son, Adam.'

Emma looked questioningly at Wilby for a second but he met her gaze unblinkingly.

'Adam knows what's going on,' he explained. 'Everything.'

Emma nodded and stepped back to allow the two men inside, ushering them into the kitchen.

Neither said a word when they saw Tate's body lying in the pool of blood that surrounded it. Wilby merely slipped off his coat and jacket and laid them across one of the worktops.

'We'll need your help cleaning this up,' he said.

Emma nodded. 'Pete and Jo left,' she said quietly. 'About an hour ago.'

'We know,' Wilby said. 'You don't have to worry about them. You don't have to worry about *anything* any more.'

Emma understood.

She watched as Adam Wilby rolled up his sleeves, glancing down impassively at the body of Nick Tate.

'Adam came to me because of his wife,' George Wilby explained.

'You told me she was paralysed,' Emma said.

'Will be for the rest of her life,' the younger Wilby announced. 'But that doesn't stop me feeling the way I feel about her.'

'He was frightened of his feelings,' George Wilby said. 'He isn't any more.'

The three of them looked at each other and something unsaid passed between them.

'We'd best get on,' the older Wilby insisted. 'There's a lot to be done.'

Emma began filling a plastic bucket with hot water. It would be the first of many.

The itching hadn't stopped. Not even when she'd washed her hair for the third time that day. Now, Lisa McQuillan stood before the bathroom mirror, her face ashen, her eyes red-rimmed.

She picked up the nit comb and dragged it through her hair with such ferocity that it raked the flesh from her scalp. She looked between the steel prongs, running the comb beneath the hot tap to wash whatever may be stuck there into the sink.

There was nothing, and yet she could still feel that maddening, unstoppable itching around the crown of her head.

She pulled open the door of the medicine cabinet and looked in.

Her eyes settled on the safety razor.

She had always used it to shave her legs and beneath her arms, preferring to remove the blade after each task. A fresh one could then be inserted before the chore was carried out again.

With quivering hands she began unfastening the screw that held the blade in place, finally sliding it free.

Lisa studied the razor blade for a moment, its sharp edges glinting in the light.

She felt the itching again. Annoying. Maddening. Unbearable.

Gripping the razor blade between two fingers she cut into the flesh of her forehead, just below the area that was giving her so much trouble. Moving the blade backwards and forwards in a sawing motion, she worked it through her flesh, ignoring the blood that ran down her face. She reached the part of her head that itched so badly and continued cutting. Through the thicker skin of the scalp itself.

She tugged hard on the hair and the skin began to come free in a large lump.

Lisa slid the blade beneath the raised flap of skin and hair and sawed once more until she had removed a piece of skin the width and length of her thumb. She held it up before her and saw something moving in the hair. Something that had burrowed deep into the flesh of the scalp.

Something small and white.

It was a maggot.

Exactly how long it had been there, digging into her flesh, she had no idea. Precisely how that vile, swollen fly that had invaded her home had managed to deposit its eggs in her flesh, she could only begin to imagine. But now all that mattered was that the itching had stopped.

She looked at the maggot again, still writhing in the clump of hair and flesh.

What if there were more of them? More that hadn't hatched yet?

She felt another twinge above her left ear but this time she didn't hesitate. Almost oblivious of the pain, Lisa cut into her scalp again, more blood spattering the white enamel of the sink.

If she had to remove every single piece of flesh on her head, she decided, she would rid herself of these parasites. She continued to cut.

Brick dust came away from the wall of the shaft that led down to the mine, shaken free by the rumbling that rolled through the tunnel like water breaking on the shore. Unheard by any human ears, a sound like asthmatic breathing filled the tunnel. Harsh and mucoid, it grew louder.

94

Emma Tate lay in bed, gazing at the ceiling of the bedroom. She could feel her eyes closing. Despite the fact that dawn was clawing its way into the sky outside, she could barely stay awake.

It had taken longer than she'd expected to clean up the mess in the kitchen.

George and Adam Wilby had left less than fifteen minutes earlier and she had retreated to bed immediately, completely drained by what had happened.

All she wanted to do now was sleep.

She turned on to one side, facing the pillow where her husband had slept the night before.

Emma reached out a hand as if to touch him and she realised that she would never feel him close to her again. The thought brought a tear to her eye but she brushed it away quickly, allowing herself to slip into the welcome oblivion of sleep instead.

And, this time, there were no dreams.

95

The mine was silent. The door of the winding shed swung gently back and forth, banging against the wall every now and then when the wind caught it, but apart from that, nothing moved.

Even below ground it was quiet.

Apart from a low, rattling breathing that filled the tunnel and the shaft.

A vile, wheezing, sucking sound that, every so often, was interrupted by what sounded strangely like a soft, breath-less laugh.

'Madness is the gift that has been given to me . . .'

Disturbed

HELL TO PAY

Shaun Hutson

Roma Todd's relationship with record company boss David is rife with deceit and deception, and the only thing that holds them together is their daughter Kirsten. And though Kirsten may seem like any other child, she suffers from an extraordinary illness, one that without her medication can unleash a bizarre and deadly trail of horror.

Nikki Reed knows only too well what the ominous knock on the front door means – the loan sharks want their money back, and if they don't get it, they're going to get nasty. But Nikki and her husband Jeff can't pay . . . until Nikki's brother John comes up with a dangerous and high-risk scheme that could make them all rich.

All desperate people running out of time. When their worlds collide, there'll be hell to pay . . .

NECESSARY EVIL

Shaun Hutson

It was to be a routine job. Matt Franklin and his companions would rob the Securicor van. Simple. Until the job turned into a nightmare. Two of them are shot dead and another fatally wounded. But who is trying to wipe them out, killing not just them but their families too? How are the government and the British army implicated? What lurks within a secret research establishment in the English countryside? Franklin has to find out. Finally the only one left alive, he tires of being the prey and decides to become the hunter.

Aided by a detective, Franklin becomes embroiled in a series of events that lead to a terrifying climax in the London Underground, where he comes face to face with the answers he has sought.

Like all of us, Franklin was told monsters don't exist. He's about to find out someone was lying . . .

Time Warner Books titles available by mail:

❑	Assassin	Shaun Hutson	£6.99
❑	Captives	Shaun Hutson	£5.99
❑	Erebus	Shaun Hutson	£6.99
❑	Heathen	Shaun Hutson	£6.99
❑	Hell to Pay	Shaun Hutson	£6.99
❑	Hybrid	Shaun Hutson	£6.99
❑	Knife Edge	Shaun Hutson	£6.99
❑	Lucy's Child	Shaun Hutson	£6.99
❑	Necessary Evil	Shaun Hutson	£5.99
❑	Nemesis	Shaun Hutson	£6.99
❑	Purity	Shaun Hutson	£6.99
❑	Relics	Shaun Hutson	£5.99
❑	Renegades	Shaun Hutson	£5.99
❑	Shadows	Shaun Hutson	£6.99
❑	Slugs	Shaun Hutson	£5.99
❑	Spawn	Shaun Hutson	£5.99
❑	Stolen Angels	Shaun Hutson	£6.99
❑	Victims	Shaun Hutson	£6.99
❑	White Ghost	Shaun Hutson	£5.99

*The prices shown above are correct at time of going to press.
However, the publishers reserve the right to increase prices on
covers from those previously advertised, without prior notice.*

TIME WARNER
BOOKS

TIME WARNER BOOKS
P.O. Box 121, Kettering, Northants, NN14 4ZQ
Tel: +44 (0) 1832 737525, Fax: +44 (0) 1832 733076
Email: aspenhouse@FSBDial.co.uk

POST AND PACKING:
Payments can be made as follows: cheque, postal order (payable to
Time Warner Books) or by credit cards. Do not send cash or
currency.

All UK Orders **FREE OF CHARGE**
E.E.C. & Overseas 25% of order value

Name (Block Letters) _____

Address _____

_____

Post/zip code: _____

❑ Please keep me in touch with future Time Warner publications

❑ I enclose my remittance £_____

❑ I wish to pay Visa/Access/Mastercard/Eurocard

Card Expiry Date